DARK HEART

THE PURGATORY OF LEO STAMP

snowbooks

Proudly Published by Snowbooks in 2011

Snowbooks Ltd.
email: info@snowbooks.com
www.snowbooks.com

British Library Cataloguing in Publication Data
A catalogue record for this book is available from the
British Library.

978-1-907777-09-7

For Lesley, the strongest person I know.

He who fights monsters should look into that he himself does not become a monster. When you gaze long into the abyss, the abyss also gazes into you.

Friedrich Nietzsche

PROLOGUE

Reuben palmed steam from the mirror so he could see his face, gripped the bone-handled dagger and drew the blade across his wrist. Blood spat from the gash and whirled round the basin in pink rivers. He studied the reflection of his eyes, longing to glimpse a flicker of the old Reuben, but they were stagnant pools. Dead and dark. A droplet of sweat grew fat on the tip of his nose, seemed to fall in slow motion. The ceiling fan in the bedroom turned pointlessly. The air-con unit whirred close to useless.

He rinsed the blade and set it down on the towel beside the basin, bandaged his wrist with a handkerchief and pulled a tight knot with his teeth. How many times had he done this? When had he stopped counting? He took the dagger through to the bedroom without the answer.

On the bed were two blocks of wood, a concaved imprint of the dagger carved into each. Reuben laid the dagger into one of the halves and placed its mirror-twin on top, entombing it like a pharaoh king. White light pulsed along the seam for a moment, then blinked out, leaving only a solid block of ebony, roughly the same size as a shoebox.

He wrapped the box in parcel paper and attached an airmail sticker to cover the two-thousand mile journey from Cairo to Suffolk, England. He bit the cap off a marker pen and wrote the address, taking care not to drip blood, but tutted at the expanding red full stop after the name: Leo Stamp.

There was a knock at the door.

'One moment,' Reuben called, smoothing a wad of crumpled banknotes against his leg. He placed the cash on the parcel and stepped back into the steaming bathroom. 'Come in.'

A young Egyptian boy entered, carrying a bottle of red wine and a glass. He set the tray on the bedside cabinet. 'Your wine, sir.'

Reuben looked over his shoulder, shielding his wrist. 'See the parcel?'

The boy nodded, brown eyes wide.

'See the money?'

The boy scooped the cash from the parcel, his eyes growing wider as he fanned the notes.

'It's all there,' Reuben said. 'Do as I've asked and you'll never see me again. Deviate, and I'll be the last thing you ever see – goes for your friend, too.'

The boy swallowed. 'The hotel courier is my cousin – a good man. His share will feed his family for six months.'

'And your share?'

'PlayStation,' the boy said, and produced a leather pouch from around his neck. He poked the notes inside and dropped it back beneath his robe.

Reuben stared, half hoped the boy would double-cross.

'Are you well, sir? You look very pale.'

'I'm fine, but I'll be sleeping late tomorrow and don't want to be disturbed.'

The boy bowed, took the parcel and left.

Reuben untied the dressing and pumped his fist over the basin, his arm tingling with pins and needles. He went to the wine and filled his glass, paused to inhale the bouquet and downed half in one gulp. He grabbed the bottle with his failing hand and headed for the balcony, leaving trails of modern art on the marble floor as he went.

The sun burned white over Cairo, but couldn't warm the unnatural chill settling into his bones. A chorus of car horns and ranting natives drifted up from the street below, seemingly oblivious to the view that never failed to take his breath. Jutting from the horizon and the cityscape of unfinished buildings, were the two larger of the three pyramids that formed Orion's belt. He toasted the tombs and collapsed to his knees, dropping the bottle but saving the glass. One last mouthful and that too found the tiles.

Reuben slumped onto his side and waited for the darkness that could not be rushed but always came, wondering how many hours would pass before the dagger was in his hand once more, and the killing started all over again.

CHAPTER 1

Leo brushed aside the gravel concealing the house brick. Beneath the brick was the spare key to the barn. He unlocked the front door, nudged it open with a knuckle and buried the key as before. Palms down on the welcome mat, he stretched his hamstrings. After a ten count he let his head drop, stared upside-down between his legs at the country road he'd left behind. He checked his watch: six miles in forty-two minutes. Not bad. He stood and breathed in a rare moment of tranquillity.

Through the open door, his eyes were drawn across the polished oak floorboards and towards his new rug. Contrasting the immaculate white sat a dog turd the size of his fist.

'You little bitch.'

A familiar red cloud began to stain his Zen-like calm, like blood being poured into a freshly-drawn bath.

'Where are you, Mutley?' he called, and stepped inside.

Mutley wasn't the Bichon's real name, just one Leo used to piss his dad off. But since Daddy was dead, he could start calling her Cotton, her given name – only there was always a chance the old man could hear him from the grave.

The chocolate leather sofa was dog-free, as was the folded blanket by the breakfast bar: Cotton's bed. Only one more place to check.

Leo bounded up the oak staircase to the mezzanine level of the barn, leaving sweaty handprints on the glass balustrade as he went. He pushed open the door to the spare bedroom and dropped to his knees. Even before he lifted the duvet he could hear her growls, but thrust his hands under the bed, anyway.

Cotton bit his hand, but he still managed to grab her by the scruff and pull her out. She hung like a cub, a feral reverberation coming from somewhere deep inside her teddy-bear façade. The thought of rubbing her nose in her own gunk flashed in his mind for a second, followed shortly by the logistics of getting a shit-caked dog upstairs to the bath without her shaking faecal matter over the gallery-white walls. Instead, Leo marched her downstairs at arm's length, trying not to think of the different kinds of infectious bacteria now swimming around in his bloodstream.

He opened the front door, already regretting what he was about to do, but helpless to see sense through the blood cloud fogging his brain. Cotton twisted in the air and landed cat-like before skidding to a stop which was punctuated by a sneeze and shake of her curly coat. He slammed the door behind her.

After dumping the soiled rug into a black sack, Leo went in the kitchen and scrubbed his hands with antibacterial soap, the stink of shit already eating into his pores. He repeated the process three times, dried his hands and took a deep breath. The blood cloud had cleared, leaving only Cotton's little face.

'Christ, you're an arsehole,' Leo told himself. '*I'd* bite me.'

He grabbed a handful of BaconBite dog treats and opened the front door, but the only thing on his drive was the postman, and he was carrying a parcel roughly the same size as a shoebox.

2

Leo put the parcel on the desk by the sofa and read the address. Sure enough, it was for him, but when he saw that the airmail sticker's origin was Egypt, he checked his name again. This time he noticed a rusty-red full stop after his name, and his morbid mind saw blood.

He tore away the brown paper and ran his hands down the sides of the black box, turned it over and around trying to find a marking or a catch that would open it, but it was smooth on every side. He held it to his ear and shook it. Nothing. Maybe it wasn't a box. Maybe it was exactly what it looked like: a solid block of ebony.

The wrapping paper had no return address or any clue as to who might have sent it. It certainly wasn't for him. He didn't know anybody from Egypt, unless his dad had taken a trip out there before he died and the delivery had been delayed somehow. There would still be a note, though, a "Happy 35th, Son! Here's a lump of wood. I hope this makes up for my being a neglectful arsehole all your life." No, it definitely wasn't for him.

Despite its apparent uselessness, it was attractive, seemed to fit in with the minimalism of the barn. And besides, it was a guarantee that if he dumped it, someone would knock on his door asking for their lump of wood back. For now it could be the dining table centrepiece, at least until he could think of somewhere better, or until he got that knock on his door.

He took the block through to the dining area, stood it on its end and stepped back from the table. It put him in mind of Arthur C Clarke's monolith, albeit a miniature version. It made him think of the ape creature that had wielded a bone in that movie and used it to crush the skull of another of its kind.

From there, Leo's mind jumped to a more disturbing memory, where he was just a boy, and the bone was his to wield.

3

He ate scrambled eggs at the breakfast bar, the front door open so Cotton might smell the food and return. The sofa was closer to the front door, and better placed for scenting the outside air with egg, but at the breakfast bar his back faced the *Dr No* movie poster. As long as he didn't look at him, Bond usually kept quiet. Usually.

Cotton still hadn't showed by the time he'd washed and dried his breakfast things to a gleam. He slid the bone-white plate to the bottom of an identical stack of five, so that each plate never went more than a few days without being cleaned, then filled Cotton's bowl with biscuits and leftover egg and placed it on the porch.

'Cotton!' he shouted. 'Come on girl, you can shit anywhere you like.'

She's not coming back, you know.

Leo glanced over his shoulder at the *Dr No* poster, wondering how Connery had managed to keep quiet for this long.

'Stay out of this,' he said. 'She'll be back.'

Sure she will.

'*Dr No*, not *Dr Doolittle*. Stay the fuck out of this.'

You hurt my feelings, Shtamp.

'You're not real. You don't have feelings.'

I shee: it's okay when you *want to talk?* Bond held him with his eternal cocky stare.

Leo shook his head. 'I wish I'd never thought of you.'

You could always try unthinking me.

'Believe me, if I could—' Leo caught movement in the corner of his eye and turned towards the woods opposite the

12

barn. A tall man with blonde hair and a long black coat was staring at him from within the trees.

Although the childish urge to stare right back was strong, the man unnerved Leo, making him crouch and fuss with Cotton's bowl purely to break eye contact. But when he looked up again the man was still staring, so Leo stood tall and headed down the driveway to see what the guy's problem was. At the gate, with only the road and couple of metres of low brush between them, Leo tilted his chin to invite a response. The man remained statuesque.

'Can I help you?' Leo called across the road.

The man turned his head and looked up the road. Leo did the same. A National Express coach came thundering around the bend and whooshed between them, leaving a swirling, grit-filled wind in its wake. Leo pinched his eyes against the grit, but when he opened them again, the man was gone. Leo scanned the woods for movement, studied the road left and right. Nothing.

He walked back up the drive, calling Cotton's name the whole way.

4

Leo slouched at the dining table, his chin resting on the backs of his hands. He'd been staring at the ebony block for more than thirty minutes, but his mind had grown bored and transformed the block into a gravestone. It wasn't long before his thoughts turned to the only book in the barn.

He went into the lounge and stood eye to eye with Bond, slipped a finger round the back of the frame and released a catch. The poster swung out on hidden hinges, revealing a wall safe. He punched in the date *Dr No* was made – 1962 – and the door clicked open. He removed a large, leather-bound book and closed the safe, swung Bond back against the wall.

Put it away, Shtamp.

'I want to look at it.'

You already feel bad about the dog.

Leo sat on the sofa and opened the book. On the first page was a newspaper clipping from 1991 – a headline. It read: SCHOOLBOY MISSING IN MUNDEY.

You've looked. Now put it back.

The clippings on pages two and three were smaller: STAMP BOY STILL MISSING and MUNDEY POLICE FEAR WORST.

Close the goddam book!

'I like to remember.' He turned the page. The headline read: MUNDEY MOURNING. 'Always thought that was clever. Mundey mourning – Monday morning.'

Fantashtic.

'Do you think my dad wished it was me instead of Davey? If I'd been the one molested, had my throat cut and was buried in the woods – think he'd have been happy? Do you think he would have loved me if I was dead?'

Close the fucking book.

The pages kept turning. ANOTHER CHILD MISSING – MUNDEY MOTHER'S PLEA – MERCER BOY FOUND IN SHALLOW GRAVE – SERIAL KILLER IN MUNDEY.

The scrapbook slipped from his lap as he slumped back on the sofa. He stared up, into the vaulted ceiling of the barn, watched dust particles ride the sun beams cutting through the Velux windows.

'Did I ever tell you I knew the Mercer kid?'

Only a hundred times.

'He was thirteen – but young for his age. He used to bring an Action-Man figure to school everyday.' Leo smiled. 'He took shit over that, but it never stopped him bringing it.'

I think you've reminisced enough.

'I caught two kids picking on him in the toilet one break time. They were dangling his Action-Man over the pan.' Leo laughed, his shoulders doing most of the work. 'He had a frogman's outfit on, for fuck's sake. The two kids were telling him he was going toilet diving. Mercer was sobbing, the kids

14

were laughing. I smacked them around a bit and gave Mercer his frogman back.'

You did the right thing – now put the book away.

'That kid followed me around for a week. Come Friday, I'd had enough. I told him to fuck off.' Bond started to blur in front of his eyes. He closed the scrapbook to keep the clippings dry. 'He never made it home that night, and a week later they found his body in some woods not two minutes from his house – his Action-Man buried next to him like the punchline to a sick joke.' Leo doubled over, his face hot and wet in his hands.

You weren't to know.

'That's got nothing to do with it.'

Davey had only been dead two months.

'I didn't care that Davey was dead.'

Yesh you did.

Leo snatched up a sofa cushion and stood. He could feel a different heat burning his face now as his fingers dug into the fabric. 'I liked seeing my dad in so much pain.'

He loved you, Leo, jusht didn't show it.

'No. He loved Davey, and he loved his fucking dogs, but he didn't love me. I'm glad the old bastard is dead – just sorry I wasn't there to see him check out.'

Put the book away now. I'm tired of lishning to your crap. You're not as bad as you think.

'You have no idea what I think.'

So tell me. Let's shtart with you-know-when.

Leo's fingers bit deeper into the cushion. 'Let's not.'

5

In the woods across the road, the tall blonde man edged his way out of the shadows and into the spring sunshine. As he watched the barn, a little white dog emerged from beneath a bush, shook its curls free of debris. The man crouched, gave a short whistle. The dog's ears pricked as it turned.

'Here, Cotton,' the man called softly.

The dog trotted down the gravel driveway, its tail flickering with delight.

6

Leo twisted on the sofa, knew he was dreaming, knew the two bodies on his bed weren't real. He'd walked through this sick play more times than he could count, but knowing how it ended didn't make it any less horrifying. He stood at the foot of his bed, staring at the kitchen knife in his bloodied fist, red up to the elbows, T-shirt plastered to his belly. The bodies were glossed dark – almost black in the half-light – their faces hideous contortions of pain and disbelief. As always at this point, Leo drifted.

The room began to fill with blood. It burst through the window, exploded through cracks in the walls. Geysers erupted from the chests of the bodies, thick and viscous and suffocating, hitting the ceiling like a water canon. He was engulfed, the feeling of drowning euphoric and terrifying at the same time. Before long, the room was no more, consumed by an oil-slick ocean. He couldn't see his hand in front of his face, couldn't tell up from down. Then he breached the surface like a bubble in hot tar and swam through the bituminous gloop to the wooden raft which was always waiting.

A thick mist entombed this place, prevented him from seeing any distance but also hid him from condemning eyes. He drew comfort from the desolation, the isolation. Being alone in here was different to the loneliness of the waking world. He curled up on the raft, let the lapping of the black water rock him and regress him to a childhood memory of his mum and Davey standing on the beach at Shingle Street.

7

The screech of car tyres jolted Leo awake. The scrapbook hit the floor with a slap.

You're shweating. Bad dream?

'Same dream.' Leo picked the scrapbook off the floor and put it back in the safe.

Want to talk about it?

'Not this time.' He walked into the kitchen and pulled a tablecloth from one of the drawers.

Call them. They're shtill alive. It's jusht a bad dream.

Leo draped the tablecloth over Bond. 'I said not this time.'

8

Cotton's food hadn't been touched. Leo's nearest neighbours were four-hundred yards in either direction, a hundred miles away for a dog that never left the house.

'Looks like she's cut off her nose to spite both of our faces, Dad,' he said, and closed the front door.

He remembered how upset his dad had been leaving Cotton behind: a complication with the Spanish airline about quarantine. Leo had made a snide remark about there not being enough room on board for both dogs – meaning Barbara Shields, the bitch his dad had replaced his mother with – but his dad didn't rise to it. He kissed Cotton with tears in his eyes and handed her to Leo, got in his taxi and drove away.

From that day on, Leo and Cotton lived separate lives of mutual disrespect. He refused to walk her, and she refused to shit in the garden. She never chewed the furniture or barked at night, but she never met Leo at the front door with a wagging tail, either. All he wanted was for Cotton to jump into his lap and fall asleep; they had both been abandoned by the same man, after all.

On the desk, a number two flashed on his phone. Leo hit play to hear the first of the messages.

'Hello, love, it's Mummy—'

He stopped the message mid flow. The drunken drawl of Barbara Shields was all too familiar. She'd plagued him on and off for over a year, trying to screw him for money she thought she was owed for nearly marrying his dad. She'd become bitter and abusive since Leo's solicitor sent her a letter stating she wasn't entitled to a penny of Ronald Stamp's estate and that she should be grateful Leo hadn't pushed for the Spanish villa. The calls from Spain became less frequent, but Leo guessed that after a few sangrias there was no stopping the big-mouthed bitch. He deleted the message and waited for the next. It was John.

'Are you avoiding me? If you don't get back to me soon I'm going get myself a new best friend. Call me. We need to drink beer, lots of beer. I've forgotten what you look like. Maybe poker round mine this week; Sadie's out with her folks this Thursday, so let's go for then. P.S. You're a gaylord!'

A grin played on Leo's face, but not for long. Hearing Sadie's name always sent him inwards. He didn't like the way John talked about her, as though he was glad to be getting rid of her. Why get with her in the first place if he wasn't going to worship her for the rest of his life?

He breathed deep, felt the blood cloud dissipate as he pushed away the echo of his nightmare. Things would be simpler if he didn't love her, if he didn't love them both. Hate didn't grow in apathy's garden.

9

The following morning, Leo shaved a whole minute off his time. He didn't set out for speed, just had an angry kick in his step that wasn't there the day before. The Mundey country roads were normally a great place to dump negative energy, but today they clung like barnacles. Finding the untouched tuna in Cotton's bowl didn't help much either.

I sense unrest in that watermelon you call a head.

Leo went into the kitchen and filled a glass from the tap, turned his back on Bond and drank deeply. Twenty-grand's worth of toughened glass made up most of the south-east corner of the barn and looked out onto a grassy hill. His dad used to walk the dogs on that hill with Davey. He never once took Leo.

Well?

'I need a shower.' Leo rinsed and dried his glass, held it up to the window before returning it to the cupboard in the exact position it was before.

Talk to me.

Leo stalled at the foot of the stairs.

Shtamp? What happened on your sixteenth birthday? That's what all this is about, isn't it?

Leo hung his head, debated fetching the tablecloth but found himself replying instead. 'That was the start.'

The start of what? It wasn't jusht your birthday, was it? It was mine too. What happened? What did you do?

Leo got moving, one heavy foot after another.

Don't walk away from me, Shtamp! What did you do?

10

Reuben floated in the vast darkness, the souls of the damned reaching out for him to prolong their inevitable judgement. The ghostly soul of a woman drifted close, her arms stretching for Reuben's face, her mouth dripping open in a whispered scream. Reuben pushed her away, felt her despair run up his arm and scratch at his throat. He recoiled, gagging from the touch, but it passed quickly. He pitied the wretch but couldn't help her even if he wanted to. Judgement could only be avoided by the few: Dark Hearts... and himself, of course.

Souls swam over and under Reuben. Often he thought he would be washed away in their current, and could feel himself being sucked into the undertow. Other times he felt their despair so potently he allowed himself to be taken by the stream, swept along in the torrent of their damnation. He sought the oblivion of darkness and would willingly succumb if oblivion would take him with open arms. Thankfully these impulses were only symptoms of unearthly cabin fever. The hazard of being in a place with a timeline so warped.

It had once taken Reuben as long as six months to re-emerge into the waking world, but had felt like a single beat of a hummingbird's wing. Other times he seemed to float here for an age, only to be spewed onto the earth a day later. Crossing over was fickle that way, especially when only a Dark Heart's body would do.

A silent scream filled Reuben's mind and he shifted in time to brush aside another damned soul. The old man's fingers touched his hand momentarily, but it was enough to fill Reuben's veins with echoes of the old man's sins. Reuben didn't feel sorry for this one.

The old man's time was up, it seemed. He was ripped from the darkness, but not before treating Reuben to a crusty middle finger. Reuben smiled and waved him goodbye, thinking if it weren't for the dagger, he too would be joining the old man in Hell.

CHAPTER 2

There were no photographs on display in the barn – no hand-me-down items of furniture or trinkets of memorabilia – nothing to stir nostalgic daydreams of a past life. Leo knew a family history was something that should be looked back on with a warm heart, but for him, it was something to be locked in a dark room without windows.

Before his dad moved to Spain with the Shields slut, he signed over the barn. He called it a leaving present – a thank you for keeping the business running in his absence. It was a blatant attempt to ease his conscience, but Leo wasn't about to turn down a half-million-pound property, even with the ghosts that came with it.

His first night alone in the barn had been a sleepless one. He wandered from room to room, switching lights on, switching lights off. The dark was scary, the emptiness more so. His dad had shipped most of the furniture over to Spain by then, but still every room was a tormenting reminder of what had been torn from his life.

Davey's room was untouched – a shrine from the day he was killed. His Spiderman duvet smoothed over his bed, his War Hammer soldiers arranged in battle on his desk, a poster of Jean-Claude Van Damme on the wall. Leo could almost smell the sweat from when they used to wrestle, and then his buttocks tingled as he recalled the slap he always got for making Davey cry.

Mum's room made his head ache and his skin clammy. The drab clothes hanging in her wardrobe reminded him of a gallows. Her single bed was stripped clean and looked like an autopsy table. The linen chest in the corner became a coffin. Everything a reminder of her gruesome death.

He couldn't go in his dad's room.

It took four months to eradicate the country home in which he'd grown up, and transform it into the contemporary barn conversion it was now. Leo saved a bottle of his mum's favourite perfume, Davey's Spiderman pillowcase and all the photos he could find that didn't show his dad. He burned the rest.

He kept those precious things in a wicker basket under his bed, but didn't look in it often. The last time was about six months ago. He had taken out a picture of his mum and Davey holding hands on the beach at Shingle Street and pinned it to the fridge with a magnet. After two hours of avoiding the kitchen, he put the photo back in the basket.

2

With Cotton missing, Leo felt more alone than usual and found himself kneeling by his bed. He pulled the basket out, took the photo of his mum and Davey and went downstairs.

What do you think you're going to do with that?

'I'm going to try again,' Leo said, walking around in circles with the photo held out at arm's length. 'Somewhere different this time.'

We both know it'll be back in the basket in under an hour.

Leo went through to the dining area and noticed the ebony block. 'Not this time.' He stood the photograph against the block and returned to the lounge.

The picture isn't the problem.

'Then what is?'

Your dead mother and brother.

He went to the front door and opened it. The dying sun had turned the sky lilac and the belly of the clouds golden. Cotton's bowl was still untouched.

You can't accept that they're dead, and until you do, you'll never be able to think about them without your gut swelling with self-hatred. You don't grieve for them, you grieve for yourself.

'You're talking shit.' Leo slammed the front door, strode into the kitchen and yanked open the tablecloth drawer.

Sure, sure, conversation over.

'Fuck you, I'm going to bed.'

Don't forget your photograph.

Leo paused at the stairs, willed himself to put a foot on the first step but couldn't. He went into the dining area, snatched the photograph from the ebony block and went upstairs without looking back.

Nite, nite, Shtamp.

3

Leo slept clutching his pillow, his tears drying on Spiderman's faded face, lavender perfume in his nostrils. He dreamed of three years ago, the last time he ever saw his mother alive.

She was humming as she packed the last of the corned beef sandwiches into the hamper. She looked different. It wasn't that she wore a yellow summer dress instead of her usual grey cardigan, or that her hair hung free to her shoulders where it was normally pinned close to her head. She was smiling. Not broadly, but subtly in her cheeks. Youthful and beautiful.

23

'You look nice,' Leo said.

'Thank you, darling.'

'Why?'

Her eyebrows crinkled but the smile stayed. She placed a bottle of white wine in the hamper and fastened it with a tartan cord. 'Aren't I allowed to look nice?'

'I just wondered why today.'

'Your father is taking me on a picnic.'

'Well, isn't he the wonderful husband.'

'Don't be like that, Leo.'

'New dress?'

She turned sideways, her hand pressing against a trim stomach. 'Do you like it?'

'It's probably second-hand,' Leo said and cocked his ear to the opening door behind him.

His dad walked in and placed an empty mug in the butler sink 'Cotton's in her bed, and I've shut the dining room door,' he told Leo without making eye contact. 'Don't go in there, even if she barks.'

'What if the house catches fire?' Leo said.

His dad looked at him then, heavy lids half covering cold grey eyes. 'Let's go,' he said, and walked out the back door.

His mother struggled with the hamper before Leo lifted it from the worktop and carried it to the back door.

'I can take it from here,' she said.

He kissed her cheek, her lavender perfume deep in his lungs. 'The dress is beautiful.'

Her smile returned, but not as before, and then his dad blasted the Jag's horn, and she turned and walked away.

In his dream, Leo reached out to her, tried to scream for her to stay, but the kitchen had already filled with the dark water and robbed his lungs of air. He floated in a silent rage, and in the midnight of his mind could still see his mother struggling to the Jag with the hamper. His head throbbed from lack of oxygen, but he was soon on the surface of the black gloop, sucking down air. He scrambled to the raft and heaved himself on board, rolled onto his back and stared up into the mist, dry sobs pulling at his lungs.

4

The Mundey countryside appeared colourless under the inky morning sky. Leo ran up his driveway as the first raindrops kissed his hot skin. He doubled over when he reached the porch, his lungs on fire. Thirty-nine minutes – two minutes faster than yesterday. He grabbed Cotton's bowl and threw it down the driveway – dog biscuits and tuna flakes trailing behind like a comet's tail. He took the key from beneath the brick and let himself in.

He filled a glass at the sink and drank, catching his breath between swallows.

Good run?

Leo didn't look up; he could sense the sarcasm.

I told you the dog wouldn't come back.

'Not in the mood,' he said, and reached for the tablecloth drawer.

Just like your mother. Are you sensing a pattern?

Leo hurled the tablecloth across the breakfast bar. It fell short of Bond. 'Shut your fucking mouth! You don't help me anymore.'

Is that what you want? I thought you enjoyed your self-pity.

'You think I enjoy feeling like this? Help me… Like you used to.'

Bond laughed. *I never used to help. I jusht gave you sympathy.*

'So why don't you anymore?'

Because I'm sick of your whining.

'I can't go on like this.'

Agreed. So what are you going to do about it?

'I don't know.' He offered Bond his palms.

You're not ready for my help.

'Please.'

Bond didn't speak for the longest time. All Leo could hear was the wind combing the trees across the road. It sounded like the ocean.

It's the simplest thing in the world: Forgive yourself.

'It's not that simple.'

Yeah, yeah, your sixteenth birthday. Well if you want my help, stop blocking me out. Tell me what happened.

'You're right,' Leo said, heading for the stairs. 'I'm not ready for your help.'

That's right, Shtamp, bottle it up.

'I need to think for a while.'

Of course you do. It's worked so well for you up to now.

5

There was no thinking to be done in the barn. When the rain stopped, Leo climbed the back fence and hiked up the hill. He reached the peak and turned around. Beyond the barn, he could see a good deal of Mundey: the spire of the town church, the BT tower in the distance, and more woodland than he'd ever noticed driving through its streets. He could see why his dad had moved here from London. He must have thought it was a good place to bring up a family.

Leo filled his lungs and bellowed into the wind. He'd come to the top of the hill to clear his head but only found his thoughts growing darker. He looked down at the barn, tried to pull a good memory out of the murk, and then his eyes turned to the road.

A rusted red Beetle slowed up outside his driveway. It was Sadie's car. A strange anxiety knotted in his chest. Part of him wanted her to turn onto his drive, and another part wanted her to accelerate away. He set off towards her.

Twenty paces down the hill, and she was still idling outside his gate. Leo stopped. What did he plan to do, tap on her window and invite her in for coffee? What the hell was she doing here anyway? She hadn't been to the barn since that fucking night: Ground Zero.

Gears crunched and Sadie drove away, up the country lane towards Mundey. Leo's breathing kick-started again, and he turned for the barn. It was then he noticed the blonde guy step out of the trees and watch Sadie disappear around the bend.

'Hey,' Leo shouted.

The guy turned around, took one look at Leo and fled into the woods. Leo didn't think. He ran after him.

At the bottom of the hill, he slipped on the wet grass, slid into the fence, and cracked his shin on the lower strut. Before the pain could claim his leg, he rolled under the fence and darted across the road. He was through the low brush and in the shadows of the woods in no time, slapping branches out of his face as he gathered speed.

The guy was fast. The tail of his long black coat whipped from side to side as he weaved through the trees and bushes. Leo felt sure-footed on the soft, peaty floor – jumping felled branches and ducking low limbs; he couldn't believe he wasn't catching up. It was all he could do to stay within twenty yards.

A clearing loomed ahead and Leo was sure he could gain ground in a flat-out sprint. The guy hit it first, stood tall and gathered speed. Leo crashed through a holly bush seconds later, scratching his face and hands, but he barely registered the razor cuts. He broke into top speed and began to close distance, then noticed the end of the clearing; it was corralled by fallen trees and dense thicket. By the time the guy figured a way through, Leo would be on him. Whatever was going to happen was going to happen soon.

With nowhere to go, the guy slowed. Leo did the same. In the back of his mind it had something to do with the guy being much taller than him, not to mention wider. Maybe chasing him wasn't such a great idea. Leo stopped.

The guy turned around at the bank of downed trees, didn't seem out of breath in the least.

'Why the fuck…' Leo could hardly talk, 'are you… watching my house?' His lungs burned, lactic acid stung his muscles.

The guy stepped into a shaft of sunlight, turning his blue eyes dark and his blonde hair gold, then eased onto his front foot as though getting set to sprint. But instead of bolting forwards, he shot up through a gap in the canopy, dead leaves and twigs dancing in his wake. Leo's breath caught somewhere between his lungs and his lips as he watched the flapping coattail turn ninety degrees in the sky and disappear in a black streak above the treetops.

A time passed before Leo noticed the birds resume their chatter. Then he started to run.

6

Leo burst through the trees and onto the road in front of his driveway, glimpsed a red car to his right but couldn't stop. The Audi left three feet of burnt rubber on the road; Leo left sweaty handprints on the bonnet. The driver shouted something as he pulled away, but Leo couldn't process it. He headed straight for his double garage, the electric door already opening. It closed behind him with a metallic clang that echoed in the vast, clinical emptiness, with only a wall of aluminium shelving units and an Aston Martin Vanquish to absorb the sound.

Engine oil and Turtle Wax filled his nostrils as he panted. His hands shook as he fumbled his keys from his pocket, shook worse when he thumbed the button on the fob. The lights on the Vanquish winked, and the central locking clicked. He got in.

It took a minute before his heart stopped kicking against his chest – just needed a moment alone to get his shit together. He switched on the overhead light and stared into the rear-view mirror. His eyes looked huge, not his own. He drew closer, blinked several times and dragged his lower lids down to reveal the pink jelly. He didn't know what he was expecting to find. Maybe nothing. Maybe a contagious rash of different coloured spots. He stuck out his tongue. It seemed normal. Had to be his brain.

He banged his head against the headrest. *Dumph, dumph, dumph.* His palms went to his temples, tried to dampen the pounding inside. The last frayed strand holding onto his sanity had just snapped in those woods. He'd seen a man fly into the fucking sky. Normal, healthy people didn't see men fly into the fucking sky.

He left the garage through the side door, shuffled backwards to the barn whilst keeping a suspicious eye on the sky the whole time. He let himself in and threw his jacket at a barstool. It missed and fell to the floor.

'Okay, I'm ready. What do I have to do?' Leo paced, chewing on a knuckle as he did so. Thirty seconds passed, a minute. He stopped and stared at Bond. 'Did you hear me?'

I heard you. Jusht wanted to shee how long it took before you picked your jacket off the floor.

'Fuck the jacket. I need help.'

Finally ready to talk about your sixteenth—

'You're not my therapist.' Leo hung his head, tried not to lose it. 'I don't want to talk about the past. I need you to tell me what to do. Physical things. Actions.'

Deep breathing exercises aren't going to work here.

'You know what I mean.'

Do I?

'You've thought about this, I know you have.'

Maybe I have, maybe I haven't. Maybe you'll come back from your run tomorrow morning and have it all figured out for yourself.

'That won't happen.'

The first part's easy, Shtamp, but you'll have to go deep eventually.

Leo picked his jacket off the floor, shook the creases out and hung it in the cupboard below the stairs, then took a seat on the sofa and looked up at Bond. 'Tell me the first part.'

CHAPTER 3

In one of the dark and dusty corners of Leo's mind, he knew that forgiving John was the way forward; he just needed Bond to shine a light on it, to scatter the tiny spiders of doubt and send them scurrying to other dark and dusty corners. The trouble with forgiving John was that it went hand in hand with giving up Sadie.

Giving her up – what a joke. She'd never been his. But then there was Ground Zero. The sample. The fucking seed which had sprouted malevolent roots like tentacles, seeking out the darkest of places to latch on and feed. It certainly didn't go hungry.

So it was just a kiss? Bond asked.

Leo hunted through the desk drawer for the details of a property he'd been sent a while back. 'More than just a kiss,' he said without looking up. 'It was heroin and cold turkey all rolled into one. It's hard to explain.'

Then show me.

'And how exactly do I do that?'

Let me in. Let me shee, let me feel.

He threw Bond a sideways glance.

I'm in your head already. Open up the memory of that night and let me experience it. I'll know exactly how you feel about Sadie then.

'Are you for real?' Leo straightened.

Bond laughed. *Do you want me to answer that?*

'What if there's stuff in here I'm not ready to show you?' Leo tapped his head.

Then don't show me; it's that simple. Come on, you said you were willing to go deep. This'll be like dipping your toe in a puddle. A good place to shtart, don't you think?

Leo rubbed his chin, sat down on the sofa. 'Now what?'

Now enjoy the ride.

At first Leo didn't feel any different, but then the room began to change. The gallery-white walls brightened, and he could smell fresh paint. Nighttime cloaked the windows, and spot lights reflected in the glass of the balustrade and polished floorboards. Static tingled his ear, then cleared to leave Spandau Ballet's *Gold* reaching into the vaulted ceiling, and somebody was talking to him... 'This place is amazing, Leo.' And Leo heard himself reply... 'Thanks. I'm pleased with how it's turned out.'

The barn was now filled with jolly faces, the smell of beer and roast pork. Mrs Shan, the lady he'd hired for the catering, was in the kitchen carving slices from a suckling pig and serving the queue of people on the other side of the breakfast bar. Every employee of Stamp & Son was here: Plumbers, electricians, bricklayers and painters. Each with five hundred in cash bulging their pockets: bonuses from the sale of the four-bed Georgian in Castle Street.

Leo stood, felt giddy. He had no control over his body, was just here for the ride. He weaved through his guests towards the kitchen with a bottle of Foster's Ice in his hand and a beer buzz in his gut. He felt good. This was no longer a memory; he was actually reliving a year ago, and in the back of his mind, he could feel Bond watching and feeling it with him.

The back door opened and Sadie entered, mouthed *hello* to a few people. Leo raised his beer to get her attention, but she turned when John's hand touched her elbow as he stepped in behind her. Something in the gesture irked Leo, but he didn't know why at the time. John loaded the fridge with his beers, and Sadie spotted Leo and walked over.

'Hiya, handsome.' She kissed his cheek and threw a glance at the buffet. 'You did that on purpose, didn't you?'

'Can never remember if it's Fridays or Saturdays you're a vegetarian.'

'Funny.'

'Besides, you could do with some meat on your bones.'

She nodded. 'I knew you were a tit man.'

Leo smiled. 'There's nothing wrong with your tits. More than a handful's a waste – everyone knows that.'

'Must be some other reason why you've never tried to get me into bed.'

Before Leo could even begin to think of a reply, John walked over, carrying a beer and a large canvas.

'John Kirkman original,' John said, and handed Leo the canvas. 'Housewarming.'

'Thanks, John. I know just where to put it. Bend over.'

'Gonna get me some dead pig,' Sadie announced, and headed for the queue at the breakfast bar.

John shrugged, his face a question mark.

'Your guess is as good as mine,' Leo answered.

'Could be the old girl that died at the nursing home last night. I think Sadie gets attached,' John said.

Leo watched Sadie grab a paper plate and stand in line for the pork, wondered where her "get me into bed" line had sprung from.

'She struggles with meat like I struggle with alcohol,' John said.

Leo could feel his eyebrows knit together as he turned to him. 'Since when did you struggle with alcohol?'

The evening moved on, and Leo became the guy on the wall. Bond was going to make him endure every minute of this memory, it seemed.

John organised a game of spoof, with a sick concoction of raw egg, Tabasco and brandy as the forfeit. Sadie stayed in the huddle of girlfriends and avoided eye contact whenever Leo looked over.

The sixty or so guests began to thin. Leo told Mrs Shan that she could go, remembered thinking he wanted everyone to go, but the younger ones were only getting started. A gruelling hour passed, and the drinking games continued. John shouted over the music for Leo to join in, but it seemed half-hearted. Sadie shouldered her way into the game with her glass held out to be filled. The group roared, and Leo headed for bed, praying that Sadie would grab his arm on the stairs and drag him back to the party, but she never did.

Leo fidgeted under the duvet, replayed the "get me into bed" conversation over in his mind. He came close to grasping it a few times, but the cheers and laughter from downstairs turned it to smoke rings. Then he heard footsteps on the stairs. John must have peaked too early and was about to crash-out in the spare room, but his bedroom door opened, and a female's silhouette appeared in the semidarkness.

'Who's that?' Leo asked, although he knew. The door clicked shut, reducing the music to a muffled din. Sadie knelt by his bed.

Leo went to sit up, but she pushed him back against his pillow.

'If I upset you somehow—' he started, but her whiskey-scented tongue cut him off.

In the then and there, Leo's heart purred with unknown joy. Within that one kiss, he'd visualised a life with Sadie. But in the here and now, his heart was being strangled by very different feelings.

I want to stop now, Leo told Bond. *You've seen enough.*

The kiss ended, and Sadie went to the bedroom door without a word.

'Don't go,' Leo whispered after her.

Don't go, he repeated in the here and now, and then to Bond: *I want to stop now.*

Sadie opened the door and the music flared. Then she was gone.

The very next moment, Leo was surrounded by trees. He was in the woods across the road from the barn, but it was a long time ago. He looked down at his chest, saw a birthday badge pinned to his T-shirt. Despite his embarrassed protests, his mother had insisted he wear it, said that a sixteenth birthday was a biggy, and that she wanted to have her boy for one last day.

Get me out of here now, Leo told Bond. *This isn't what I wanted to show you.*

He saw the hefty branch in his young hands, felt the rage course through his muscles as he wielded it high above his head, wondering if he would be sprayed by the blood.

NOW! he shouted to Bond. *Get me out of here now!*

Leo was sat on his sofa again, back in the here and now. Fingers biting into the leather, and short, sharp breaths escaping through his clenched teeth. 'You fucking arsehole.'

Thought you were ready, Bond said.

'I'll tell you when I'm fucking ready.' Leo went into the kitchen and came back with the tablecloth.

I shee what you mean about the kiss. Why would she do that and then hook up with John?

'She didn't hook up with him. They'd been together for two weeks by then.' Leo tossed the cloth on the sofa, breathed deep and released a sigh. 'John came to the barn the next day and told me. They'd kept it a secret until they were sure it was right.'

I'm sorry for taking advantage like that.

'I said I'm in the whole way, and I meant it. Just need some time before I deal with that one.'

35

2

Leo pulled up outside Jenner's Estate Agency and checked over the details of the property he hoped was still on the market. He wasn't just going to forgive John, he wanted to do him a solid. It was the least he could do for the way he'd snubbed him over the past year, not to mention a few other things he wasn't proud of.

Before they had even met Sadie, John laboured for Stamp & Son to earn his bread, but it wasn't his dream. He was an artist – good or bad, Leo didn't know – but he'd been impassioned enough to take a year out and travel to Italy. John said Rome was the capital of world art, and if he didn't come back transformed by the experience, he had no business holding a paintbrush. Leo hated himself for thinking it, but he hoped John *would* come back uninspired. John's passion made Leo feel insignificant. Leo had no dreams or ambitions. He'd inherited a business he hated, from a father he hated. He was hardly master of his own destiny.

When John returned from Rome, he walked back into his job at Stamp & Son. He told Leo that he'd met a couple of Scandinavian girls in the first week and spent the rest of the year drinking and screwing. The closest he'd come to art was a faded *Mona Lisa* print in his hostel's lobby, and a *Guns N' Roses* tattoo that each of the girls had stamped on the small of their back.

Leo sat outside Jenner's, thinking about why he'd taken such pleasure in John's news that day. He shook his head.

'What an arsehole you've become,' he told himself. 'No wonder you're fucked in the head.' He checked the paperwork one last time and climbed out of the Vanquish.

3

Jenner's was an independent agency that Stamp & Son used from time to time. Before his dad left for Spain, he had told Leo to stick with the smaller firms. They were more susceptible to cash deals and didn't get sniffy when you offered a bribe. Leo took the company business elsewhere the first chance he got. The thought of taking after his dad in any aspect of his life felt like a witch's fingernail tracing down his spine.

The door bleeped as he entered, and Leo noted the lack of enthusiasm his presence roused: it barely raised a head from the three agents manning the front desks.

An attractive woman in a navy pinstripe came out of a door in the back and approached Leo with a smile. With any luck, her name would be Angela.

'Can I help?'

'Angela?' he asked.

She cocked her head, her smile turning crooked with apparent concern.

'I don't know if you remember us,' Leo started, 'but we bought the four-bed Georgian in Castle Street through you… about eighteen months back?'

'I do.' She seemed pleased with herself. 'That one's hard to forget. You didn't give me the resale you promised. It went for just over a million, didn't it?'

'Something like that, I can't remember the actual fig—'

'Very nice job, as I understand. Stamp and Son, isn't it?'

'Yeah, and I apologise if my dad—'

'No need to apologise. We're only talking two percent, after all.'

Leo kept his mouth shut. More to come, he guessed.

'I think it was your first offer of four-ninety that was accepted, wasn't it? Thirty grand under the asking price?' She moved closer. 'That wasn't luck, you know.'

Leo thought he'd squirmed long enough. He didn't know his father as a son should, but he knew how he had done business. 'If memory serves, Angela, I think you did okay financially… on a personal level.'

She straightened, tugged at the hem of her jacket and ushered him to her desk without another word. Leo took the papers from his jacket and sat opposite.

'What can we do for you, Mr Stamp?'

'Leo's fine.' He passed her the papers. 'You sent me the details for this shop a while back. Is it still on the market?'

Her lips moved as she read in silence, then she opened the filing cabinet beside her. 'I'm sure it is. It's been on for quite a while, I think.' She fingered through files. 'Not in this one,' she said. 'I'll check out back.'

She reappeared a minute later with the details. 'I thought your name was Ron for some reason.' Her face was brighter now, and Leo could smell perfume that wasn't there a moment ago.

'That was my dad.'

'Of course, sorry, how is he?'

'He was murdered last year.'

'My god, how tragic,' she said. 'I'm so sorry.'

'Don't be, we weren't close.' There was an awkward silence Leo felt obliged to end. 'Do you think I could take a look at this today?'

She glanced around the office, then back to Leo. 'Look, one hundred and eighty thousand is a bargain for a freehold like this, but if you're thinking of converting it into a residential dwelling, the application's been turned down three times in two years. As far as keeping it as a shop, the location isn't great, and it needs a hell of a lot work. I wouldn't want to waste your time, or my client's.'

'I'm looking to open an art gallery. As long as there's enough room out back to paint and somewhere out front to hang 'em when they're dry, it sounds perfect.'

4

Leo threw the tablecloth over Bond the moment he got back. He wanted to hear himself think for the next few hours.

The shop wasn't perfect, but it would be after he'd put his team on it for a month. He told Angela the deal was as good as done; he just needed to speak with his partner. If all went as planned, he'd make a cash offer in the morning.

He rang John's mobile and he picked up on the first ring.

'Yessir, Boss,' John answered in his Deep South Negro voice. 'I's workin' like a mule, Boss. Yessir.'

Leo hated this voice, hated that he found it funny. John liked to do it in front of the workforce when Leo arrived on-site for the timesheets. John would cower and walk a pace or two behind until Leo grew irritated and kicked him away, exactly what John wanted. "Doan' whip me, Boss. I's workin' haard, yessir". The site would erupt into fits of laughter, even Mick. The voice was so good that Leo wondered if John had been black in another lifetime.

'Are we still on for poker tonight?' Leo asked. 'And answer me in your normal voice, or I'm putting the phone down.'

There was a pause, then: 'Eight o'clock... Bring beer... Boss.'

'Tell Mick I'll pick the timesheets up tomorrow.' Leo grinned despite himself. 'Now get back to work, nigger.'

'Yessir, Boss. Like a muule, yessir.'

5

With the tablecloth folded neatly back in the drawer, Leo stood outside his bedroom door, leant over the glass balustrade. He was deciding where to leave the photograph of Davey and his mother.

You're going to be late.

Only a stud wall separated the main living area from the dining room, but from up here he could see the ground floor as a whole. 'I'm leaving the picture out tonight.'

Do you think that's wise?

'I feel good. Haven't felt this good in a long time.' He glanced at the ebony block. 'Hopefully I'll come in drunk and forget the picture's there.'

And realise in the morning that the world is shtill turning.

'I may even take a trip out to the cemetery tomorrow, leave some flowers for Mum and Davey.'

He went downstairs and stood the photo against the ebony block.

There'll come a time when you won't need me anymore, Shtamp.

Leo didn't answer, just swung his jacket on and headed out the front door.

CHAPTER 4

John rented a grade two listed cottage on the other side of the field to Leo. It had an ancient grey thatch and a white picket fence, but the chocolate box ended there. John was no gardener. He'd left the half-acre plot to govern itself, and now wild grasses and poppies cast the majority vote. It baffled Leo as to why he would move to such a place, until Mick told him that over a hundred years ago it used to be a pub: the beer monster lurking within John must have been drawn to it. At least it wasn't far from the barn. If the cottage was as filthy as the last time he'd been there, he might have to hike across the field to his own bed.

He reversed the Vanquish onto the small muddy drive, grabbed the case of beer from the passenger seat and walked around the side of the cottage. John never used the front door; it opened directly into the lounge and took up too much living space to give it access. The side door was ajar and led into the kitchen. Leo shouldered it open and stepped inside.

'Come in, mate. Just got to finish washing Mr Winky.'

The gate-like door at the end of the passageway banged shut, sending out a plume of steam to dissipate on the low flaky ceiling. Leo set the case on the draining board, cringed at the gunge around the taps, and peered out the small window. Through the crud on the glass, lush countryside rolled on forever, and floating above the green were the blackest of clouds. He took a beer from the fridge and cracked it with the opener that lay on the tea-stained counter, smiled at the four bent caps beside it, then adjusted all of John's bottles so the labels faced out. He ducked under the kitchen doorway and again to step into the lounge.

The cottage looked much the same as the last time he'd been here. Sadie had tried to brighten the place up, but despite the flowers in the window and the candles on the mantel, the room still screamed of old people. The grotty carpet didn't reach the walls, and a concrete floor grinned around the perimeter, lending to the illusion of shrinkage. But shrinkage implied washing of some kind. As far as Leo could tell, it was in the same awful state it had been when John pulled it from the site skip four months ago. Leo could feel the dust mites crawling up his legs just standing on it. Tonight, he would definitely be sleeping at home.

The armchair and two-seat sofa were stacked against the front door, making room for the round table which now dominated the space. Green baize covered the table, and an aluminium case lay open, displaying poker chips and playing cards. Leo sat down and picked up the deck.

The cards felt good in his hands, and the butterflies dancing in his stomach made him feel normal. It was encouraging to feel anything that didn't stem from something negative. He and John hadn't played poker in over a year, hadn't done much together since Ground Zero. He hoped that would change.

John glided past the doorway in a towel and returned a few moments later with a bottle of beer vacuum-sucked to his bottom lip. It gave him a gummy grin that could've looked sinister, but instead made Leo squirt beer out his nose.

Ten minutes later, John sat down with fresh beers for both of them.

'Thanks for sorting the fridge out,' John said. 'You've no idea how much better the beer tastes when all the labels face front.'

'Don't take the piss.'

'There's a name for that, isn't there? Pills you can take?' John grinned.

'Liking things clean and in good order isn't a condition that needs medicating. On the other hand...' Leo screwed his face up and gave the room a once over. 'Are you up to date on your tetanus shots?' He stared at the carpet. 'I feel like I should be wearing wellies.'

'Your condition goes way beyond cleanliness. It even bugs you that I wear my watch upside-down, doesn't it?' John twisted his wrist back and forth to show the reversed strap. 'Can hear your teeth grinding already. It's like nails down a blackboard for you freaks.'

The watch thing did bug Leo, but he smiled and ignored it. 'One big clean, and then it's just ten minutes a day to maintain. I could lend you my lawnmower, too.'

'Thanks, but I pay to sleep here, not work here.' John held out his bottle.

Fifteen minutes in this dirty little cottage, and Leo felt changed; he should've listened to Bond sooner. His heart was lighter, his shoulders loose, a beer buzz fizzed in the back of his head like sherbet. He clinked John's bottle with his own.

'Leo Stamp,' John said. 'Back from the dead.'

2

The blonde man sat cross-legged on top of the hill. He watched the two men toast with the beer bottles, then laid the binoculars in his lap. He checked his watch. Not long now.

He turned his collar up to the gathering darkness, reached into his coat for the Gameboy. A moment later, his face was lit with moving colours, his shoulders swaying as the digital broadsword cut down the first of the lurching zombie horde.

3

Three hours later, all the beer in the fridge had gone. John reloaded with Leo's case.

'That is poor beer management, old boy,' Leo called out. 'I refuse to drink warm lager. My tolerance level for alcohol may have dropped, but my standards have not, and I also raise "all in".' He pushed his entire chip-stack into the centre of the table. 'Fold, pussy.' He licked his fingers and groomed imaginary whiskers. 'Meoow.'

John came back in and checked his cards, pondered a moment before pushing all his chips in. He didn't have many. 'I call and raise—'

Leo quit preening his whiskers. 'You can't raise an "all in". Call or fold.'

'Hush now, my darling.' John squashed a finger to his own lips, hiccupped, and opened a small trunk that was on the floor behind his seat. The trunk wouldn't have looked out of place on a pirate ship, with iron strap hinges and black studding on the curved lid. He lifted something out but kept it hidden under the table. 'I raise this.' He placed a hipflask on the baize.

'Haven't seen that in a long while,' Leo said, and leaned closer. Back in the days when he and John drank regularly in Mundey, this hipflask kept them topped up on the walk home, but that wasn't its primary function. John used to say that when the bars stopped serving, having your own supply of liquor was like walking a puppy through the park, and he was right. They attracted more girls on the way home than they ever did standing at the bar. Leo thought it was genius. 'Full?'

'Of course.'

Leo pondered the hand. He had a pair of kings, and the flop was garbage. Realistically, he was only beaten by aces, but he still had nothing left to call with. Then he remembered the envelope. He stood and pulled it from his back pocket and threw it on the stack of chips. It had *John Kirkman* written on it.

'I call,' Leo said.

'With what?'

'Well, if you can beat these, you can take a look.' Leo turned his cards over.

John stared at the kings. 'Beats me,' he said with a flat smile, and folded his cards to the bottom of the deck.

'Knew you were bluffing.'

'Had to try.' John shrugged and nodded at the flask. 'It's yours.'

'You sure?'

'You won it fair and square.'

Leo took the flask, wondered if John knew how much he'd loved the thing.

'Now what's in the envelope?' He picked it up but Leo snatched it from him.

'You lost.' Leo took the envelope to the mantel and slipped it under one of the candles. He'd tease him for a while before handing it over.

'But it's got my name on it.'

Leo unscrewed the cap on the flask, took a long hit and offered it to John.

'Your prize,' John said, and headed for the kitchen. He came back with two shot glasses and a bottle of Jack Daniels.

Leo slid the flask into his back pocket to test the fit. Felt good.

Thunder rumbled in the distance. John cocked his ear to the sound and set about lighting the fire. When it was good and going, he sat back down, poured two fingers of whiskey into his glass.

'So,' he said. 'You seem like your old self. What's changed? – and don't lay the family tragedy on me.' He gulped his whiskey, held his fist over his mouth and winced. 'I mean, it's fucked up what's happened to you, Leo, but it's got nothing to do with how you've been acting towards me.'

The night sky flashed white in the window. It was going to be a bad one. Leo put the flask on the table and sat down. Was it even worth bullshitting?

'Are you really going to make me say it?' Leo said.

John shook his head and filled both the shot glasses, pushed one over to Leo. 'Not if you don't want to.'

Leo felt acutely sober, aware of himself and his surroundings. Rain smattered the window despite the low thatched eve, the embers of the fire grinned at him between the logs.

'Do you love her?' John asked.

'I did.'

'But you don't now?'

'I love you both.'

'That's not what I mean.'

'Look, it's never going to happen.' Leo downed his whiskey, banged the glass on the table harder than he meant. 'She chose you, and instead of being happy for you both I behaved like a dick for a while.' He grabbed the JD and filled both glasses, handed one to John. 'Come on, I'm trying to make good here.'

John stared at the glass before taking it. Leo chinked them together and drank his in one. John set his down in front of him, rotated it in quarter turns on the baize.

'But it wasn't just *a while*; it was a whole year. That's a long time.'

'I suppose.'

'Nothing is self-sustaining – even the sun will burn itself out eventually – so what stoked your fire for a year? Something you want to tell me?'

'What are you talking about?'

'I didn't see you from one month to the next, and when I did, you acted weird. Just wondered if it was a guilty conscience.'

'Something's gone on between me and Sadie? Is that what you're getting at?'

John shrugged.

'I would never do that. You're like my brother.'

'Brother? Yeah, right – Yessir, Boss.' John saluted.

'Fuck you. I'll tell you what stoked me for a year: I thought she felt the same way.'

'What gave you that idea?'

'You remember the party I laid on for the guys – hog roast, last year?'

'Vaguely.'

'I went to bed early – don't know how long I'd been in bed before Sadie came in. She kissed me.'

John stared past him, seemingly not registering the words at all.

'The next morning you told me that you and Sadie had been at it for two weeks, so technically I did do you wrong, but how the fuck was I supposed to know?'

John raised his hands to his face, knocking over his glass with his elbow. The silent shudders and the soft repetitions of breath were telltale, but Leo didn't sympathise. If John had come clean in the first place about getting with Sadie, none of this would have happened. Why shouldn't he taste a little discomfort? Nothing compared to the psychological broken glass Leo had been walking on this past year.

John sucked in a heaving breath, slapped his hands down on his lap and turned his red face up to the ceiling. 'What a fucking idiot.' He started laughing and shaking his head.

Leo sipped his whiskey and tried to shake off his annoyance at misreading two very different emotions. Didn't much care for the 'fucking idiot' tag, either. The laughter continued. Loud and non-infectious. He straightened John's glass, filled it slow and deliberate, and set it in front of him. John wound it down in stages before reaching for it.

'What's so funny?' Leo asked.

John gulped his whiskey and flicked the empty glass away. It fell on its side and ran round in a circle. He seemed under control again, just the faintest of smiles playing on his flushed face.

'That night she came to you,' John said. 'It was me.'

'I would've noticed the beer gut.'

'I mean, I sent her to you.'

'And why would you do that?'

The light flickered and sent them into momentary darkness. They both watched the bulb brighten again.

'You went to bed didn't you?' John said, his eyes lowering from the naked bulb to Leo's face. 'Well, we all stayed up drinking and messing around, and someone suggested we all play spin the bottle, so we did.'

'You're still not making any sense.'

'After wading through all that silly truth shit, your fat plumber – Steve I think his name was – chose me to kiss his girlfriend. Everyone was paired up with someone, and Sadie didn't seem to mind. She was goading me like everyone else. As the game moved along, the people who'd had action got excluded – fat Steve's rule, because nobody was choosing him. Sadie hadn't been picked yet, and that was just fine with me, but it was going to happen. Anyway, it spun on Sadie, and I could see all their tongues hanging out in anticipation, and it made me feel sick to think of any of those monkeys kissing her, but I'd been playing, so I had no choice but to pick someone, so I sent her upstairs to you. It made perfect sense at the time, but if I'd known what it was going to do… well, fat Steve would have had his turn.' John laughed as he unscrewed the bottle and splashed whiskey in his glass and on the baize in equal measures.

Sobriety hit Leo like a cold axe to the head, the world around him sharp and clear and spiteful.

John was trying to drink between breaths, but his juddering laughter shook most of it down his front. He sucked his

48

whiskied fingers to a soundtrack of sickening slurps, then managed to find his mouth with the elusive shot glass. He drained it. Stared into the bottom of it – a jeweller grading diamonds. 'What a stupid prick you are,' he said.

The blood cloud gathered quickly at that remark. Leo's fist landed with a dull crunch, bursting John's nose like a squib. John covered the mess with his hand, the other one raised out in front of him.

'I didn't mean—' John started to say through bloody teeth, but Leo cut him off with a shove to his face, sending him backwards. Only his legs hitting the underside of the table stopped him from toppling completely.

Leo snatched the bottle of Jack in his blood-smeared palm and headed for the doorway. The thought of using the bottle sparked in his mind for a second but was replaced by a thud from the low doorframe. Blood trickled down his forehead but he didn't grab for it; the pain was at the back of a long queue of emotions and would have to wait its turn. He glanced back at John. He was teetering on the hind legs of the chair, blood pissing from his nose, eyes glassy and wide. Leo left through the kitchen door, slammed it behind him with all the power his contorted muscles could muster. It shuddered half open and stayed that way.

The rain hit his face but didn't cool him, and as he turned for the Vanquish, he heard John lose his battle with balance.

In Leo's haste to get away, he drove off in the wrong direction. He didn't care. Home was the last place he wanted to be. Why rush back to sleep in a bed that had been the stage for the most humiliating night of his life?

He sucked down the last of the Jack Daniels and tossed the empty on the back seat. Blood and tears mixed in his eyes, creating a stinging cocktail that blinded him from the snaking road. Wipers slashed left and right against the torrent, a couple of beats behind his heart rate. The country road was deserted, at least; only the trees leaned in to mock him. He had a near miss on the left, the bushes slapping the side of the Vanquish. His knuckles bleached white against the steering wheel as he fought to hold the centre of the lane. Still he accelerated.

The alcohol was working again, the road appeared in snapshots instead of moving pictures, and the tyres squealed for him to stop, but he ignored them. As the road straightened, he stamped down harder on the accelerator.

He pulled his right hand from the wheel to wipe his eyes; it came free with a tearing sound that warped his stomach. John's blood, he thought, and wanted to puke.

The rubbing made his vision worse; it was hard see anything at all. A few blinks and it was better. He saw something up ahead in the middle of the road. A figure. Leo blasted the horn; he wasn't slowing down. More blood drizzled into his eyes, and he pawed it away. When he looked back at the road, the figure had gone. He eased off the accelerator until he passed where the person had been. Floored it again.

He was thinking how Bond would react to this when the figure reappeared in the middle of the road. The man strode towards him, waving his arms, his long black jacket reflecting the headlamps, making Leo squint. There was no time to brake; the man was only metres away. Leo ripped the steering wheel to his left; the man's golden hair imprinting itself on his retinas as it flashed past the driver's side window.

The Vanquish hit the verge and corkscrewed into the night, rotating Leo's world in slow motion until it struck water on the other side of the hedge. He was instantaneously ejected from his seat and smashed against the upholstered roof of the car. He lost consciousness on impact.

It took twelve and a half minutes for the Vanquish to fill with water. Leo Stamp was dead inside of nine.

CHAPTER 5

Reuben had emerged in some strange places over the centuries, and more than a few times underwater, so the only shock was the cold. He couldn't taste salt, so he wasn't in the sea, and his eardrums told him he wasn't deep, but there was still no cause to linger. He orientated himself in the murk and soon realised where he was.

The car was upside-down, and it took a moment to find the door handle. He felt it unlock on the first pull, planted his feet on the window and pushed. The pressure inside the car had balanced with the outside, and the door opened easily. He grabbed the keys from the ignition and swam out into the dark.

He breached the surface like an alligator: eyes just above the water. Lightning lit the sky, illuminated trees and bushes in every direction. Headlights appeared to his right: a road. He swam to the bank and scrambled out, sat on the edge to let the residue of troubled thoughts pass from the Dark Heart's mind.

At first Reuben thought he'd emerged in the wrong body; he was getting the name Bond from the memories. He panicked for a second but soon found the name he was after. He smiled. Leo Stamp's mind was a wonderful mess. Occasionally the Dark Hearts Reuben used were like this. Schizophrenics. He pitied them in a way.

Reuben closed his eyes, concentrated on the trivial things in Leo Stamp's mind: where he lived, how to access his money. The memories didn't last long, but he gleaned as much as he would need for his stay here in… *Mundey?* The name was familiar to him, but he couldn't think why.

Thunder quaked above, shook him from his thoughts. He glanced over the surface of the lake; it appeared to boil under the heavy downpour. The car wouldn't be found anytime soon, and by then it would be too late, the blood already spilled.

With the keys tight in his fist, Reuben clambered through the hedge and turned left towards his new home. He jogged up the road a hundred yards or so and stopped at a road sign: MUNDEY. At that moment he remembered why he'd recognised the town's name. He'd been here before.

2

Leo drifted in a silent darkness, cradled in a peace he hadn't known since he was a child. As he floated, he felt his mother's arms envelop him, but when he turned to see her beautiful smile, he was met with the screaming face of a young man, which made Leo recoil in horror.

The young man's skin had a jellyfish translucence. Cheeks and jowls trailing loosely behind dead eyes and transparent gums. *Help me,* the young man pleaded, but his lips didn't move. Leo heard the words directly in his head, as though born there. He kicked and flailed, but the young man held tight, fed more thoughts into Leo's head. *I killed the bitch,* Leo heard deep within his mind, and then images rushed in also. The young man was stood by an elderly woman's bed, crimsoned face with spittle on his lips. He was pressing a pillow over the woman's face. She scratched at the murdering hands, writhed feebly. Leo could feel the hate in the young man's heart, the euphoria when the old girl stopped twitching.

Leo kicked out again, freeing himself from the hellish embrace. The young man's skin returned to opaque decay. *I killed my own mother*, the voice planted in Leo's mind. *My own mother.*

The young man reached out one last time, misery weighing heavy on his tattered face, and then he was ripped away, engulfed in the nothingness.

Leo floated in the vacuum of darkness for some time. Weightless. Senseless. Nothing but a mind in the void. And then from nowhere, light began to drip through the black, and soon after, shapes and shades began to form in the distance. Images jostled and whirled into focus, and Leo realised he was now an observer, a witness to a play, of sorts…

The cobblestones were wet from the recent downpour and shared a blurred reflection of the moon which hung above the descending street. Footsteps echoed off the sun-bleached render that lined the narrow street, and in the distance, the thrum of Latin guitar, muffled cheers and laughter.

The silhouette of a man meandered down the cobbles, the straight line eluding him. A low voice drew the man's attention to a shadowy doorway, and then the glint of a blade emerged from the darkness. The man stumbled back against the wall and held out a hand in defence. He grumbled and reached for his back pocket, offered his wallet to the shadows. A scruffy young native stepped into the moonlight and slapped the wallet away, sending it tumbling down the street. He held the man against the wall and pushed the curved blade under his ribcage. The man didn't make a sound.

A light came on in the window above, and Ronald Stamp's face was visible for a moment before he was allowed to fall to the floor. The young native crouched beside him and whispered something too faint to decipher, and then Ron Stamp's chest rose one last time.

The young native closed Ron's eyes with thumb and forefinger, and the light from the window above blinked out also, returning the scene to a shadow puppet show. Clouds drifted over the moon until all light was drained, and Leo could no longer distinguish shapes or shades. The sounds of the guitar and the laughter faded, following the light into the darkness...

Leo reached out to his father, wanted to hold his hand, but the images dissolved, along with the memory of the scene.

The atmosphere around Leo had either changed, or his senses were returning. He was wet. Cold. Panic seized him when he realised he was underwater and needed air. How long had he been without it? His pumping head told him too long. He tried to swim up, but contradicting senses told him he was swimming deeper. Unconsciousness pulled at him – a mercy perhaps, to drift into oblivion. How long did he have left? Twenty seconds? Less? His head throbbed, his heartbeat chimed through his whole body, and then he felt something tugging at his collar.

The next thing he knew was exquisite oxygen exploding into his lungs, burning his throat and setting brain cells ablaze. The sudden rush of air sent him into a dizzying freefall. Leo puked hard.

With his vision blurred, it was difficult to make sense of where he was, but he could feel wood beneath his palms; some sort of jetty, he thought. He blinked, could make out the vomit beneath him, blinked again and caught flashes of the crash and the events leading up to it. John's nose was busted for sure, along with their friendship. And Sadie? Maybe drowning would have been the best thing, all round.

Though fitting, he couldn't stay in this dog's position forever. He lifted a head that felt double its normal size, and for the first time noticed the worn black boots stood in front of him.

'Better out than in, ja, Leo?'

Leo was too weak to look up any further and dropped his head back down to his puke puddle. He retched.

'I think you're all out.'

The floor swayed beneath him. He glanced at the boots again. They had shifted apart and were twisting back and forth on the balls.

'Nein! Nein! So close! I used the ice spell on the Black Queen, but still she will not fall. AAAAGHH!

A man's hand appeared in front of Leo's face. He took it and allowed himself to be pulled up. He felt giddy on his feet and staggered as the deck or jetty swayed. The man's grip tightened and held him steady.

'Easy does it, Leo. It'll pass soon enough. Then you'll just feel dreadful.'

The man seemed familiar, but Leo was still sorting through the broken pieces of his mind and couldn't place him. Freaky tall, though.

'Better, ja?' the man asked, his clean blue eyes probing for a response.

'I think so.'

The man smiled and released Leo's hand.

'Thanks for saving me. I was gone for sure,' Leo said.

'You're a little ways from saved, but I'll do what I can.'

Leo detected an accent but couldn't place it. German would have been his best guess, especially with all that blonde hair.

'What more is there to do? I may feel like shit, but I'm alive, and that's thanks to you.' Leo scanned the surface of the water, expecting to see his Vanquish protruding from somewhere, only then did he notice his surroundings.

A dense fog shrouded the area; anything beyond thirty metres was gone, and although it was dark, it wasn't night. There was a haze behind the fog that suggested sunlight, but he couldn't pinpoint a source. And it was silent; no birds, no rain, no traffic in the distance or wind in the trees, and even though he could see the black water moving, he couldn't hear the plinking and plopping that usually accompanied the images. Then he recognized what was keeping him afloat. Thick, uniform logs of bleached driftwood tied with a handmade twine, exactly how he would imagine a raft to look, how a child might imagine a raft to look. *It can't be*, he thought.

'Where am I? Leo said.

'You don't recognise this place, Leo?'

'What's to recognise?' He scanned for headlights in the mist that would point him in the direction of the road, then caught the oddity in the blonde man's question. 'How do you know my name?'

'Truly, you do not recognise this place?'

'Of course I know where I am,' Leo said.

The blonde guy nodded and tilted his head forwards.

He actually wants me to answer, Leo thought. *What's next, how many fingers am I holding up?*

'I'm in the Suffolk countryside, somewhere on the outskirts of a town called Mundey – on a fucking lake – by the fucking road – and somewhere underneath me is a-hundred-and-twenty-grand's worth of Aston fucking Martin. Now if you don't mind, I need to get home.' Leo chose the side that didn't have a banana skin of puke to slip in and went to step off the raft, but before his centre of gravity made it over the water, he was grabbed from behind and thrown on his back. He struggled, but the blonde guy had him by the scruff of his shirt, pinning him easily. Leo could sense the physical power and stopped struggling. He was still exhausted from the near-fatal drowning.

'There's no need for that kind of language.'

'What?'

'The cussing. Using vulgarities to vent your anger is unnecessary. Emphasising a different word in the sentence works just as well, or try substituting the nasty word for a nice one. How about 'fluffy' or 'fudge'?'

'Okay,' Leo said, still too weak to do any more than lie there. 'Get the fluffy-fudge off me.'

'I can't let you go back in there, Leo. Not without explaining some things first. Hear me, and if you still wish to go back in, I won't stop you.'

The guy's blonde hair shrouded his face in shadow, making it impossible for Leo to read his features. He sounded serious, though. Leo nodded and was hoisted to his feet.

'You say you don't know this place, and yet it's your own creation,' the blonde guy said.

'I appreciate what you did for me, but I need to go home. If you could help me paddle this thing to the edge somehow – I mean, you're actually dry – you surely don't want to jump in with that jacket on. Looks expensive. And it'll ruin your phone.'

'There's no edge to swim to, and I don't own a phone.'

'But I heard you talking to someone while I was puking my guts up.'

'You heard me bellyaching to myself.' He reached into his coat pocket. 'It's this infuriating game.' He waved a Gameboy at Leo. 'Do you want to try? I can't get past level three.'

'I gave up video games when I was a kid. Bit childish, don't you think?'

'Childish?' The blonde guy made a finger-and-thumb gun, aimed at Leo's head with one eye sighting down the two-fingered barrel. 'You mean like idolising a fictional spy, Mish Funnyfanny? That *is* why you're riding around in an Aston Martin, ja?'

Lucky guess, Leo thought.

The blonde guy lowered the gun and smiled. 'Have you read any of his books?'

'Bond?'

'Fleming.'

'Don't read.'

'That's a shame.'

Leo could feel his neck collapsing under the weight of his head. He looked left, then right. He was ready to jump again.

'Don't do it, Leo.'

'How the fuck do you know my name?'

'Close your eyes.'

'I don't want to close my fucking eyes; I just want to go.' Leo started looking around again, he was getting impatient and a little freaked out. 'HELP! CAN ANYBODY HEAR ME?' he bellowed into the fog.

'Leo, trust me. Close your eyes.'

The last thing he wanted to do was close his eyes, but he was tired of this game and wanted to go home. He closed them.

'Now, can you feel where you are?'

'No.' Leo sighed.

'It frightens you, this place, and yet at the same time comforts you, ja?'

Leo shook his head.

'You wish you could leave this place, and yet you dare not.'

Leo didn't want to admit it, but he did recognise this place; he had dreamt of it many times. It was *his* place, *his* raft, but that still didn't make it real. He opened his eyes. 'Can I go now?'

The blonde man pointed at him, a smirk on his tilted face. 'Ja, you recognised it.'

'This is bullshit – no – this is a dream.' *That's it*, Leo thought. *That's how he knows my name. That's how he knows about Bond. But it seems so real.*

'You know this isn't a dream, and you know this isn't the lake you crashed into.'

'If it isn't a dream, it has to be the lake. I'm just disorientated by the mist. Concussed or something.'

'Then how do you explain your clothes?'

'My clothes?'

'You're dry, Leo. Clean. Is that by accident or subconscious design?'

'I don't know what you mean.' Leo gazed out over the black water, looked at his hands. They were clean and dry, just like his clothes. Always the same in this place, but never as lucid.

'The thing is, Leo…'

'Don't say it.'

'You're dead.'

Leo shook his head, fever-sweat prickling his skin. 'I remember hitting the water, and the next thing you're pulling me up. I can't be dead. You saved me.'

'As I said before, you're not beyond salvation, but the life you had is gone.'

A word echoed in Leo's head, but he didn't dare repeat it out loud. 'Is this…?'

'Hell?' The blonde guy smiled. 'Nein. A Way Station. All Dark Hearts have them.'

'What the fuck's a Dark Heart?'

The blonde guy winced at the F-word.

'What's a Dark Heart?'

'Neither good nor bad, yet both. You're unworthy of Heaven and undeserving of Hell. So when you die, you come here, to a Way Station.'

'So this is Purgatory?'

'Nein. Purgatory is the world as you know it. Each of us walks a path through life – some go up, some go down, some just wander round and round.' He smiled again.

'But I haven't done anything wrong. I shouldn't be here.'

'I don't make the rules, Leo, but you must have done something.'

'But I didn't do it.'

'Do what? – Don't answer that,' he said, waving his hands. 'It's none of my business. Why did you think this was Hell?'

Leo felt his legs weaken and the giddiness return. He squatted on his haunches, one hand on the deck for balance. 'So what now?' he said, cuffing the fever-sweat from his forehead.

'Now you go back, but not how you think. You'll be reborn… literally. As an infant, you'll have no knowledge of your previous life, no knowledge of this. You'll have the chance to choose a different path.'

'Why can't I have my old body back?'

The blonde guy threw up his hands and mocked a scream. 'Just once I want to get through this process without someone asking that blasted question.'

'It's a fair question,' Leo said, and stood up. 'I was getting on top of things before I crashed, and I know I can make it up to John and Sadie. Just give me the chance.'

'Reuben,' the blonde guy said.

'Reuben?'

'Reuben is the name of the spirit who now has your body. That is why you cannot go back.'

'Can't you get Reuben out? Stick him in a fucking baby.' He watched the blonde guy roll his eyes at the F-word but ignored it. Leo was finding his feet; this was far from over.

'Believe me, if it were possible, it would be done. Reuben's too cunning to be lured out of a body once he has control of it. He'll only leave when he's good and ready, and he's never good.'

'There must be another way. I can't go back as a baby. I have money, a lot of money, and it could be put to good use.'

'It's Reuben's money now. Whomever you returned as, it would always be Reuben's money.'

'So it *is* possible? There *are* other ways?' Leo stepped closer, tried to press his advantage. 'Who are you anyway?'

'My name's Michael, and I'm *supposed* to aid your passing.' His shoulders slumped, and he began muttering under his breath. Leo couldn't hear much, but got the impression he was berating himself.

'Michael?'

He turned to Leo, a look of frustration on his face. 'Ja?'

'What are the other ways?'

Michael shook his head, started muttering again as he stared off into the mist.

'Michael?'

'Only one way,' Michael said a little sulkily. 'Much the same as Reuben, you wait for a body to pass over. If the time is right, you can take control. But there is no way of knowing where or whom; I can only help you with when.'

'Better than the baby option you gave me.'

'I'm not sure that I'm giving you this option.'

'Why wouldn't you?'

'Let's say I help you, and you return with full knowledge of who you are, what's stopping you continuing along the path you seem to have chosen for yourself? What if you return and find yourself in the body of a beggar, or perhaps an old woman, or someone who's physically or mentally handicapped? In your own life, you were blessed with health and wealth, and yet you still grew bitter and resentful and even violent towards the ones who loved you. I can't see you being dealt such a hand and viewing it as the blessed second chance it would be. I'd be doing you a disservice to give you such an option.'

'No you wouldn't, I promise you I—'

'Nein, Leo, I have made my decision. It's time for you to return.' Michael moved forwards.

'Wait, please, just listen to me.' Leo held up his hands and was surprised to see him halt. 'I understand your reasons for sending Dark Hearts back as babies, but what about the ones who'd have bettered themselves without your intervention? Wouldn't they be truly deserving of Heaven then, rather than being steered like sheep?'

Michael looked away, obviously giving Leo's words some thought, but returned with a blank expression that didn't encourage.

'I've thought of that many times,' he said, 'but by the same token, if I were to send you back with full consciousness, knowing what you now know, wouldn't you be choosing the right path out of fear of damnation? How would this be any different?'

Leo opened his mouth, found he had nothing to say. The strength in his legs seemed to ebb, and the giddiness rushed him from behind. He dropped to his knees at the edge of the raft, cupped the gloopy black water and watched it bead and roll from his skin like raindrops off a lotus leaf.

Why did you have to mock me, John? Leo thought, and then Michael's hands were on his shoulders, and he wilted to the touch. 'But I can turn it around.'

'Do you honestly believe you can find the right path?' Michael whispered.

Leo bowed his head and nodded, prayed for it to be a dream.

'Stay away from Reuben.'

Michael's foreign tone buzzed in Leo's ear as he shot forwards from the push. He struck the water face-first, and in that moment he remembered were he'd seen Michael before. Then he was gone.

CHAPTER 6

Reuben closed the front door on the storm. It felt good to be out of the rain, although he preferred it to the heat he was used to. Perhaps later if the weather was still to his liking, he would wander the garden with some wine, if he could find some, and gather his thoughts. But first things first.

He threw his keys on the desk and switched on the lamp, looked about the room for that spark of recognition in the Dark Heart's memory – something associated with the ebony box. Nothing came immediately, but it always came.

Reuben never used to get down to business so quickly – the novelty of being in another's body held little fascination anymore. No longer did he stand hypnotised in front of mirrors and glass, studying his new host's features like a child seeing fire for the very first time. The body was just a vessel for the soul, a fragile sack of blood and bones.

He saw flashes of the box in the Dark Heart's mind. It was close. Reuben stood facing a vibrant modern painting which hung on the partitioning wall dividing the living area and the... the... dining room? Yes, the dining room. He walked around the wall and discovered a large wooden table, and in the centre of the table was the ebony box. Propped against it was a photograph of a woman and a child. Reuben held the picture and was suddenly struck numb with the Dark Heart's turbulent emotions. This Dark Heart was a real mess, he thought, and laid the photograph facedown on the table.

In the living area, Reuben sat on the sofa with the box on his soggy lap. Apart from some new travel scars, it looked the same as ever: no markings, no decorations or symbols, but when he ran his hand over the top, a configuration of nubs and buttons emerged from its surface. His fingers danced over the protrusions, causing a seam of yellow light to dissect the box, giving a top and bottom to what was once solid. He lifted the lid.

The dagger's handle was made of bone; to be more precise, it *was* a bone. A doctor would identify it as the right humerus of an adult human male, at least half of it. Only the 'distal end' remained, forming the handle. The other end, what would have been the 'proximal end', was now a vicious looking blade which curved like an Arabian Jambiya. There was no distinct join between bone and metal; they bled into one another like some freak creation of an insane vivisection experiment. The bone felt as familiar in these new hands as it always did: unholy. Reuben dug the tip into his palm and twisted. The pain was delicious.

2

The crushing pain in the back of Leo's skull eclipsed all other senses. He tried to sit up, but his hair was stuck to the carpet with what he assumed was dried blood, if the throbbing was anything to go by. He lay still for a moment, let the invisible world slow its spin on the other side of his eyelids. Had he been sick?

When he opened his eyes, it was dark, apart from the odd lightning burst in the window opposite, and the fading embers of a fire to his left. The sound of the storm was a surprising comfort. He concentrated on the pitter-patter of raindrops committing hari-kari against the windowpane, tried not to hear the Velcro tear of his head peeling from the carpet.

Another flash from outside momentarily silvered his surroundings. He gasped, then laughed at himself. He was in John's cottage, so he'd dreamt the fight, the crash, and the trip to 'his place'.

He clambered to his knees and then to his feet with the aid of a toppled chair lying next to him. He righted the chair and slid onto it, felt the back of his head. There was no pain at all now, only dry tufts of matted hair. He groped further to find the cut but there was nothing at all. Not even a lump.

Perhaps it wasn't blood. Perhaps it was Balti, only he couldn't remember ordering takeout. And then hoped he hadn't. The thought of lying unconscious in curry was less appealing than the thought of lying in his own blood. And hats off to John; at least he'd managed to crawl into bed.

As bed entered his mind, so did a multitude of other thoughts, confusing thoughts. He was thinking – no, remembering – being with Sadie, having sex with her. It was absurd, but the image was in his head, nonetheless. He was lying on a bed in a room he didn't recognise. Sadie was riding him, and he was kneading her breasts, sweat glossing her hot skin. This couldn't be a memory; he'd never seen Sadie naked, let alone had sex with her. As she rode him, his eyes wandered past her head and to the Africa-shaped stain on the ceiling. Where the fuck was this? Then the image changed, and he was looking at himself across the poker table, a confusion of emotions running through his head and heart: Love, betrayal, disappointment and... jealousy. Jealousy? How could he be jealous of himself?

The strange thoughts began to fade – not forgotten – but discarded, abandoned as useless. His conscious rationale drifted to the surface once more, picking the fruit from reality and the here and now.

If it's not Balti, and it's not blood, then he'd been lying in his own sick, or worse: John's. He did feel remarkably clear headed, and it wouldn't be the first time a good puke had spared him a hangover. Leo had a vague flashback of being sick on all fours. It had to be puke, and if he didn't wash it off soon there would be an encore. He could already feel his gag reflex limbering up in the wings from lying on that disgusting carpet.

He went to the light switch, but the electric was out. The lightning must have blown something. The shower room had a battery-operated light above the basin, he was sure. He stepped into the dark hallway, forgetting to duck under the doorframe, but this time only grazing the top of his head. He felt his way along the hall and lifted the latch on the toilet door, eased it open in case John was on the loo, or more likely, on the floor, but it was empty.

The small space had just enough room for the shower, toilet and hand basin, and the carpet had the faint aroma of piss. Leo stood in front of the basin, groped for the pull cord and found it.

The brutal glare blinded at first, and a mixture of panic, fear and confusion threw him backwards onto the toilet seat. A neon negative of John's bloody face was repeating itself over and over beneath his eyelids, as if he'd been tricked into staring at the sun. He tried to open his eyes but couldn't, didn't need to. His hands told him what he had feared the moment he regained consciousness: that it had been no dream or alcohol induced delusion, that Michael had been as real as his own death.

Leo pawed at a beer gut, then clawed at one. He ripped open his lurid shirt, sending buttons flying, and pounded the fatty mound beneath with John Kirkman's fists. The horror of the situation frenzied Leo. The pure dizzying terror shook him. The toilet seat broke and spilled him to the damp carpet, where he writhed to escape the skin in which he was trapped. The sound of his screams made it worse, as they didn't sound his own.

Eventually he tired. The screams became sobs and his limbs became still. Through the shower room door, he could see down the hall to the kitchen, to where the door he'd slammed earlier hung open. He pinched his eyes to the pain taking hold of his chest, to the ache of emptiness and loss. The feeling conjured memories of his mother and Davey, and the pressure in his chest multiplied, and he thought his heart would stop beating. He prayed it would.

Cool air drifted along the hall and stroked his new face, soothed him momentarily before repulsion slipped over him like snakes. How dare he take comfort from anything in this world. He was evil, had known it forever, and now he'd murdered his best friend. He lay on the moist carpet, the taunting aroma of piss in his nostrils, and wished he could change places with Davey. If Leo had been murdered when he was a boy, he couldn't have grown into this beast. He would have died pure. He would have gone to Heaven. Now only one place awaited him, and his wicked soul deserved it.

Somehow he got to his feet and made his way to the kitchen. His arms and legs ached painfully but otherwise felt natural. There was no awkward phase of getting used to John's body, not in the physical sense. Mentally he was all over the place, a newborn foal. But though his mind wobbled, he never lost sight of the one clear thought in all the carnage.

Leo hunted through the kitchen drawers, could only find one knife that wasn't for spreading butter. He tested the blade on the worktop. It wasn't sharp, but it would have to do. The thought of slitting his wrists calmed him and chilled him at the same time. This was it; the slate would be clean once and for all. If Hell was his destination, so be it. He couldn't bear himself any longer.

Through the hall window, Leo noticed the rain had moved on, and the orange glow below the horizon spoke the promise of sun. How cruel, he thought, that the sun should rise at this moment. The whole universe was celebrating his imminent departure.

He rattled open the grimy cubicle door and turned the shower on, adjusted the temperature to a tolerable heat. It wasn't quite how they did it in the movies – no roll-top bath, steaming and full – but at least the water would wash away the blood, and spare John the indignity of a gory discovery.

Leo closed the toilet door.

3

The sun was just breaking free of the horizon when Sadie entered the kitchen. She heard the shower running and saw steam rising up from under the door. She quietly lowered her bag to the floor and stepped into the lounge.

The poker table was still out, and so the armchair was perched on top of the sofa to make room. She searched under cushions, delved her hands down the sides and back of as much sofa as she could reach around the upturned armchair, but only felt crumbs and coins and something gummy she guessed had fallen from the top of a pizza. John's trunk had the usual stuff inside, but not what she was looking for. She padded along the hallway and slipped into John's bedroom, huffed at the mess as she checked the bedside cabinets, the wardrobe, under the bed. Maybe she hadn't left it here, after all.

Steam billowed from the shower room when she cracked the door and stuck her head inside.

'John, the front door's wide open.'

No reply.

'John?' she sang again, opening the door fully. A frosted silhouette sat on the floor of the shower tray. 'I hope you haven't pissed yourself again. It was funny the first time, but…'

She rattled open the cubicle door.

4

As the door opened, Leo dropped the knife.

'I couldn't do it,' he sobbed. 'I tried, but it wasn't sharp enough, look.' He held out his wrists, showed her the bloodless scratch marks. 'I have to go back to the Way Station. I don't want this. I shouldn't be here.'

Sadie killed the shower and knelt down in front of him, her cheeks rosy from the steam. She reached for his face, but he recoiled. Her compassion would be unbearable. If she knew the things he'd done, the things he'd imagined doing to her and John, she would grab the knife and kill him herself.

'You've read it, haven't you?' she said.

Leo stared at her, his brain limping along. He didn't know what she was talking about.

'They're only words,' she said. 'They don't mean anything. Sometimes you have to get them out there to see how ridiculous they sound.' She held his face in both hands. Made him look at her. 'We're fine, and we're going to get through this together. We'll burn it together. Do you hear me, John?'

The sound of John's name brought him round to a degree. She didn't see Leo, she saw John.

'Did you hear me, John? We'll burn it, okay? Where is it?'

'Where's what?' Leo answered reflexively, his brain still sludge.

She let go of his face and wiped her own. She was sweating. 'What do you think I'm talking about?' she asked.

He didn't have a clue what she was talking about. Didn't care. Pills and booze, he thought. Satisfy her that everything's okay and get her out. Later, when she's gone, do the job right.

'My artwork?' he said. It sounded ridiculous in his ears, but it was the only John-related topic he could think of.

'You haven't worked on a piece in over a year.'

It was physically painful, but he tried to focus on the situation and not on his dead friend. He gathered himself, and then: 'I know. I spoke to Leo last night, and he said I was wasting my life, and I thought about it and he's right. Then I got pissed and we had a fight. I ended up in here with a blunt knife. I wasn't serious. Just being melodramatic.'

She wrapped her arms around him, kissed his cheeks. 'You silly sod,' she said. 'Come on, out of these wet clothes.' She grabbed a towel from behind the door and threw it over his head. She rubbed vigorously with one hand and undid what was left of his shirt with the other.

She walked him to the bedroom and towelled his chest dry, unbuckled his belt and tugged his jeans down, started drying the backs of his legs. Leo only realised he was hard when Sadie took him into her mouth and pushed him back onto the bed without missing a stroke.

He almost gave into the pleasure; he'd dreamed of moments like this, but as he lay on the bed he noticed the Africa-shaped stain on the ceiling and knew it was all wrong. He pushed her off and wrapped the towel around his waist.

'I can't do this,' he said.

'Mr Winky looked like he was up to it.'

'I've got the mother of all hangovers, and I haven't slept all night.' He took her hand and helped her up. 'Mr Winky's got jetlag.'

Sadie shook her head and smiled. 'Get into bed. I've got Paracetamol in my bag.'

Ten minutes later, Sadie planted a kiss on his forehead and told him she would see him tomorrow night. Leo rolled over and buried his face in John's smelly pillow, stifled a sob. He wouldn't be seeing her again.

When he heard the kitchen door close, he expected the tears to come, but he was too weary even for that. He would sleep as long as he needed in these filthy sheets and then get the job done. Every minute he breathed air was an insult to John.

The theme from the *Rockford Files* eased Leo out of his sleep, but the sight of the Africa-shaped stain brought him to fully awake at a staggering velocity. He wrapped a towel around his extended midriff and followed the ringtone.

The phone was on the poker table but he didn't get to it in time. He picked it up and it buzzed in his hand. A text message from Sadie: R U OK? He replied: Fine. C U 2Nite.

He put the phone down next to the deck of cards, his kings still face up on the baize. John had folded his hand at the cost of his hipflask, which lay on its side next to the stack of chips. Leo flipped the deck over and fanned the two bottom cards. They were aces.

For some reason John had wanted him to have the flask. Why else throw away the winning hand? Leo didn't think it possible to feel any worse, and was suddenly awed by the human capacity for misery.

After showering, he found something a little less 'John' to wear and spent an hour in front of the mirror exploring his face. He couldn't believe how natural it felt, and yet, how totally different. He had a tooth ache – mild, but there. His eyesight was sharper. The big toe on his right foot stung were the nail had been taken back too far. His hands were rough from labour, and there was an occasional twinge in his lower back. But most noticeably, John was unfit. His breathing was raspy, something Leo had never noticed before, and he suffered from a general, overall feeling of unwell.

The search for drugs was fruitless. He found a new box of Piriteze allergy tablets and a half-empty bottle of Glycerine lemon and honey cough syrup. Likewise, the hunt for booze was dismal. Only beer left in the fridge, and something stronger was traditional in the movies. It looked like his last few hours on the right side of dead would be spent shopping, if only he could find John's money.

Forty minutes of ransacking the cottage, and all Leo found were three soggy tenners in John's jeans. What the hell had John been living on? Where were the bankbooks and credit cards? While the ten pound notes dried out in the oven, Leo formulated a plan. He doubted he could buy enough drugs over the counter anyway, so he would have to cross shoplifting off his 'things to do before I die' list.

CHAPTER 7

Schofield's Newsagents was a throwback from the seventies and run by Old Man Schofield, who was a throwback from the fifties. Davey had a paper round there for a while but had got the sack for swiping chewing gum. Davey denied it, and Leo backed him up, told his dad that Davey hadn't liked chewing gum ever since he'd convinced Davey it would curl around his heart and kill him if he swallowed it. His dad believed Davey about the stealing but smacked Leo for scaring his brother. Leo thought Old Man Schofield owed him one on that score.

The doorbell tinkled as Leo entered, and an old woman pushed him out of the way to leave. The bell tinkled again when the door closed, leaving him alone in the tiny shop.

He approached the counter, studied the display shelf of cigarettes and cigars, and below them, the two rows of headache tablets. He could hear Old Man Schofield through the beaded curtain that led out back, could hear grunting, boxes shifting, and a ripping fart go unexcused: Leo's cue to move. He checked the front door to make sure nobody was coming in, stepped around the side of the counter and took two deep handfuls: Codis in one, Nurofen in the other. He jammed them inside his jacket and padded to the door, stealing a packet of chewing gum for Davey along the way. The bell tinkled as he left, and he heard Old Man Schofield inform an empty shop that he wouldn't be long.

2

The walk into Mundey and back took an hour and a half, and Leo now had blisters on his feet to add to his other ailments. John's lungs didn't much care for the journey either, and wheezed all the way home.

Leo removed two bottles of vodka from the carrier bag and placed them on the poker table, unzipped his jacket and spilled the drugs onto the baize. He'd managed to grab sixteen boxes of tablets in all, but once he'd emptied the pills into a breakfast bowl they didn't look nearly enough, even with the top-up of John's antihistamines. He was also parched, and could think of nothing he wanted less than alcohol. But then he noticed the blackened stain on the carpet where John had bled-out, and it quickly put his own discomfort into perspective.

He unscrewed one of the vodkas and took a deep hit, then another. He wanted to be half-cut before starting on the pills, and also wanted to die in a tidy room. He put the poker chips and baize in the trunk and folded the table away, took the armchair down from the sofa and placed it in front of the TV set.

Bond should be here, Leo thought, as he sat on the musty sofa, strangling the neck of the vodka bottle. *Bond should at least know I'm going. I could tell him everything now, make him understand.* Leo reached for the bowl of pills on the cushion beside him and tweezed one out, crunched it like a Dorito and chased it down with Russia's finest. He thumbed the TV remote and the old set crackled with static. Misery loved company.

A feeling of detachment took over as he watched the six o'clock news with no interest, and the first patters of rain lifted to the window on a gust. Somewhere out there a spirit called Reuben was walking around in *his* body, and Leo didn't give a fluffy-fuck. He dropped a pill and washed it back.

He stirred the pills with a finger, knew it was time to get on with it. He grabbed a handful and dropped them into his mouth, chased them with vodka before the bitter chalk could trigger his gag reflex. He had another fistful poised over his mouth like beer nuts when he heard Michael's German accent fill the room.

'What are you doing, Leo?'

Leo dropped the pills back into the bowl and snapped his head towards the lounge doorway, a mixture of fear and embarrassment burning his face. He expected to see Michael bearing down on him, but he was nowhere to be seen.

'Can you not hear me, Leo?'

'Clear as a soap bubble,' Leo said, and switched off the TV. 'Are you speaking from the *other side*?'

'You didn't answer my question. What are you doing?'

'I should've listened to you. Just leave me be.' He took a violent gulp of vodka, his knuckles white around the neck of the bottle.

'Let me in,' Michael said.

'What, take over my body so I can't harm myself? I've made up my mind; you can't stop me.' He could feel himself slurring, his words like butter in the sun.

'Please let me in, Leo.'

'Why should I?'

'Because I am getting wet.'

'Getting wet?' Leo muttered, wondering from what strange realm he was being contacted. Then there was a knock at the front door. He went to the window but couldn't

75

see anyone. Another knock, and he noticed the letterbox. He ducked down and saw Michael's blue eyes peering at him. A strange realm indeed.

'You'll have to come round the side, we don't use the front,' Leo said, the word 'we' playing in his head a second time.

The letterbox snapped shut.

Leo fell into the sofa, flipping the bowl of pills. Tablets disappeared down the sides of the cushions and onto the floor. He tried to stop them, but his reactions were ghosting his intensions.

Michael ducked into the lounge, took the armchair and gestured for the vodka. Leo passed it and was surprised to see him take a swig, even more surprised when the bottle came back. They both sat watching the dead TV, Leo feeling as though the silence would kill him before the pills.

'You practically beg me for a second chance at life,' Michael said, 'and this is how you repay my generosity?'

'If by generosity you mean trapping me in the body of my dead best friend, then fuck you very much.'

Michael faced him. 'I had no control over whom you would enter, only when.'

'So you're telling me you had no idea I'd end up here?' Leo banged the vodka bottle into his chest, dousing his shirt. 'And don't think I don't remember you watching my house – flying into the fucking sky.' More vodka sloshed from the bottle as he threw his hand into the air.

'You forget I'm only supposed to guide you. I've already exceeded my duties by giving you this choice in the first instance. It puzzles me also that you have journeyed to your friend.'

'I killed him. I fucking killed him.' He took a vicious swig and his stomach twisted. From the pills maybe.

'Language, Leo.'

Leo rolled his eyes and gulped more vodka.

'You could not have killed him.'

'Have you seen the blood over there?' Leo pointed.

'If you meant to kill John, you would not have been met by me.'

Leo stood, presented himself arms wide. 'Well he's fucking dead, and he didn't kill himself, so what does it matter if I meant it or not? Maybe this is Hell, my sick punishment. Poetic, don't you think? Every time I look in the mirror, I'll see *his* face.'

'Murder guarantees no man passage into The Pit.'

'If killing a man doesn't get you into Hell, what the fuck does?'

Michael dipped his eyelids on 'fuck'. 'The act of murder, in itself, is not significant. It's a common misconception.'

'Get to the point. I don't feel great.'

'Consider this: A police officer shoots a suicide bomber on a train – saves hundreds of lives – still murder, ja? Lawful or otherwise.'

Leo blinked a yes.

'Same scenario: The officer misses. The bomber triggers the device, killing himself and many innocent bystanders. Murder, ja?'

Leo blinked again. Swayed.

'How can the two murderers by judged in the same way? The answer is that they cannot.' Michael leaned back in his chair, steepled his fingers. 'At that moment, The Lord judges the man's heart. If He finds it black within, then the fiery Pit for him. If the heart is pure and white, He guides the soul up to the light. But if He finds the heart is dark, again the soul must walk the path. '

'Doesn't even rhyme.'

'Did you wish him dead?'

'Course I didn't wish him dead. He hurt me; just wanted to hurt him back. Fucking lashed out without finking again.' Leo's head swam.

'At the Way Station, I believed you could change your course. I still believe it. Look at yourself. You don't have murder in your heart.'

'Wouldn't be so sure.' Leo fell onto the sofa, brought the bottle to his quivering lips. 'Surprise myself capable of... ' he slurred. The bottle slipped from his fingers and Michael caught it with spooky speed and stood it on the mantel.

'You can hardly speak, let alone think.' He hoisted Leo up and tucked his head beneath his arm. 'We both need time to think on this one.' He walked Leo through the door and along the hall to the shower room.

'D'you fink I'm evil?' Leo asked. His whole face felt post-dentist.

'Nein. Why would I think you are evil?'

'Sumfin' someone told me once, when I's a kid.'

'Children are very impressionable.' Michael kicked open the shower room door.

Leo looked under his arm, tried to focus on Michael, or was it Malcolm? He was losing track. 'You are a very handsome man, Malcolm.'

'Why thank you, Leo.'

The next thing Leo knew, his head was being lowered to the toilet, and Malcolm or Michael's fingers were in his throat.

CHAPTER 8

A year after Davey was murdered, Leo's dad grew a second shadow. His name was Simian, and he was the one who gave Leo the idea he might be evil.

Simian had only been on the scene for three months, but they were long months. He would mostly arrive late, after the pub closed, come guffawing through the front door ahead of Leo's dad, who liked to piss against the house instead of walking the ten feet to the toilet. They would then disappear into the study, smoke cigars, drink Courvoisier, and whisper. Leo didn't know what he hated most: the foul cigar smoke drifting through his bedroom floorboards or the whispering.

Simian's last visit had been on Leo's sixteenth birthday, the only time they had ever spoken. But that conversation played in Leo's head often. Even now, as he lay on John's stinking sheets, a plough gouging ruts in his head, Simian's words echoed again: *You'll go to Hell for that, Leo. Even little boys go to Hell.*

'Who's Simian?'

Leo cracked open an eye. Michael was sitting cross-legged on the bedroom floor, battling his muted Gameboy.

'Simian?' Leo croaked, his throat raw. 'You know Simian?'

Michael shook his head but didn't look up from the screen. 'You said the name a few times in your sleep.'

'He's nobody.' Leo sat up, squinted at the digital clock.

'You've been sleeping for ten hours.'

'And you stayed?'

Michael looked up from his game. 'Couldn't have you trying to kill yourself again.'

'You can't babysit me forever.'

'I don't intend to. If a man wishes to kill himself, he'll find a way.' Michael stood, put the Gameboy in his coat pocket. 'Give it a week. If you still feel the same after that... do as you please. But I don't think this is a coincidence.'

'Divine intervention? Give me a break.'

Michael went to the door. 'I believe I already have.'

2

Divine intervention wasn't such an absurd theory, not after Leo scrutinised it from every angle. He'd seen things – irrefutable things – had died for fuck's sake. But the most profound thing of all was that he'd been judged and found not to be the evil soul he'd feared for so long. He was a Dark Heart. Neither good nor bad, and yet both. If God was willing to give him a second chance, perhaps he should do the same. Maybe God would show him the righteous path, give him a higher purpose.

'One week,' he told the Africa-stain on the ceiling. 'What harm could it do?'

Two days in bed had left Leo's stomach barren – a rocky wasteland in need of vegetation and rainfall. There was a glass of water by his bed, but it tasted dusty and made him want to brush his teeth. It was then Leo realised that even spending a week in John's body would require some preparation, and a toothbrush was just the tip of the grime-smeared and fetid iceberg.

He pulled on jeans and a white T-shirt and headed for the kitchen. There was half a mouldy white loaf in the cupboard, no tinned food, and a sauce for every day of the week – ranging from red and brown, to barbecue and fiery hot chilli. The fridge contained the leftover beers from poker night, a jar of pitted green olives and a wedge of Cheddar that now looked like Stilton's long lost cousin. In the one drawer of freezer space were five more beers, all frozen solid, and a tray of ice cubes. He closed the fridge door, his stomach gargling acid, then realised where John kept his food supplies.

The familiar painting of a bowler-hatted gentleman with a large green apple obscuring his face had been immortalised as a fridge magnet and now gripped a Chinese take-away menu to the door. Leo wondered if the irony of the fruit had been lost on John.

Nothing to eat and only pennies left from the cash: not the start he wanted, though it was the start he deserved. He searched the cottage again, emptied the trunk, looked on top of the wardrobe, inside the toilet cistern – anywhere John might have hidden his bankbooks and credit cards, but nothing turned up, not even a bank statement.

To taunt him further, he found the envelope he was going to give John on poker night. He slid it out from under the candle and tore it open. Inside were the details of the property he'd intended to buy for John.

Although the studio was meant to be a partnership, he wanted John to have full ownership of the building, so no matter what happened between them, he would always have somewhere to paint, somewhere to be an artist. John had no need of a studio now, or the one hundred and eighty-grand cheque made out in his name. Leo *did* need the money, but until he found out where John banked, it was just a piece of paper. Couldn't spend it. Couldn't eat it. It was funny how even the most complex emotional problems had to get in line behind money and nourishment.

He paced up and down the hallway for twenty minutes, sifting his brain for an idea. When it finally came, he didn't want it; there had to be another way. He paced some more, but all roads ended at the same spot.

'What choice do I have?' Leo asked himself. 'Gotta go back to the barn.'

CHAPTER 9

Michael had been very clear about Reuben. He was not to be approached. So knocking on the front door and asking to pop in for a few things was not an option. The spare key should still be under the house brick, so access wasn't a problem. Five minutes on his computer would be time enough to copy all his business files onto disc, and the cash in the wall safe would keep him afloat until he got some real money in John's account. Just because Leo was going to be walking the righteous path, didn't mean he had to do it poor.

Michael hadn't been as clear on Reuben's mental state, but gave the impression he was closer to demonic than angelic, and that gave Leo a healthy fear. Who knew what Reuben was capable of if confronted with the former owner of his newly acquired body?

The view from the field was impressive. The last time Leo had seen the barn from up here was when the toughened glass had just been installed. He'd wandered to the top of the hill with his digital camera, thinking he would send his dad some pictures in the hopes of pissing him off. He never sent them.

Lying in the damp grass made him feel like a sniper. He'd even picked out a green jumper from John's wardrobe for camouflage. At this distance, Leo could barely make out the figure in his kitchen and thankfully was too far away to see his own features. If that disturbing day never came, it would still be too soon.

Reuben appeared to be making something to eat, shuttling backwards and forwards between the fridge and the hob. It made Leo feel his own hunger more acutely. There was nothing he could do now but watch and wait and hope that Reuben wasn't staying in for the day.

Two hours passed with little interest. Leo was damp from the grass and his neck and spine ached. He wanted to roll onto his back to relieve the pain but feared he would fall asleep or miss Reuben leaving.

Dark rain clouds were bringing the day to a premature end, and the seriousness of getting wet hit home. Walking drenched through the barn would result in foot puddles on the floorboards. If Reuben came back and found evidence of an intruder and no sign of a forced entry, he could only assume insider knowledge. And that would lead him where? Without reading Reuben's mind, it was impossible to say if he knew about Leo's rebirth into John, but it couldn't be ruled out. If he did know and thought that Leo was messing in his business, whatever that business may be, Leo could end up with an unwanted visitor himself, with more sinister things on his mind than retrieving cash and bank details. Rain was bad.

The desk lamp came on, followed by the strips beneath the kitchen units. It seemed Reuben was staying in for the night after all. Leo wondered what to do. He couldn't camp on the hill all night. But then, as if hearing his thoughts, Reuben swung his coat on and switched the kitchen lights off again.

Reuben closed the front door, walked down the gravel drive and turned right towards town. At two hundred yards, Leo finally lost sight of him. He waited ten minutes, battling with the idea of a premature return, then headed for the barn.

It was almost dark as the first drops of rain began to fall, making stealth redundant. Leo vaulted the low fence which separated his property from the field and ran for the porch, wincing at the gravel crunching underfoot. He pressed his back against the front door, catching his breath in controlled respirations while listening for footfalls on the driveway. John really was unfit. Once his breathing calmed, he lifted the brick and grabbed the key. The clouds unloaded, and Leo slipped inside.

In the darkness, the barn took a breath, exhaled the familiar creaks and groans of the oak beams – sounds that went unnoticed most of the time, but were now a macabre orchestra. He hugged the wall and sidestepped to the chimney breast, trying to stay out of the desk lamp's glow.

Perhaps it was the dark, but Bond didn't say anything when Leo swung the poster aside and punched in the combination to the safe. He grabbed the bundle of cash and stuffed it inside his jacket, fought hard not to delve in again for the scrapbook. He closed the safe before he could change his mind and swung the poster back against the wall.

I'd say you were making good progress. Bond's voice filled Leo's head.

'Haven't got time for this.' Leo went to the front door, lifted the letterbox and peered down the drive.

Leaving the scrapbook, Shtamp? That's an impressive display of self-control. What's next: leaving me?

'I've got no choice.' Leo headed for the stairs. 'It was listening to you in the first place that got me into this.'

Wasn't me that killed John.

'Fuck you,' Leo whispered, all spit and teeth.

So you've got a different face – big deal. Could be jusht the change you need.

Leo trotted up the stairs, glanced back over the glass balustrade, then opened the study door. The computer was on as always. Tropical fish swam backwards and forwards in never-ending laps of the screen. He brought up the Stamp & Son employee document, took a disc from the drawer and loaded it. He eyed the crack in the door while the file copied in what felt like slow motion, the bright green bar dragging its heels to spite him. The creaking beams seemed to grow louder in the rain. A ghost ship in a storm.

The disc finally ejected, and he slipped it inside his jacket, stepped onto the shadowy landing. He tried to muster the nerve to go into his bedroom and retrieve the photograph of Mum and Davey, but his legs wouldn't move. He looked at the front door, cocked his ear to the gravel driveway, but all he could hear was the damn beams crying and moaning.

You've got plenty of time, Shtamp. You get the picture; I'll listen out for Reuben. Bond laughed.

Another step. He had time to get the photo.

I can hear Reuben coming up the drive.

'Shut up. You can't hear anything.'

Bond laughed again. *You'll have to come back for it, come back for me.*

'I've got time.' Leo checked the door again, took another couple of steps.

If Reuben finds you here, he'll kill you. And if you die, Shtamp, you'll go to Hell. That's what you think, isn't it?

'Be quiet.' Another step and Leo was at his bedroom door, his fingers on the handle.

After all you've learned, you shtill think you're going to Hell, and I know why.

'You know shit. I'm a Dark Heart.' He turned the handle, but froze. He could feel Reuben's breath on his neck.

I listened in on your conversation with Simian, and I watched you in the woods as a boy.

The beams were growing louder, the creaking becoming unbearable. 'I didn't show you that. I wouldn't.' Leo released the door handle and headed downstairs.

Sometimes I know what's besht for you, even when you don't know it yourself. Share the burden, Shtamp.

Halfway to the front door Leo stopped. 'You don't know anything, do you? You're just fishing.'

I know you'll be back for me.

Leo closed the front door on Bond, pulled the collar up on his jacket and stepped out into the rain. At the top of the hill, he remembered the photograph hadn't been in the basket anyway. It was on the dining table with the ebony block, and he was damn sure Bond knew it, too.

3

By the time he arrived back at the cottage, the rain had petered out. He paid the taxi driver and lugged the shopping bags to the kitchen door. Michael was waiting for him, his jacket pulled up over his head to keep the video screen dry.

'Where have you been?' Michael said, shrugging his jacket back onto his shoulders.

Leo looked down at his bags. 'Food?'

Michael pocketed the Gameboy and took a bag from Leo. 'Let's go inside.'

The taxi's lights swept an arc in the night, revealed a momentary band of fine drizzle before disappearing.

'Thought we were done,' Leo said, taking the bag back and pushing the kitchen door open with his foot.

'You should think about getting the lock fixed.'

'Soon as I get something worth stealing.' Leo dumped the bags on the draining board. 'You can come in, you know.'

He started loading the fridge with food, and Michael stepped inside.

'How are you feeling, Leo?'

'Okay, considering.'

'I see by the food you mean to see out the week. Any thoughts of beyond?'

'Let's see how the week goes.'

'Have you thought about Sadie?'

Leo stalled, a loaf of brown bread in each hand. 'What's there to think about?'

'John and Sadie have a relationship, ja?'

'*Had* a relationship.'

Michael clasped his hands together, his eyebrows rising.

Leo set the loaves down. 'You're not suggesting I take over *every* aspect of John's life?'

'You love her. What better way of honouring your friend than to take his woman as your own.'

'What better way of disrespecting him, you mean?'

'The Book of Deuteronomy states that if two brothers live together, and one dies, leaving no children, it is the surviving brother's duty to take his dead brother's wife for his own.'

'That misses me on so many levels I don't even know where to start.'

'Symbolically it's perfect.' Michael took the loaves and put them in the fridge. 'John was like a brother to you,' he said, 'and Sadie like a wife to John.'

Leo took the loaves back out of the fridge. 'Does it say anything in that book about killing your best friend and stealing his body and girlfriend?' He set the loaves back on the side. 'We didn't even live together.'

'You did for a while.'

'It's immoral.'

'It's an expression of your love for both John and Sadie.'

Leo palmed moisture from his forehead.

'Distancing yourself from Sadie will only cause you pain. You love her, and she loves you.'

'She loves John.' Leo slammed the fridge door. 'She never loved me.'

Michael took him by the shoulders, stared into his face. 'Let her.'

Leo shook free, went back to his bags and rummaged for nothing in particular.

'God wishes all men to live in love,' Michael said.

Leo heard the kitchen door close. When he turned around, Michael had gone.

4

It seemed John's body craved Chinese food like Leo's body craved hygiene. Despite the well-stocked fridge and a hunger ache he had never known, Leo was happy to wait the extra forty minutes for the delivery meal. He'd ordered from the menu with belly small and eyes large, and was now surrounded with half-eaten foil containers from Mr Wing's Chinese takeaway. If he didn't feel as though a piano had been sewn into his stomach, he would start cleaning right away, but for now, slobbing in the armchair and watching the local news was all he could manage.

A twelve-year-old local boy named Billy Walker had been missing for two days, and half of Mundey were out looking for him. The police officer giving the statement said there was no truth in the rumours that Billy's disappearance was in anyway connected to the Ryan Oliver case. Leo wasn't familiar with that case. If it wasn't happening to him, it wasn't happening.

The officer went on to say that Billy would probably turn up safe and sound as soon as he was hungry and that it was too early to assume anything else.

'That's what they said about Davey.'

Leo peeled himself from the armchair and switched the TV off. He needed to clean.

5

The kitchen floor was bare concrete, but Leo swept it and scrubbed it nonetheless. He emptied and cleaned the cupboards and washed the walls and surfaces. When the entire kitchen was scented with lemon disinfectant and the crockery and cutlery squeaked to his satisfaction, he emptied the fridge and set to work again.

As he scoured, images of Sadie and him together pushed to the forefront of his mind. They cuddled on the sofa, walked Cotton along the beach at Shingle Street... made love. He drove the thoughts away, only for his mind to fill with images of John, lying on that filthy carpet, blood seeping from his head, life draining from his eyes.

The same old story, Leo thought. Without light, only darkness survives.

6

Reuben walked around Mundey in the dark and rain. He remembered some streets better than others, noted changes here and there. Nineteen years was a long time, but it was all coming back.

He headed down the thoroughfare, past the knick-knack shops and second-hand booksellers. Up ahead on the left was an alleyway that led to the main road. It was well lit now, but nineteen years ago it had been dark. He'd killed a woman in that alley.

At the top of the thoroughfare was a crossroads. Reuben turned right into Church Street, walked up the hill to St Mary's and the churchyard where he'd once left a young man's body cold and dead against a headstone.

The further he walked, the clearer his bloody memory became, but the murders that were most vivid were the young boys and their shallow graves. He could still recall one of the headlines: MERCER BOY FOUND IN SHALLOW GRAVE

– SERIAL KILLER IN MUNDEY. Reuben shook his head. He wouldn't make the same mistakes again.

The rain eased, but his bones were cold. He turned down New Street and headed for home, passed the familiar red Tudor house and another of the town's old pubs. Why was he here again? Was the world so small that he had to revisit old ground, or was it something else? Questions he meant to ask Simian, the next time he saw him.

CHAPTER 10

Despite not going to bed till gone three, Leo was up early. He threw together the leftover Chinese and warmed it in a battle-scarred (but very clean) wok. Just the idea of such a breakfast should've had his stomach recoiling in horror, not rejoicing in hunger, as it was. The side effects of body swapping, he supposed, but genetic or poetic, he didn't know.

He leant over the stove and ate straight from the wok, shaking his head with every disgusting, satisfying spoonful, and almost choked on a noodle when Sadie opened the kitchen door.

'Flying visit. Your phone's switched off.'

He lurched over the sink and coughed. She slapped his bare back.

'Six years in nursing, and I've only performed the Heimlich Manoeuvre once. An old guy called Lonny. Three good yanks and he spat a boiled sweet across the ward and broke a vase.'

Leo caught his breath and stood up. Sadie wrapped her arms around his chest from behind, performed the mock procedure using her hips. He could feel her breasts in his back.

'Suppose you want a bed bath, now?' she breathed into his ear.

'Is that what Lonny got? Must have had a boiled sweet epidemic.'

'Lonny was ninety-three. He was dead a week later.'

'Nothing to do with the bed bath, I hope.'

Sadie let him go. 'Have you cleaned in here?'

'A bit.' He could still feel her hands on his chest.

'A bit? I can actually see through the oven door.'

Leo took a mug from the cupboard and filled it at the sink. Drank half trying to hide his nerves.

'I thought we'd go out for dinner tonight,' she said, 'and don't worry, I've been paid.'

'I've got money.'

'Sure you have, but I don't fancy Kentucky. I've booked us a table at the new veggie restaurant in town. I'll pick you up at seven. Wear something clean.' She stepped close, and he backed up to the sink. She held his chin and thumbed food from his bottom lip, kissed him long and slow. Leo died and was reborn in that kiss.

2

With all that was going on in Leo's head, the last person he wanted to talk to was Bond, but he needed someone to give it to him straight. He waited for Sadie's rusted Beetle to pull away, then grabbed his jacket and headed for the field.

He crouched on the brow of the hill and looked down towards the barn. Reuben wasn't in the kitchen or lounge, but that didn't mean he was out. He decided to walk past the front gate. From there he'd be able to see through the dining room window, rule out another room at least. He dropped back behind the hill a ways and walked to the road, climbed the fence and headed along the grass verge towards the barn. At around twenty metres from the gate, a black Toyota Pickup rounded the corner. Leo recognised it immediately and turned as if to tie his laces. He heard the truck swing onto the driveway, then heavy boots splashed the gravel and marched toward the barn. The double garage obscured Leo's sightline, but he could hear Mick knocking on the front door.

At that moment, Leo realised what a reckless idea it was trying to get back into the barn. He had no idea what Reuben was capable of, and for that reason couldn't leave Mick here alone.

Leo trotted back up the road and climbed the fence, squatted on his heels when he reached his spot on the brow. Mick was kicking the bottom of the door, and Reuben had appeared from somewhere and was now standing in the middle of the lounge.

'Walk the fuck away, Mick,' Leo said under his breath. 'I don't want to have to come down there. I can't.'

Reuben took a step closer to the door. He was holding something behind his back.

'Fuck.' How *would* it go if he went down there and Reuben opened the door? Would he realise that one of the two guys in front of him knew more than he should? Would he just kill them both and not even think about it?

Leo took his phone out, praying John had Mick's number saved. He did. Leo dialled and it started to ring. He held the phone to his chest and cocked his ear to the barn. More shouting from Mick, and Reuben had stepped closer to the front door, but no ringtone.

'Fuck.'

He put the phone to his ear again. Still ringing. Must be on silent, or maybe in the truck. He cut it off and was about to shout something, anything so long as he didn't have to go down there, when Mick backed away from the door, and Reuben did the same.

Mick turned for the truck, his hand in the pocket of his Donkey jacket. Leo backed down the hill, keeping both Mick and Reuben in sight, and then the phone rang in his hand.

'Mick?'

'You're not dead then, boy?'

'Dead?'

'Where are ya?'

Leo watched him climb into the truck. 'At home.'

'Right. Don't move, boy. I'll be there in two minutes.'

The phone flatlined, and the Toyota's engine gunned. Leo started sprinting back to the cottage.

3

Reuben watched the black truck pull away. Laid the dagger back in the ebony box.

CHAPTER 11

The day Leo's dad told him the company name was changing to Stamp '& Son' was only a good day in hindsight, and only then when he erased the morning.

'Don't you look all grown up in your work uniform?' Leo's mum handed him a thermos and a plastic lunchbox with Roger Moore as James Bond on it.

'For Christ's sake, woman,' his dad shouted across the kitchen table. 'Jeans and an old T-shirt isn't a fucking uniform.' His dad banged his mug down on the table and stood. 'And he's not taking that lunchbox. Wrap his sarnies in foil or something – Jesus Christ.'

His mum went to take his lunchbox back.

'Don't worry about it now, we haven't got time. Go wait in the car, Leo.'

Leo kissed his mum on the cheek and walked out with the thermos, heard his dad say "this isn't going to work" in a low angry voice.

Leo opened the Jag's passenger door and climbed in. 'Fucking arsehole,' he muttered under his breath.

'Such a nasty word for such a young boy.'

Leo jumped in his seat, lurched forward and turned. Simian was sitting in the back.

'Did I scare you?'

Leo didn't have the breath to answer. Couldn't bring himself to turn back in his seat, either.

Simian wore a tweed suit and a shiny gold necktie. His dark hair was longer than Leo remembered and was slicked back in a ponytail. Handsome, if you didn't know him.

'Could you push that button on the dash for me?' Simian pointed with a fat cigar.

Still frozen, Leo glanced at where he was aiming.

'That's it. The one with the smoking cigarette on it.'

Leo pushed the button.

'Marvellous.' Simian produced a small gadget from inside his jacket and snipped the end from his cigar. 'Beast of a smoke, it really is.'

Leo jumped again when his dad opened the door and climbed in.

'Simian? What the hell are you doing here?'

'Long time, Ronald.'

The lighter popped.

They drove in silence. Filthy cigar smoke poured into the front of the car. Leo was relieved when they pulled onto the dusty driveway of a near-derelict house and his dad told him to get out.

His dad rolled his window down. 'There's a big Irish bloke in there called Mick. He knows you're coming. Don't embarrass me.'

The Jag crept away, and Simian gave Leo a two-fingered salute with his cigar. It looked as though he was being chauffeured.

Leo walked up the dusty drive and stood at the open door. He could just make out a radio playing in between the buzz of power tools, and then a grizzly bear appeared in the doorway wearing a Donkey jacket and hardhat.

'How ya doin', boy?' The bear held out a giant paw. Leo mirrored it, watched his hand disappear up to the wrist. 'Mick,' the bear said.

Leo followed him into an empty room on the left, and Mick shouted for everyone to 'down tools'.

'We got a shite-load to do today, and I can see you're itchin' to rough-up those beautiful hands o'yours, so I'll quickly introduce you to the lads, and we can get crackin', okay, boy?'

Five men huddled into the empty room, and Leo shook another five hands.

'Well, that's everyone, boy, but there's one more thing you should know.' Mick glanced across at his men. 'All those who can't tap dance are poofs!'

At that moment, all the blokes in the room, including Mick, started doing some sort of jig, kicking dust in the air and tapping their feet on the wooden floorboards. It looked like a barn dance as they swung each other around by the arm and 'yee-haw'd'.

It took a while for the penny to drop, but when it did, Leo discovered he could tap dance just fine and was soon kicking dust into the air and swinging his thermos in a do-si-do.

'He ain't no poof, lads. Look at him go.' Mick was laughing, and for some reason it made Leo happy. 'Go on, boy! Show 'em how it's done!'

2

He made it back to the cottage just as Mick pulled up in the Toyota. Leo flung his jacket into the bedroom and ducked into the toilet, panting like a sheepdog. He waited for Mick to appear at the kitchen door.

'It's open, Mick,' Leo shouted, then closed the toilet door.

He felt giddy from the run and thought he might puke. He splashed water on his face and took deep breaths until the dizziness passed. Then he opened the door.

'That better be the plague you're sweatin', boy.'

Mick's ruddy complexion deepened. Even the wiry grey hair sprouting from beneath his flat cap looked angry. Mick took his phone out of his pocket and held it to his ear. 'Hello, John, how are ya doing, boy? Oh that's too bad, the flu, you say? No don't apologise, boy, that flu bug can be a real tinker. At least I know now that you've been poorly and not off taking the piss out of ol' Mick.'

How could he have forgotten about Mick?

'Well, boy? Are ya going to tell me what you've been doing for over a week? And don't give me no shite now, 'cause I'm not in any mood for it.'

Leo could account for a few days, but as for the rest of John's time off work, he could only guess... or make it up.

'I thought Leo told you?'

'Told me what, boy?'

'Sadie and me are having problems, and I needed some time off to sort it. I squared it with Leo, and he said take as much time as I needed.'

'I honestly don't know what that boy is playing at.' Mick stepped out of the way and Leo entered the kitchen. 'You know him better than most. Has he said anything to you? If something is going on, you better tell me, 'cause I got ten fellas who ain't getting paid this week.'

'I don't know what you mean, Mick. Are you talking about Leo?'

'Course I'm talking about Leo. Who else?' Mick opened the fridge, grabbed a beer and bit the cap off. Then, as if he'd forgotten his manners, he gave Leo the beer and repeated the process for himself.

'He didn't turn up on Tuesday for the timesheets, and he ain't been returning my calls. So I went round his place just now to find out what the fuck is going on.' Mick gulped his beer to empty and belched into the back of his hand, opened the fridge and took another. 'Now get this: I knock on the door, and I can see him through the obscured glass, right?'

Leo nodded.

'And he just stands there looking at me through the glass, still doesn't open the door, but just stares. Now I'm thinking he's having a bit of a laugh, but I'm not in the mood, right? So I bang on the door again and tell him I'm not in the fucking mood, and he just stares at me. Five fucking minutes I stood there banging on that fucking door – was all I could do to stop myself from booting the thing in.' He bit the cap off his second beer.

Leo had never heard Mick run-off at the mouth like that: everything was usually short and sweet. It was more than just work getting to him.

'Well, boy?' Mick asked.

Leo took a long, slow slug of his beer, looked down the neck of the bottle for no reason other than to occupy his shaking hand. 'I think it's finally hit him – about his dad, I mean. We played poker Thursday night, and it all came out. I didn't know he was this bad, though. He must be hurting if he wouldn't even see you. You were more of a dad to him than that other prick.'

Mick sniffed and looked away. 'He's a good lad.'

'Look Mick, I'll go and see Leo and find out what's going on. He did joke about me taking over for a while. Perhaps he wasn't joking.'

'Well, I ain't got a problem with it. I just want to know that the boy's all right. He seemed a long way away.' Mick headed for the door and turned, inspected his empty bottle. 'What is this shite?'

Leo smiled. 'I'll get round there as soon as I can. Got a couple of things to do first, but I'll call you tonight with an outcome?'

Mick nodded and swapped bottles with Leo, proclaimed the beer as shite and walked out the door.

Reuben sat at the breakfast bar, slicing wedges from a green apple. Fruit still felt like a treat, even after all this time. He speared the segments with the tip of the kitchen knife and fed himself one delicious piece after another.

As he ate, he heard footsteps on the gravel, mail being pushed through the letterbox. He waited until the postman had gone before fetching the letters; he'd already had one unwanted interaction this morning – no need to chance another.

At the breakfast bar, he sifted through the bundle until he found an A4 envelope with handwriting he recognised. He tore it open and pulled out the contents.

Inside was a single white sheet with a photograph attached. He detached the photo and pored over the tiny writing that filled the page. It was everywhere: up and down, right to left, upside-down in some places and lines between lines in others. It was a mess he'd learned to decipher years ago. He filtered the details he needed: Name, address, habitual patterns. The rest was a meaningless fountain of ink that only served Simian's sick mind.

Reuben held up the photograph, stared into the old man's eyes. 'Well, Mr Fudickar, you have lived a long life. You should be thankful of that, at least.'

He laid the photo down, picked up the knife and the apple, and cut out a jagged chunk.

CHAPTER 12

As long as Stamp & Son ran smoothly, Mick had no reason to knock on Reuben's door again. And as Leo had no intention of giving Reuben a one-to-one on the finer aspects of property development, he needed a computer for more than just running the disc with John's bank details on; he needed to get on-line and get the team paid. But his urgency for a PC was none of these reasons. He'd thought of a way to talk to Bond.

The taxi driver helped him in with the last of the boxes and the large picture frame, then loitered in the kitchen for his money. Tarik, who was named after his grandfather, had bored Leo shitless about his family's passage from India into England, all three generations. It was as if he were trying to justify his presence here.

Tarik wore an Ipswich Town football shirt stretched over a beach-ball gut and spoke with the thickest of Suffolk tongues. He couldn't have been more British. Leo thanked him with a twenty and told him to keep the change.

Leo opened one side of the drop-leaf table and installed the laptop, printer and scanner, but it was only temporary. As soon as he'd constructed the flat-packed desk he'd bought and organised a phone line, it would all be relocated in the spare room. The new clutter was already a constant static of irritation.

He removed the *Dr No* DVD from the carrier bag and laid the cover facedown on the flatbed scanner. Within moments, he had an A4 sized image of Bond on the laptop. It took some fussing, but he managed to zoom in and print off different segments, and sixteen sheets later, had a James Bond jigsaw puzzle. He tore the protective film from the picture frame and set about assembling it.

The image was grainy, but it was Bond. Leo stood his patchwork Picasso on the mantel and sat down on the sofa opposite, frightened to talk. If this didn't work he was out of ideas.

I suppose you think giving me a new face is funny?

Leo took an easy breath, let Bond's words hang in the air for a moment.

So what now? You bleat on about your problems and I say 'there, there'?

'There *is* something I need to talk about, yes.'

No.

'What do you mean, no?'

Quid pro quo, Clarice. You tell me something I want to know, then we'll talk.

'You mean show you something?'

Yesh.

Leo closed his eyes, pinched the bridge of his nose. 'Fine. Just get on with it.'

Instantly, Bond began to change in front of his eyes. At first, Leo thought he was back at the barn, but the picture was too small. It was a mass-produced poster with a similar poster next to it, only this time it was Roger Moore – identical poses, but with Moore in a white dinner jacket and Connery in black.

Below the posters was a chest of drawers with a TV and video cassette recorder on top. Birthday cards stood next to the TV, tin badges still attached. Leo was suddenly lying on a bed – remote control in one hand and a video cassette of *The Spy Who Loved Me* in the other. He turned to his bedroom door.

'Vince has gone missing,' his mum said. 'Come and help your dad find him.'

'I was just about to watch a film. He's probably on the hill.'

'He's not. We've looked. Now come on – your dad's frantic.'

'If I went missing, he wouldn't care.'

'Think how pleased your dad'll be if you find him. Come on. They're in the woods already.'

'They?'

His mum's face screwed up just a little. 'Simian.'

The pale blue walls of his bedroom tore away. Trees and branches shot into the sky, ripping through the carpet and jagging out from under his bed. Leo was now standing in the woods across the road from his house, his breath white in the cold air. He could hear his dad shouting for the English Bull Terrier.

'Vince! Come on, boy!'

Leo followed the calls and found his dad traipsing amongst the fallen leaves.

'Don't need you, Leo,' his dad said without looking round. 'Go back to the house.'

'But Mum said…'

'Go watch your films. You're not needed.'

Leo's cheeks burned, despite the chilly air. He walked away, but not back to the house. He didn't want to disappoint his mum or do what his dad had told him. Instead he went deeper into the woods to find the stupid mutt. He wanted his dad to choke on the thank you.

At some point, his dad had stopped calling Vince. Leo hoped he'd found him but wasn't ready to go home himself. He was going to stay out here a while, let his dad wonder where he was. Pinholes of sun were sinking beyond the trees. It would be dark soon. What would his dad do if he wasn't home by then? Nothing – that's what. Davey was an only child in his dad's eyes, and now Davey was dead.

The cold finally bit too hard, and his cheeks were sore from the tears. He was only spiting himself and his mum by staying out. With the sinking sun at his back, Leo threaded his way through the trees, and before long, he heard a car pass up ahead and knew he was close to the road. He stopped and cuffed his face dry, thought of Davey in his shallow grave and wanted to cry again. That was when he heard the groan. He startled at first, then looked about him. Nothing. The groan came again, and he saw the white against the rusty leaves. He moved closer.

His dad was lying facedown on the ground, blood leaking from his ear, his left foot bound in a root. He groaned again, but Leo could see he was a long way from conscious.

The blood cloud gathered silently, unexpectedly. He paced around his prone father.

In some faraway world, Leo squirmed on the sofa. *Have you seen enough?* he said, knowing Bond would never let him leave now.

Round and round he circled, kicking leaves and cursing through gritted teeth. 'You wish it was me, don't you? You wish it was me in the ground and you had your Davey back. Say it!'

Leo turned away, sobbing and trembling. Then he saw the branch on the ground, and it was in his hands before he could think.

No, no, no, Leo echoed from the sofa, but his younger self would never hear.

He gripped the branch tighter, the weight of it almost too heavy for his scrawny arms.

No, no, no!

He hefted the branch high with both hands, his dad's head before him on the ground. 'You love him so much, then go to him.'

A wailing cry tore from his young chest and his muscles coiled…

'You're not about to do what I think you're about to do, are you?'

Leo staggered back, rejecting the branch more than dropping it. Simian was leaning against a tree in a sharp suit. A flick of the wrist, and a chunky silver lighter spat out a long orange flame. He infected his cigar with it.

'My father was an arsehole, too.' Smoke poured from Simian's mouth. 'That's why I killed him.' He took another pull on the cigar. 'Beast of a smoke.'

If Leo had bent his knees at that moment, he would have dropped like a corpse. He felt close to blacking out.

Simian aimed the cigar butt at the branch on the ground. 'Finish up. I won't tell.' He stared at Leo, then his lips parted in a humourless smile. 'Only kidding. You head back to the house. I'll take care of Ronald.'

Leo took a step, stared at his dad.

'Go,' Simian said.

One step turned into two. Two into a run.

'Leo?'

Leo skidded to a halt and looked back.

'Talk to you later.'

2

What did you talk about later?

Leo sat hunched on the edge of the sofa, face in his hands.

Come on, Shtamp. You didn't do it.

'But I would have!' he shouted.

Could have.

He got up and opened the window, the breeze soothing his skin but not his mind.

And that's when I came along, I suppose?

Leo crossed his arms and stared sidelong at Bond. 'Quid pro quo.'

3

If you love her then be with her. This Michael's right.

'But it feels morally wrong.'

You've had a shit life by anybody's shtandards. If you pass up this opportunity to be happy, you're a fucking idiot. Now what did Simian want to talk about?

Leo took the picture down from the mantel…

Wondered when that was coming.

… and slid it behind the sofa.

CHAPTER 13

Bond had made him feel a whole lot better about his decision to be with Sadie: this was his chance at happiness. He would sacrifice his life to bring John back if he could, and knowing that eased his heart. But John was gone, and he was here. Live for love or die for nothing? Leo chose to live.

He held fire on loading the disc with the bank details in favour of setting up the new plasma he'd bought. It was too late to pay the cheque in today, and there was no point calling Mick with no news, so he might as well get the TV operational. He took *Dr No* from John's trunk and loaded it into the DVD player. The surround sound circled the room and made the hairs on the back of his neck stand up.

The self-tuning facility located the five terrestrial channels while he stomped and folded the empty boxes. By the time he'd dumped the rubbish out back and returned, the main news was passing over to the local teams. Topping the bill again was the young kid who hadn't made it home from school. There was nothing new to add to the investigation other than a possible sighting and a plea from the police for any info on his whereabouts. Leo rooted for Billy.

At half six he cracked a beer and stood by the window, waiting for Sadie's Beetle to pull up. When seven-fifteen rolled by, he knew the phone ringing in his pocket wasn't going to be good.

'Sadie?'

'Hi, darling, you okay?' she asked, sedately.

'Fine, just hungry.'

'God, I'm sorry. Gonna have to cancel. We lost Jim tonight.' She said this as if he were supposed to know who Jim was.

'Oh no – you okay?'

'Tired. We stayed with him all day. He hasn't got any family, and I felt somebody should be with him when he… you know?'

'You did the right thing.'

'I can't think of anything worse than dying alone.'

Everybody dies alone, Leo thought. 'Get some sleep. We can go out tomorrow night.'

'That would be nice.'

'Sleep tight,' he said, but she'd already gone.

Later that night, after a few beers and the Bond film, Leo knew he'd feel the sting of shame for finding another emotion he couldn't be proud of. But until then he was content with hoping ole Jimbo had not gone peacefully.

2

The aroma of frying eggs and bacon coaxed Leo from a particularly unpleasant dream: Jimbo's maggot-riddled corpse was sat in the armchair with the remote control aimed at the new plasma. His bony thumb, barely dressed with flesh, stabbed buttons in a lazy tempo, the changing channels keeping in time, but with every new scene the same: A demonic figure, half man, half goat, was throwing naked men and women into a fiery pit. Those who'd dare protest were lifted into the air on the prongs of the beast's pitchfork and thrown like hay bales into the flames. Jimbo's wet cackling only ceased to periodically turn towards Leo, to check he was watching the show, and then the laughter would resume with a shower of maggots being spat from his nostrils like a giggly schoolboy losing his milk.

Leo sat up as Sadie walked into the bedroom with what smelled like a mug of coffee. He patted the empty half of the bed.

'Not even if those sheets were clean,' she said, and walked out again.

'Smells great,' he called after her.

'That's more than can be said for those sheets.'

Leo sniffed the sheets but couldn't detect anything nasty. Maybe John's biology had something to do with it. He couldn't remember bleaching the toilet before bed, either.

'I thought you were skint?' she shouted.

The smell drifting up the hallway was exquisite. Leo hadn't eaten a thing last night, and it felt like his stomach had grown teeth. 'What do you mean?' He pulled on a pair of jeans.

'The TV and laptop?'

Shit, he thought. 'My mum sent me some money.' He winced and held his breath, readied himself for more lies.

'Come and eat,' she shouted again.

'No need to shout,' he whispered into her ear.

She wriggled free of his hug and took two plates through to the lounge. Leo folded the laptop away so she could set them down.

'Meat eater this morning?' he said, noticing the bacon on her plate.

She ignored him.

'What's all this in aid of?' he asked.

'I can't make dinner tonight, so I thought I'd make you breakfast instead.'

Leo tried to hide his disappointment, but not too hard.

'The girls have organised a few drinks at the home for the residents, then we're going into Ipswich.'

'Like a wake for Jimbo? Thought they had to bury'em first?' Leo broke into his yolk, and it took him back to his dream.

'Wasn't me that organised it. Can't really say no, can I?'

'Suppose not.' Leo tried the bacon. Egg was off the menu.

'We'll do something next weekend, I promise.'

'What's wrong with tomorrow?'

'Mum's Ann Summers' party. I told you weeks ago.'

'Oh yeah.'

An engine revved outside. Sadie went to the window. 'Is this Sky van for you?'

'That was quick.'

'Christ, how much money did she give you?'

The Sky guy knocked on the front door.

'Round the side,' Leo shouted, avoiding Sadie's question. He got up to meet him at the kitchen door, and Sadie followed with her plate of uneaten breakfast.

'Stay. Eat your meat,' Leo said.

'Not hungry anyway.' She pecked him on the cheek, shouldered her bag and opened the door for the Sky guy. 'I'll call you.' She smiled and left.

Leo saw no warmth in that smile, so thought it best to leave it there.

3

Because the cottage was listed, Sky Guy fitted a Metronic transparent satellite dish, and for an extra twenty in cash, extended a phone line into the spare bedroom where Leo had built the flat-pack desk using Sky Guy's cordless drill.

John had used the spare room as a mini studio, of sorts, and it was littered with canvases. Leo counted over forty, all stacked against the walls with no care, it seemed. It was hard to see from where he'd drawn the inspiration; the spare room was as dingy and musty as the rest of the cottage, apart from the cheap laminate covering the floor.

The new desk and laptop looked out of place in this room, but it was John's empty easel that drew the eye. It stood by the window, as though waiting for its true master to return. Knowing that Leo was an impostor. A fake.

The laptop screen gave birth to colour, breaking the easel's spell. Leo loaded the disc, brought up John's details and printed a copy.

4

The day was warm and bright, so Leo walked into Mundey. He paid the cheque in using a Lloyds paying-in slip, as he still couldn't find John's bank stuff, and it was only now, whilst enjoying his third pint, that he realised he should've ordered a new card and chequebook in the bank.

The Cross and Crown was not the finest pub in Mundey, with its grimy, quarry-tiled floor and stained pine panels trying to pass for oak. But if people-watching was your thing, you could do no better. It was situated on the corner of a crossroads at the top of the thoroughfare and enjoyed views up and down Church Street and all the way along Cumberland Street opposite. Sitting in a booth by the window, Leo could see everything and everyone. Mundey moved on by, oblivious to his circumstance, and he took a strange comfort from it. Then John crept into his head and turned the beer sour in his mouth.

The night beat back the day, and the hordes could no longer be held. His booth filled up with unwanted locals. Their clothes and complexions gave them away as students, along with the malnourished look they all seemed to actively seek.

One of them – wearing a Green Day T-shirt and a Norwich City scarf – appeared to recognise Leo, or more accurately, John, but before the youngster could engage him in awkward conversation, Leo relinquished his post in favour of a barstool.

He sat at the bar for a while, trailing his finger through beer dribbles on the oak counter, then moved again to find another hiding place, away from the crowd. He thought he would finish his beer and head home, could feel a channel flicking session coming on. Then something caught his attention at the bar, but it wasn't something, it was someone.

The guy had his back to him, which didn't make him instantly recognisable, but nevertheless, he was more than just familiar. Perhaps it was somebody John had known, and there was some residual memory being triggered – another biological echo. But when the man turned around, it was clear why Leo had found him so familiar. He'd been staring at himself.

5

Reuben carried a large glass of red wine to the bar area Leo had moved from earlier. Christ, if Leo hadn't moved he would have been sitting at the very next table.

At first Leo couldn't decipher his feelings, then found he was gauging them at something like terror, and if he didn't take control right away he would go running and screaming into the street. He gulped a mouthful of beer, the glass shaking in his hand as though struggling with a mild case of Parkinson's. He slid off his chair, praying he would not fall straight to the floor, and made his way to the haven of the toilet, on legs that for the first time truly didn't feel like his own.

He barricaded himself into the pub's only cubicle and slammed down the seat.

'Get a fucking grip,' he said, low and guttural. He took a couple of deep breaths and noticed his hands were still shaking. 'Shit!'

Climbing out the toilet window was an option for a second, before sanity slapped him and he regained some composure. There was no need to run from this man. There was no reason to think that he would even recognise John as Leo, or even recognise John at all. The only pictures at the barn were of Sean Connery and his mum and Davey, so why should he be afraid? It was Michael building Reuben up as some evil demon that had done the mind job on Leo. Who was Reuben, really? He'd just walked into a pub and ordered a glass of wine. Hardly demonic behaviour. Maybe this would be a good opportunity to observe him.

'Now, just go back in there, drink your pint, and chill the fuck out.'

He opened the cubicle door, splashed his face with water at the basin. 'Be cool,' he told John's reflection.

The bar had gotten busier, but he could see Reuben through the crowd. Leo sat back at his table, wary of making eye contact, and surveilled him with stolen glances.

Reuben's stare did not falter. He was watching someone too. At first it was unclear who he was interested in, but then an old gentleman stood and took his empty glass to the bar. Reuben's eyes never left him.

The old man looked comfortably into his eighties and an obvious regular. The young barmaid had him another whiskey on the bar before he reached it, and he thanked her by name, which was Tina, and tottered off to his table, where he sat out of sight again.

Reuben had picked out the drabbest of clothes from Leo's extensive wardrobe: a long brown jacket he hadn't worn in years, a khaki work shirt, faded jeans and old boots. Perhaps he was trying to be inconspicuous?

The pub continued to fill, and Tina was joined by another bartender: a tall young man with long, dry black hair tied back in a messy ponytail.

Ponytail came around to the other side of the bar, switched on the jukebox and punched in a code without looking through the albums. Tina rolled her eyes. Ponytail shrugged and mouthed: *what?*

The opening guitar riff to The Cure's *Lullaby* poured from the speakers.

Reuben stood and weaved through the crowd, finally breaking eye contact with the old man. Leo thought he must be going to the toilet, but instead he walked out of the pub. He watched him pass the window to his left and head down Church Street toward the old theatre, not the direction of home.

He could have sworn Reuben was waiting for the old man. Why else the interest? Leo started to panic. Maybe he *had* waited for him. He'd been so engrossed in Reuben, the old guy had probably got up and walked out without him noticing. But before Leo could give himself fully to his cerebral carnage, the old guy stood up from the crowd of young drinkers, buttoned his coat and tipped his cap in Tina's direction.

A gap appeared at the bar and Leo dived into it, ordered a pint from Ponytail. The old guy turned his collar up and went out the door. Leo took his pint and sat in Reuben's empty seat, pushed the untouched wine away with his fingertips and watched the old guy shuffle up Church Street towards the churchyard, the opposite direction to Reuben. Once the old guy was out of sight, Leo relaxed, dug coins from his pocket and went over to the jukebox.

6

Reuben stood in the darkened doorway of an antique shop and watched Christian Fudickar leave the public house and head up Church Street towards St Mary's. He waited until he was almost at the top of the hill before setting off after him. If he'd timed it right, he should catch the old man in the churchyard.

CHAPTER 14

Sadie called and said she'd be over at seven with a couple of films for them to watch.

'Is it me you want or my plasma?'

'If you've got any of your mum's money left, you could buy some new sheets. Whoever stimulates me the most gets to take me to bed.'

'I don't think the aerial will reach that far. Looks like I win by default.'

'Get some decent wine. And I don't want to drink it out of a mug. Veggie curry from Mr Wing's is fine.'

'Thank fuck for that,' he laughed. Sadie had put the phone down laughing too.

Leo buzzed around Mundey, working through a mental shopping list. He picked up everything he would need for the perfect evening, including new sheets. He thought it might be a good idea to buy condoms too – not knowing who was in charge of contraception.

He made his way up the thoroughfare, thinking he'd buy them from the gents' vending machine in the Cross, but as he turned the corner he noticed the commotion at the top of Church Street.

An ambulance was backed up to the gates of St Mary's Church, and two squad cars had converged in a V across the road and pavement. A crowd was being held back by tape. Leo pushed open the doors of the Cross, an unpleasant sensation swelling in his guts.

There were only half a dozen customers, but the atmosphere was undoubtedly sombre. Leo approached the bar and ordered a beer from Ponytail, noticed Tina sitting on a crate by a doorway marked 'Staff'. She had a tissue scrunched in her fist and her eyes were red. Ponytail handed Leo his change, and Leo cocked a thumb at the church.

'They found a dead body this morning in the churchyard…'
Ponytail glanced at Tina and then back to Leo. 'A customer.'

Leo didn't need to ask who. He left his beer and headed home.

2

He couldn't get the old man's face out of his head and wished he had more chores to occupy his mind. After putting the new sheets on the bed and the old ones in a black bag, he opened the good wine so it could breathe. He washed the new glasses to remove shop dust and polished them until the act itself lost all meaning. He twisted them at the window and the sun filtered through the crystal angles and projected colours around the kitchen. That would have to do, he thought, and polished for a little longer.

With nothing left to do, he flopped into the sofa (as the armchair reminded him of a tombstone since his dream of ole Jimbo) and thumbed the remote. Channel bouncing stole twenty minutes of his life, and whether he knew it or not, he was only passing time until the news came on. He wanted to know if the kid had been found, amongst other things.

With a solemn face, the same policeman told the East Anglian viewing public that they were following a number of leads. They were also looking into the possibility that Billy's disappearance *was* linked to that of Ryan Oliver's, but the officer didn't elaborate. Too early to hear anything of this morning's events. A good thing, perhaps.

Leo gave the cottage one last look over and put on a clean shirt. Despite this morning's development, he was getting excited about seeing Sadie, and before long, he could think only of her. He grabbed a beer from the fridge and poured suds over the butterflies in his stomach. The combination of fluttering wings and alcohol reminded him of something his mum had once told him: Happiness was the anticipation of good things to come. He hadn't understood what she'd meant at the time, but he understood now.

3

Early signs were good. Sadie had brought an overnight bag. Leo poured her a glass of wine and offered it with his pinkie out.

'Crystal.' She looked impressed.

He beckoned her along the hallway and opened the bedroom door to reveal the new sheets. 'Would Madame care to take her for a spin?' He stroked the small of her back, tried to coax her through the door but caught a painful flick to the nose for his efforts.

'Stimulation!' she reminded him.

He sat patiently through the first of the Hugh Grant films, massaging Sadie's neck and shoulders as she sat between his legs on the floor in front of him. But once the film ended, his hand wandered down towards her breasts.

'Uh, uh, uh,' she said, and smacked his wrist.

'What was that for?'

'Pass me the control.' She held her hand up behind her head.

Leo didn't oblige.

'You like Hugh Grant.' Sadie moved out from between his legs and crawled towards the TV and ejected the film.

'Oh, yeah. He's the greatest character actor of his generation.'

'Since when did you have an opinion on the thespian craft?' She hooked her head around, one eyebrow raised. 'Well, we've got another film yet, and you've got another bottle of wine to open.'

'Thought you were only joking when you pitted me against the bloody plasma,' he muttered, and went into the kitchen.

'Don't be like that. There's plenty of time for *this* later.'

Leo craned his neck around the doorway and saw Sadie rubbing her tightly-jeaned arse. Checkmate. He was watching *Four Weddings* and liking it.

When he re-emerged from the kitchen, the news was just finishing.

'Have you been watching the story on the missing kid?' he asked, and sat down next to her on the floor.

'Haven't seen it, but the girls are talking about it at work. Why?'

'Another kid went missing a while back, and the police think there maybe a link. Sounded like a big deal, so I wondered if you remembered anything.' He filled her glass.

'What was the other kid's name?'

'Ryan Oliver.'

'Nope. I can ask Sandra at work if you like; she's doing most of the talking about the Walker kid. She'd know if anyone does.'

'Yeah, thanks. Don't forget, though.'

'I won't. Now shush, Hugh's on.' She grabbed his wrist and draped his arm around her neck, placed his hand on her breast.

Leo took it away. Happiness was the anticipation of good things to come.

Reuben was meditating cross-legged on the floor when the phone began to ring. He counted the digital warbles, and on the fourth the phone died. He stood and hovered by the desk. The phone rang again, and he snatched the receiver from the cradle.

'Where's the boy, Simian?'

'Hello, Ruby.'

'Answer me.'

'I've no interest in the boy. I said you could have him, and have him you shall.'

Reuben breathed. Relaxed. 'Why are we here?'

'Aaahh, a philosophical question.'

'You know what I mean. In Mundey.'

'The world has become a smaller place, and we've been in it a very long time. It was going to happen eventually.'

'No. It feels wrong.'

'Did Fudickar go quietly? Was there lots of blood?'

Reuben didn't answer.

'I'll have another one for you soon, but until then, just relax. Tomorrow, why not get your wonderful tattoos done.' Simian laughed.

'I mean it, Simian. Give me fair warning when it's time to leave. I need plenty of time for the boy. I don't want a repeat of last time.'

'Get some sleep, Ruby. It's late.' Simian was still laughing when Reuben hung up the phone.

CHAPTER 15

Leo woke early, curled Sadie's hair behind her ear and watched her sleep. How he wanted to kiss her freckles. It seemed like they'd made love all night, but he felt charged and fresh. Looking at her now, breathing gently in his bed, he was satisfied he loved her – satisfied his love was honest. He kissed her shoulder and slid out from under the covers.

He glimpsed himself in the wardrobe mirror as he pulled on jeans. It was no longer John Kirkman he saw; it was Leo Stamp, a new Leo Stamp. Not quite good, but the journey had begun. He closed the door and left her to sleep and was drawn to the spare room on his way to the kitchen.

The easel was still looking out of the window for its master, and an overcast morning looked in. Leo thought about turning it to face the room, or even putting it away, but he didn't want John, wherever he was, to think that he was trying to forget him, or that he felt no shame for what he'd done.

He studied the many canvases leant against the walls, all the same style as the painting that hung in the barn. Abstract, he guessed, but it was only a guess. For all he knew, John might've painted them when he was nine.

In each canvas he tried to find its personality, John's personality, until he became transfixed with one in particular. The painting was dominated by orange, vivid and glowing. It spiralled around the canvas in all directions, changing shade and vibrancy as it danced. He mounted it on the easel.

'Getting the urge again?' Sadie said.

Leo was lost in the picture and didn't answer.

'I love that one,' she said.

'Yeah?' He turned, but she'd gone, then he heard the shower running.

By the time Sadie had done her womanly things, Leo was just waiting on the bacon.

'Go sit, I'll bring it through in a sec,' he said. 'I think the plasma needs some company anyway. Been sulking all morning.'

She went into the lounge without speaking, and Leo followed with two English breakfasts balanced on two mugs of tea.

'You got bacon. Didn't know if you were or weren't this morning.'

She picked up her fork and toyed with a mushroom. 'Have you been thinking of going back to work?' she said without looking up.

'What do you mean, back on site or painting?'

'Either or.'

'Dunno really.'

'Don't know about your painting, or your job on site?'

'Either or.' Leo burst into his yolk with a slice of toast and was pleased to find ole Jimbo had lifted his curse.

'How long do you think Mick's going to hold that job for you?'

'Mick's fine. Your breakfast's going cold.' He gestured for her to eat, but she laid her fork down.

'What is going on, John?'

'What do you mean?' he said without slowing the demolition of his breakfast. 'Nothing's going on. Everything's fine.'

'Got another handout pending from your mother, you mean?'

'No, course not.'

'Then please tell me how everything is fine for you, because I'm having real trouble seeing the silver lining in your cloud. You're not working, you're living off the charity of a woman you hate – and if I'm not mistaken, the feeling's mutual on her part, unless she's taken a knock to the head that's reawakened her maternal instincts – and you haven't painted a thing for ages. You know you used to have ambition, that's what I loved about you. Easy going but focused. You were an artist.' She threw a glance at the plasma. 'What are you now?'

Leo hadn't realised he'd stopped chewing; he was too busy wondering where that had all come from, and although he couldn't know for sure, he had a pretty good idea. This had been brewing for a while, long before he took over John's body. Wherever it had come from though, she didn't need to worry any longer. John's financial situation was more secure than ever. He wrapped his hand around hers and swallowed down his unchewed mouthful.

'Everything is fine. Better than fine. In fact, there's something I want to ask you.' He put his fork down and wrapped another hand around Sadie's, watched as a single tear fell from her eye, as if he had squeezed it out himself. 'I want you to move in.'

Sadie took a shuddering breath and slipped her hand out from under his, got up from the table and went to the bedroom. When she returned, her bag was shouldered.

'I think we need some time apart,' she said.

'What?' He jumped up so quickly he banged his knee under the table, sloshing tea from their mugs. 'Where the hell did that come from?'

'I need some time to think.' Sadie headed for the kitchen. '*You* need time to think.'

'I have been. That's why I asked you to move in.' He caught her before she could open the door. 'Tell me what I've done. I'll fix it.'

'I never thought you were going to make millions painting, that's not why I chose you. You used to have drive, dedication. But you've changed, John, and it's changed us.'

He could see how painful this was for her and wished he could tell her everything, but that was the price he would always have to pay.

Sadie dabbed at her tears with the heel of her hand and opened the door. 'I'm not asking you to change, John, because that wouldn't be fair. But if you don't, I have to, and that isn't fair, either.' She stepped outside and a cold breeze took her place in the doorway. Leo folded his arms to his bare chest.

'Sadie?'

'I mean it. Don't call for a while.' She turned to go but looked back. He thought for a second that she would step into his arms and everything would be okay, but she didn't.

'Please don't do anything stupid,' she said.

Leo stood barefoot on the cold concrete, replaying that last goodbye. Was that pity he'd heard? The first stage of the easy breakup, because ending it right then ran the risk of the unstable boyfriend topping himself? One thing was for sure; John wasn't going to start painting again anytime soon.

'Fuck!' he shouted, and pulled a psychedelic T-shirt over his head, caught himself in the wardrobe mirror. 'And what's with these fucking T-shirts?'

What was he supposed to do now? How long was he supposed to wait? It could be days before she called him, and what if she didn't? He grabbed his phone, highlighted her number, but thought better of it. She looked serious when she said not to call. 'Fuck!'

The quiet of the cottage was excruciating, and the thought of talking to Bond was worse. He switched on the TV. Maybe Billy had been found – at least that would be something, but he didn't even get a mention.

The headliner was the murder of a Suffolk pensioner. Mr Fudickar, an eighty-nine-year-old man from Mundey, had last been seen leaving The Crown and Cross public house at around nine-thirty on Friday evening. His body was later found in St Mary's churchyard. He'd been stabbed. Police were appealing for witnesses.

Leo wanted Sadie with him now, so they could crawl into bed and hide from the rest of the world, a world that only a few hours ago was orange. He switched off the plasma and looked out the window; it had started to rain.

There was no way he could stay here, not with just his mind for company. He grabbed his jacket and counted the last of his cash. Over three hundred. It looked like alcohol was going to be his friend for the day.

Leo strode for the door and kicked John's trunk on the way. It didn't put up much of a fight, and flipped on its side, spewing its contents.

'John, fucking, Kirkman!'

2

By the time he'd walked into Mundey, the rain had worked its way through to his skin. His back ached, the blisters on his feet had reawakened, and the dull throb in his tooth had returned. He relished the discomfort. John had died by his hand, and he'd still found the nerve to be angry with him.

In some ways he was glad John wasn't here. What could he say to him? Even worse was knowing that John would forgive him, as he didn't possess the negative biology for grudge-bearing. Leo wondered if you could die of shame: If you could feel it, then why couldn't you die from it? People died from broken hearts, or so they said. Perhaps that was how God had intended it to be. The broken-hearted deserved the release. The shameful did not.

The Cross and Crown was devoid of customers *and* staff. Leo was pleased about the lack of custom – not so about the lack of staff. He was looking to get real numb, real quick, and stay that way real long. Even the smell of keg beer – which was brutal at this time of day – wasn't going to sway him from his mission. And besides, he was wet, and his body had found new places to ache, and that seemed like a good enough reason to stay.

A polite cough and jangle of change failed to bring anyone to his assistance. He shook his jacket out and threw it over the back of his booth to claim his spot for the day, then scraped a barstool noisily across the quarry tiles and took the weight off his blistered feet.

'You know, even in this country, noon's considered very early to be drinking.'

A sigh escaped Leo at the sound of the voice behind him.

'What can I get you, Michael? I think they sell Blue Nun by the glass.'

'No thank you, Leo, but I would like to speak with you.'

Michael either didn't understand sarcasm or chose to ignore it. Leo thought his expression may give him a clue, but when he shifted around, the bar was still empty.

'Call me old-fashioned, but I'd rather do it face to face. So appear, materialise, or do whatever it is you do, because I don't want the bartender walking in while I'm talking to myself.' He slid off of his stool and scanned the bar. 'Well?'

'Well what?'

Leo turned towards his booth and saw Michael's head peering round the seat. He had a faux-puzzled look on his face that made Leo's cheeks burn. They burned hotter when Michael smirked and retracted his blonde head into the booth.

'It isn't a stupid assumption.' Leo slid in opposite Michael but didn't sit down. 'Last week I was dead, and you were waiting for me at the Way Station. I bet you didn't fly there, so lose the smirk.'

Michael didn't look intimidated, but the amusement left his face. 'My travels to other planes are merely parlour tricks. Men have been doing it for centuries.'

Leo eyed him for a moment longer, then sat.

'Have you ever heard of Astral Projection?'

Leo tried to look disinterested, but he did know a little. 'Remote Viewing.'

'Ja, ja. It's also known as 'Remote Viewing'. You've read about it?'

'Discovery Channel. Don't do books, remember?'

'But you are aware of the process, ja?'

'I'm aware of the myth: The 'Viewer' can *supposedly* project his mind anywhere in the world, see things like military bases.'

'It was used in the Cold War.'

'So was LSD. You'll probably find that all the 'Viewers',' Leo used air quotes this time, 'were stoners – say anything for the free drugs, man.'

Michael smiled. 'I'm sure for every genuine Viewer there were a dozen frauds.'

'You expect me to believe that you Remote Viewed the 'other side'?'

'Nein. My ability has evolved far beyond merely projecting my mind. I can now project my physical presence.'

Leo thought back to the Way Station, when Michael had pinned him to the raft with one hand. That had felt real enough.

Michael tilted his head. 'You don't think I can really fly, do you?'

'That was your projected self, I suppose?'

'I'm not unique. Ja, I was talented to begin with, but I've had the luxury of many lifetimes to nurture my abilities. Now I have few limits as to where I can travel. In fact, my limits are the reason I'm here. I need you to find something for me. Something in your barn.'

Leo folded his arms. 'It's Reuben's barn now, remember? And you told me to stay away from him, so what's changed?'

'Nothing has changed. Reuben continues to butcher his way around the globe, leaving behind a trail of corpses for me to follow. I ease the passing of those he takes, as I've done for centuries, but all I can do is watch. But then you are delivered to me, and I can see an end to it.'

'As long as I find what it is you're looking for, right?'

Michael crossed his arms on the table. 'Many years ago, Reuben stole a dagger. Without it, he is nothing. I believe the dagger is at the barn, and if you were to retrieve it, Reuben's reign would be over.'

'What's so special about this dagger? Even if you get it back, wouldn't he just find something else that's pointy?'

'He won't.'

'And why is that?'

'Because he has the same fear as you, Leo.'

Leo shucked a half laugh. 'Which is?'

'The fear of Hell, of course.'

Leo rubbed his face with both hands, let out a great sigh and checked for movement behind the bar. 'Sorry, Michael, this still means nothing to me. Sure I can't get you a drink?'

He got up to leave the booth, but Michael grabbed him by the wrist. Leo looked at his hand; it was firmly rooted to the table. He wondered how this would go if he decided the conversation was over.

'I apologise, Leo.' Michael released his grip. 'Perhaps my explanation lacks clarity. I'll try to do better. Please sit.'

'Get to the point or I'm out the door.' Leo rubbed at the finger marks imbedded in his wrist.

'It was always about the balance,' Michael said, when Leo was seated again, 'the constant tug of war between God and Lucifer in their game with mankind. It's a cliché because it's true. But one amazing day, that balance shifted: a child was born, and with him came the word of God. Lucifer was furious. He possessed Judas Iscariot and brought about the crucifixion of Jesus – this is all well documented, Leo. You must be familiar with the story?'

Leo shifted in his seat. 'Like I said, I don't read.'

'You have never read The Bible?'

'Not even *The Da Vinci Code*.' Leo twirled a finger for Michael to continue, and after a confused-looking pause, Michael did.

'The breaking of rules began to spiral from there. God breathed life into his dead son, and Lucifer prepared an army to go to war if God didn't rectify His madness. A war was something neither of them wanted. Lucifer would have taken it to the earthly planes, and God would have had to destroy everything he had created to stop him. God took his son back.'

'Where does Reuben fit into this?'

Michael held up a finger for Leo's patience. 'The dagger was Lucifer's concoction. They were stalemated, deadlocked, and Lucifer wanted to keep it that way. He demanded a bone from the body of Jesus so that it could be taken to The Pit and forged into a sacred dagger, both blessed and unholy. God reluctantly agreed. The dagger was entrusted to two Disciples – an angel from Heaven, and a demon from Hell – and they were granted leave and allowed to roam the earth for all days. If such a time arose that God or Lucifer fathered another mortal child, the dagger would alert the Disciples, and they would seek out the child and kill it, without fear of God's wrath or the Devil's fury, because the dagger would hide the sin.'

'So Reuben will never be judged?'

'Correct. Whomever wields the dagger can kill with impunity.'

'So how did Reuben get his hands on it?'

'The Disciples were put to work. Walking the earth till the end of days is a long time, so Lucifer proposed that the Disciples send back any sinners that crossed their path.'

'To keep them busy?'

'To give them purpose. But in the end, even that was not enough. The Disciples believed themselves to be forgotten, believed their work insignificant. They agreed to go their separate ways. They hid the dagger where they thought nobody on this earth would find it, and they were right, nobody from this earth ever did.'

'So how the hell did Reuben find it?'

'Now that's one for Sherlock Holmes – you must've read Conan Doyle?'

Leo ignored him. 'Now you think that Reuben's got the dagger at the barn?'

'Ja.'

'And you don't walk in and get the dagger because… ?'

'Because Reuben would sense that I had been there, even my projected self, and then he'd disappear again and it would take me months to find him, only to become an observer once again. You on the other hand, he can't sense.'

'What makes you think that?'

'Because you are still alive. Believe me, if Reuben knew you'd been back to your barn, you would be dead all over again.'

Holding back a gulp, Leo got up to go to the bar. Where were the staff in this place?

'Leo, sit down. There's nothing to worry about. As I told you, he can't sense you. Sit down.'

Leo did as he was told but stared out of the window at a young couple coming out of the video shop across the road. It felt like they were from another world. They looked happy.

'When Reuben leaves the barn, you slip in again. The dagger will be close at hand, I am sure. The search need only be brief.'

Leo jerked his head back and glared at Michael. 'If it only needs a quick look, then why don't you nip in and grab it?'

'If by chance the dagger is not there…' Michael made a bird with his hands as though he were performing a shadow puppet show. The bird took flight from the table and Michael followed it with his cool blue eyes until his hands separated, and the bird disappeared.

'By that, you don't mean he just…' Leo walked two fingers across the table. Not quite as graceful as Michael's bird. 'Into the sunset?'

'Nein. He doesn't walk away. He commits suicide and releases his spirit into limbo. And as nobody will come for him, he searches for another host, a new haven for his wicked soul. You can see why I am not eager for this to happen. Do you know what the world population is at the moment?'

'And the dagger goes with him?'

The muscles in Michael's jaw contorted, the grinding of his teeth, audible. 'Nein, Leo. The dagger does not go with him – a mystery that taunts me. The dagger can't cross into limbo; it is matter, as this is matter.' Michael thumped the tabletop, hard enough to make Leo blink.

'I don't know what black magic he has at his command, but the dagger seems to find him wherever he re-emerges.' He fixed Leo with a stony stare. 'You could save lives. That would not go unnoticed, I am sure.'

'I'm sorry, but nothing will get me back in the barn. You'll have to find another way.'

'You would turn your cowardly cheek?'

Leo got to his feet, could feel the blood cloud gathering. 'Listen, I don't owe you a damn thing, and as for that fucker, he stole my life. So you can quit it with the guilt-trip tactics because I'm already on the world tour.'

Michael stood and leaned close. 'He has killed once as you well know, and he will kill again,' he said.

'Some old bloke? He'd have been dead in a few months anyway.' Leo's words tore him as they came out, but he couldn't help himself; he'd had enough now. 'I didn't ask to be put in this situation, and I'm not responsible for it either.' He grabbed his jacket. It was still damp, but he slipped it on anyway.

'Think about it, Leo,' Michael called after him.

'I have. Now leave me alone.'

Reuben stepped off the bus and studied the scrap of paper he'd torn from the yellow directory. When the bus pulled away again, the place he was looking for revealed itself. He screwed up the scrap and tossed it, then headed across the road to JJ's INK EMPORIUM.

The inside smelled of sweat and chemicals, much the same as every other tattoo parlour he had ever been in, with only the degrees of pungency differing from time to time. The examples of artwork on display were equally meaningless, as ever.

'Take a look around,' a man's smoke-eroded voice called from behind a beaded curtain. 'Be with you in a moment.'

Reuben stepped through the beads.

The man beyond the curtain was stroking down surgical tape on the arm of a young girl. Apart from whatever was beneath the dressing, the girl was free of piercings and other tattoos and looked out of place in here. The artist was typically covered in ink, displaying nothing Reuben hadn't seen before. They both turned to face him.

'I told you I'd be out in a minute, so if you don't mind…'

'I don't,' Reuben said, and took the chair in the corner.

The girl handed the man some money, and the artist parted the beaded curtain for her to leave. He then turned to Reuben, still holding the curtain open. 'Shall we go back into the shop?'

Reuben rose but didn't leave. 'No need. I know what I want.' He switched to the seat the girl had just been sitting in.

The artist said goodbye to the girl and turned back to Reuben. 'Look, mate, I'm booked up all day. If you want to choose something out here, I'll try and fit you in tomorrow. Now, can you please evacuate my studio.'

Reuben put his hand inside his jacket and pulled out a brick of twenties. 'For your time.' He under-armed the wad to the artist. 'I'll wait while you rearrange your bookings.' Reuben shrugged off his jacket.

The artist fanned the notes and eyed him. 'What did you have in mind?'

CHAPTER 16

The drizzle had crept into his joints by the time he reached the cottage, and he knew he was going to be sore the next day. What he wouldn't give for his Vanquish; walking everywhere was really starting to piss him off.

He opened both bottles of the wine he'd bought, then peeled out of his wet clothes. Once he'd towelled himself dry, he hunted through his dwindling wardrobe, thought he'd got lucky with a plain white T-shirt until he unfolded it. On the front was a bright green square. Inside the square was a fist with its middle finger sticking out, and beneath the fist was a caption that read: CUBISM IS FOR ARTISTS THAT CAN'T DO HANDS. He tugged it over his head.

He filled one of the crystal wine glasses and stepped into the lounge. At first he thought he'd been burgled but then remembered punting John's trunk, something he now regretted.

The trunk looked broken: the base and contents lying beside the dark stain on the carpet. Leo put his glass on the mantel and lifted the trunk back onto its stubby legs, got confused when his hand touched the base that shouldn't have been there. He opened the lid and peered in. Smiled. It wasn't the base that had dislodged, it was the false bottom.

Inside were bank statements, a chequebook, the lease agreement for the cottage and a wallet fat with notes. Beneath that he found a diary.

It looked a little on the girlie-side with the bright yellow padding and the silver clasp, but judging by John's taste in shirts, Leo didn't give it much thought. He was too busy battling with his conscience as to whether he should read it or not. It was more a slaughter than a battle.

Without reading any particular entry, it became clear that it wasn't John's diary. The handwriting was too fine and elaborate, and above each 'I' sat a small bubble where a dot should be; a girl's hand for sure.

Leo snapped the diary shut, then opened it again to the front page to confirm what he already knew. The diary belonged to Sadie Louise Howard.

There wasn't much to look through, as it was only April, but not one entry had been missed – each beginning with 'Dear Diary', which Leo found adorable and nauseating at the same time.

There was no question that he was going to read the diary; he'd already justified it as a way of getting to know Sadie better. The thought that what he was about to do was morally wrong was a faint nipping in the back of his mind, something he had learned to tolerate a long time ago.

Leo sat in the armchair. He was about to read his first book.

It took half an hour to work his way through January and to realise there was a lot he didn't know about Sadie. Her job, for one thing, played a massive part in her life, and wasn't just a place where she earned her money. In nearly every entry, she mentioned work colleagues, but more so the patients. It was as if she were keeping a file on their progress – their mental states as much as their physical ones – and had plenty of ideas for helping those patients finding things difficult in 'this sterile environment'.

She had an appetite for books, too. In three weeks she had managed to finish four: A book on psychology that had gone over her head, a vegetarian-based G.I diet that John would never stick to, a trashy Romance novel that was boring and predictable and not a true reflection of anything based on human emotion and was probably written by a man under a female pseudonym, and a book about mockingbirds that was written by a bloke called Harper Lee, that she hadn't understood properly at school but blew her away now.

Leo gave a mental salute to DVDs: They didn't take a week to watch and had a hit rate for satisfaction that was better than twenty-five percent, in his experience.

John was mentioned numerously, of course, although her feelings for him never made the page. It was more like a written account of the times she saw him – no sense of emotional attachment – as if someone else had written it for her.

Leo nearly spilled his wine at the first sight of his own name, but it turned out to be another emotionless recall. Sadie had driven past the barn on the way to work one morning and had seen him putting out the rubbish. That was it.

He filled his glass and took a moment. It wasn't too late to stop. He had the rest of his life to discover who she was, doubted there was anything in these pages that would change the way he felt about her. But there was something nagging him that kept the pages turning.

A few weeks on, Leo popped up again. Same thing as before, only this time when Sadie had passed the barn he was doing something in the garage. Why this warranted an entry into her diary he didn't know, but felt flattered all the same.

On the last Monday in March, Sandra had told Sadie she was dating a married man. Sadie was disgusted with her. On Tuesday, Sandra told Sadie she had called it off with the married man, as Sadie had made her feel terrible about herself. Sadie had suspected it was more likely the husband had gone back to his wife. On Wednesday she stayed in and finished another book Leo had never heard of, while John played cards, wasted his money, time, and his life, and by the sounds of it, did a grand job of pissing Sadie off. The rest of the week played out much the same, until April Fools' Day. He read that entry three times, pacing the room between readings, as each time his feelings changed. First he was elated, then his gut filled with cold stones, causing elation to give way to a sickening swell. On the third reading came remorse, of course.

Leo threw the diary on the sofa and swapped his glass for the bottle, thought back to the morning Sadie had found him in the shower. He paced a while, swigging straight from the bottle as he pieced together snippets from his memory: "You've read it," she'd said. Of course, he hadn't known what she was talking about then. "They're only words," she'd said. "Sometimes you have to get them out there to see how ridiculous they sound," she'd said. "We'll burn it together," she'd said.

Leo picked up the diary and read it again.

2

The German had lived a long life, but he'd clung to the scrap he had left. Reuben could still feel the finger marks in his shoulders, even under the sting of fresh tattoos. But when the blade slipped in, the old man's eyes told a different story. He'd been ready. Expecting it almost.

Reuben switched on the desk lamp and studied the photograph of his next target. Ben Frinton was forty years of age and taught carpentry at Berrington High School. Simian had highlighted the carpentry detail for his own amusement, but the irony hadn't been lost on Reuben. The rest of the information he sifted as usual: absorbed the necessary, discarded the rest. He doubted Ben Frinton would be ready, but the eyes would soon tell. They always did.

He took the dagger and wrapped it in a cloth, slipped it under his belt and concealed it with his shirttail and jacket. The sun had been down an hour, and in another hour Ben Frinton would be running by the river. Perhaps if he knew his fate he would take in the views more fully, savour it as the last thing he would ever see in this world, but life wasn't fair like that. If it were, Reuben would not be here.

The flame from the hob ignited the corner of the photograph, and Ben Frinton's face blackened and curled. Reuben laid the charred remains on a baking tray and ran it under the tap at the sink. He left the barn soon after.

Sat on a bench by the river, Reuben checked his watch: five minutes more, ten at the most. Simian's mapping of routine was meticulous; Ben Frinton wouldn't be late for his own death.

Reuben closed his eyes and for a brief moment was on the bank of the Nile, the wind drifting gently over the surface of the water, grooming the peeks and ripples, making them sing. Then his reminiscence was broken by footfalls on the dry hoggin path, and he was returned.

The dark outline of a jogger bobbed towards him, but Reuben stayed sat on the bench where he would be lost in shadow. He unwrapped the dagger.

At last he could hear the man's breath over his footsteps, and Reuben stood and turned into his path. They collided.

'My apologies, Ben,' Reuben said, satisfied that he could now see his face.

'Sorry,' Ben Frinton said, panting. 'Do I know you?'

The bone handle creaked inside Reuben's tightening fist. '*I* don't even know me,' he said, and plunged the dagger into the hollow beneath Frinton's ribcage. The man stopped panting immediately.

As he fell forwards, Reuben took his weight, one hand beneath a sweaty armpit, the other pulling upwards on the dagger until it hit bone and would go no further. He dragged Frinton behind the bench, where they would both disappear into the blackening canvas of wild grass and crushed beer cans. Frinton never let him go.

'Look at me, Ben,' Reuben said. Frinton looked him in the eyes. 'Jesus was a carpenter – a teacher. Did you know that?'

Reuben eased the dagger free, and a viscous blood bubble spilled onto Frinton's running vest.

'Look at me, Ben.'

Frinton's eyes focused one last time before Reuben pulled him close, whispered in his ear. It was the same thing he whispered to all of them.

He left the dead man in the grass, then sat back on the bench and wrapped the dagger. When it was concealed beneath his shirt once more, Reuben closed his eyes and listened to the night. All he could hear was the river and the wind. All he could smell was the blood.

CHAPTER 17

John's biological makeup didn't allow for much of a hangover. By Leo's second cup of coffee, he felt fairly okay.

While he was waiting for the taxi, he made sure Sadie's diary was safely back beneath the false bottom of the trunk. He wouldn't need another look for some time, as the only passage of any interest he could now recite word for word. Bond would have an opinion, but until Leo had formed one of his own, Bond could stay behind the sofa

The taxi tooted, and he gave Tarik a thumb's up from the spare room window. He folded his money into his jeans and stepped out into a bright April morning. An empty easel watched him go.

2

Tarik took the twenty and made a half-hearted attempt at fishing four pounds out of an old bank bag before Leo told him not to worry. Tarik hadn't been as chatty on this trip, but he'd still made Leo pang for the tranquillity of his Vanquish.

He walked up the dusty driveway of Stamp and Son's

latest development: a contemporary barn conversion that would eventually look something like his own. His dad would have hated it.

Inside was echoey silence. Two weeks had gone by since he'd last been on-site, and sweet little had changed. Internal studwork had been erected but still needed skimming, and the first fix for the electrics looked underway, but nothing else. It was the Mary Celeste of building sites. As he walked around, he half expected John to jump out, start trailing behind him with a comic cower: *Yessir, Boss. I's workin' haard, Boss. No need for the stick, Boss.* And with that would come the laughter, but the place was empty. He was just about to shout out for somebody when he saw Mick pass by the French doors at the other end of barn.

With a mobile pressed against his ear, Mick paced back and forth, in and out of sight, reminding Leo of a tin duck in a shooting gallery, an image he'd probably taken from an old movie rather than the fond recollection of a family day out at the fairground. Mick noticed him, raised a finger and mouthed *one minute.* Leo obliged him and climbed the ladder to his right, the only way you could reach the mezzanine level until the oak staircase was installed. He found himself equally unimpressed with the progress up here. The studwork was finished but nothing else. He tried to visualize the end product, but an already overworked imagination couldn't bridge the gap from this squalid state. Under normal circumstances he would be pissed off, but these where not normal circumstances, and the best he could muster was indifference. He was only here for Mick.

The French doors opened and closed beneath him, and then the top of the ladder twitched.

'You up there, boy?'

'Yeah, Mick, don't come up, I'll come down.'

'It's all right, all me paperwork's up there anyway.' Mick made it to the top of the ladder, out of breath. Leo held his hand out to help, but Mick swatted it away.

'I'm not an invalid, you know.'

'You're telling me that beer gut isn't a handicap?'

'Watch it now, boy, you'll find yourself going down a lot quicker than you came up.'

'Why the hell have you got all your paperwork up here?' Leo asked, smiling hard.

'Some little shits broke in over the weekend and tried to smash open the site box but couldn't. Settled for a couple of shovels and a hardhat, instead. Who in their right mind would want to nick a fucking hardhat?'

'Don't worry about it; just stick them on the account the next time you're at the merchant's.'

'Anyway, that's why everything is up here. When I go home, so does the ladder. Step into my new office, boy.'

Leo followed him into what would eventually be the master bedroom. In it was the old desk that Mick dragged with him from job to job, and a chair made out of six bags of finishing plaster.

'Where is everyone? Leo asked from the window.

'Where is everyone?' Mick repeated. 'Let me see, who shall I start with?' He stopped shuffling papers and stared into the distance. 'Steve, the plumber, has taken on a private job for a week because he can't start hanging rads and putting the heating in until Terry has finished plastering. Dave the spark has done all he can until Terry has finished plastering. Pete, fat Steve, and the two Tones flew off to Spain on Saturday – thank fuck, because they've got naff-all to do until Terry's finished the plastering. And Terry has been off sick for over a week – but he hasn't, he's been working on another job – but I can't say anything, can I? He hasn't been paid for two weeks, and I don't want to get another plasterer in because, as you know, Terry is also our tiler, and we're lucky to have him.' Mick squared a mess of papers. 'And I know I could be getting on with the plastering, but if I even look at a trowel this fucking thing goes off, and I have to deal with another barrel of shite.' He threw his phone on the floor, hard enough to make Leo blink, and as if on cue, it started vibrating. 'See what I mean, boy?'

Mick jumped up and kicked his phone through the doorway. It thudded against the plasterboard wall opposite, leaving a small hole. He sat back down and continued to fuss with the paperwork, seemingly calm again, even though the phone was still buzzing in the dust.

Leo felt it prudent not to speak.

'I'm making it sound worse than it is. Tell Leo there's nothing to worry about. They're good lads. Get some dosh in their banks and everything's fine.' After a pause: 'How's the boy?'

The phone finally died, which in Leo's mind made it safe to open his mouth. 'He's better, just wants more time to himself, you know? He's put me in charge till his head's clear.' Leo pointed at Mick with a smirk. 'Which means no turning up at his door or pestering him with phone calls – he wants it all to come through me, okay?'

Mick held up his hands. 'Whatever gets the job done.'

'What about you, Mick?'

'Me? I'm all right. Just like to let off a little steam. All us paddies are the same. I'll be fine when I get a beer in me mitt.'

He handed Leo the timesheets. 'There you go, boy.'

'Cheers, I'll make sure the lads get a bit extra, for having to wait.'

'They'll be fine. Just make sure they get paid this week. Don't want them thinking they own the place. They've got it good as it is.'

Leo folded the sheets and slipped them into his pocket, stood there in the quiet. He wasn't ready to go. He thought back to his first week at Stamp & Son's. The labouring was hard, but it cleared the mind. After that week, his dad told him to pick a trade. It was an easy pick.

Watching Mick lay plaster was a thing to behold. A man his size had no business being graceful. Leo could still remember the expressions of the trades standing idle around him, all gawking at Mick when they should've been busy themselves. Leo remembered that look because he craved it himself. He told his dad he wanted to be a plasterer like Mick, and so it was. He still did his fare share of labouring, but on the days Mick was plastering, Leo would be by his side. Man and boy.

'I could do some plastering if you want?' Leo said.

Mick smiled but didn't look up. 'Don't worry about it, boy, I think I've fucked my phone anyway. I'll try and get some pink on as soon as I've gone through this lot. You get off and see that young girl of yours.'

'I'm handy with a trowel. Leo taught me when he was renovating his barn. And as you taught Leo…'

Mick looked up from his paperwork.

'Thanks for the offer, but I've seen your little efforts.' A ghost of a smile lingered on his face.

'I'm pretty good now.'

'Pretty good ain't good enough, especially for this contemporary look he loves so much. You just get them wages sorted and I'll see you in the week for a drink, okay?'

'Trowels in the back of your van?' Leo headed for the door.

'Leave my tools alone,' Mick barked. 'You get going, that's all the help I need.'

'Okay, I'm joking.' Leo backed out the door with his hands up, waited a moment then stuck his head around again. 'That plaster you're sitting on, is that all there is? Oh – don't worry, I think I saw some on the way in.' He reached the ladder and heard Mick coming after him. It was hard not to laugh.

'Don't you dare, boy, I'm telling ya. I haven't got time for this.'

Mick's face was getting redder, and he actually wagged his finger.

'I'm joking, calm down.' Leo started to laugh.

'Go.' Mick shouted.

'Okay, I'm gone.' Leo descended the ladder and when at the bottom looked up to see Mick's black cloud of a face. 'See you in the week for a beer, then?'

'Maybe,' Mick said, and then his head disappeared.

There was a moment of doubt, but only a moment. Some things were just too sweet to resist. Leo pulled the ladder away and laid it on the ground in time to hear Mick erupt above him.

'You get that bloody ladder back up here now, boy!'

3

Mick hailed threats for ten minutes, then disappeared into his makeshift office. When Leo had finished smoothing the first coat, he put the ladder back loud enough for Mick to hear, but he seemed content to catch up on the paperwork and didn't show his face until Leo was polishing the second coat.

Mick stepped onto the ladder, descended halfway and slid down the rest with surprising agility. He approached in silence, and Leo couldn't help but take a couple of steps away from the old bear.

Mick flicked his eyes around the surface of the wall, ran two fingers across it.

'I'm just popping into town for a paper and some bacon rolls,' Mick said, without taking his eyes off the wall. 'When I get back, you can make a start upstairs.' He brushed past Leo. 'Don't go mad with the polishing. Smooth is fine.'

That was all the approval Leo was going to get, even though he knew Mick was looking at perfection. Mick drove off in the Toyota, and Leo swept away the finger marks with his trowel. And then, out of pure reflex, he scratched his name in the corner, down where the skirting would hide it – a habit John had instilled in him when they had plastered the barn together. *An artist should always sign his work,* John had said, and always made Leo scratch his name.

When Mick returned, they ate two bacon rolls each and shared Mick's flask of sickly sweet tea. Mick read his *East Anglian* in virtual silence, only breaking it with the occasional snort. Leo made a start upstairs.

He found he'd missed plastering. What had once been a boring, uninspiring daily routine now felt like much-needed therapy. The mundane repetition was meditative, like running, and a welcome break from his sprawling thoughts and emotions. But as much as it was calming, it wasn't long before Sadie's diary entry invaded his peace-filled mind. He began to recite it over and over again, every word imprinted in his memory.

Dear diary, it began, as all the other entries had.

I sat outside Leo's before work again this morning. I really am pathetic. If only he had pulled me into bed with him that night, I wouldn't be feeling this guilty, I'm sure.

The jealousy game has backfired on me beautifully, as genuine feelings of love for John torture me daily, as do my feelings of love for Leo. How could I ever be with him *now?*

When Leo read it the first time, he was ecstatic, to hear that Sadie loved him. But the ecstasy didn't last. He wasn't Leo anymore – he was John.

Nevertheless, by Sadie's own admission, she still loved John, so everything was fine, wasn't it? Apart from the torturing her daily bit.

And who was *him*? Could mean Leo *or* John.

It suddenly occurred to Leo that John had read the diary. Of course he had. It was in his trunk wasn't it? How did John feel, knowing his girl loved another man, his best friend? He must have been having dark thoughts of his own.

John had lost his hipflask on purpose. It was his way of letting it all go, letting the jealousy go. He'd forgiven Leo for something that wasn't Leo's fault. Leo harboured dark thoughts for over a years before arriving at the same solution, and even then it had been Bond's idea.

Leo dropped Mick's trowel and staggered backwards into the plasterboard wall, hard enough to make the whole mezzanine tremble. That night, poker night, though the blood cloud had gathered, it was John's words that had finally pushed Leo to violence: *What a stupid prick you are,* John had said to him. *What a stupid prick.* Leo could recall every crease in John's face when he'd said it. But it wasn't Leo he was calling a stupid prick, it was himself. *I didn't mean* you, John would have said if Leo hadn't cut him off with the shove that eventually killed him. John was calling himself a prick for sending Sadie up to Leo's room in the first place. That night had been John's Ground Zero, too.

Tears formed in Leo's eyes, and he tried to pinch them back with his fingers. It was all he could do to stop the audible sobs. He didn't hear Mick's size twelves cross the mezzanine floor, but saw their distorted image in the doorway.

'You alright, boy?' Mick asked. 'I thought you were coming through the ceiling.'

'Plaster in my eyes,' Leo replied, his face in his hands.

'Stings like a bitch, don't it, boy?'

4

Mick dropped him back at the cottage around six, said he would pick him up in the morning. Leo had offered to help out with the rest of the plastering. Wasn't like he had plans.

He threw up an arm as the Toyota sped off, pushed open the kitchen door and flopped into the armchair in time for the local news.

Billy Walker was still missing, but the police had found new evidence linking his abduction with that of Ryan Oliver's four months earlier. A cloth had been discovered near where Billy was last sighted, on which forensics found traces of chloroform. Similar traces of chloroform had been found on the collar of Ryan Oliver's school shirt.

He switched off the set, and the plasma began to swim. He found tears for Davey and tears for John, for his mother and for Sadie, for Mick and Billy Walker. Even for his dead unloving father. Finally, he found tears for himself, the heaviest of them all.

5

Reuben switched off the television and threw the remote against the wall. It didn't break. He was about to rectify that with the heel of his boot when the phone rang... *three*... *four*... *silent*. He grabbed the receiver when it rang again.

'Why didn't you tell me there was another boy?' he said through gritted teeth.

Simian laughed. 'For exactly this reason. You know how you get. You can't have them all, Reuben.'

'Tell me where the Walker boy is. I'll not do another one until I know.'

'I don't think so.'

'TELL ME!'

Simian laughed again. 'You're sweet when you're grumpy. Now... I'll be sending you another quite soon. Then you can have the boy.'

'No, Simian.'

'Byeee.'

The phone went dead. Reuben finished off the remote with his boot.

CHAPTER 18

The rest of Leo's week was blessed repetition. He and Mick finished all the plastering they could have by Friday afternoon, and Mick seemed his cheery self again. He invited Leo for cold beers and legendary ale pie at his local drinking pit, The Eel's Hoof, and although Leo could think of nothing better, he declined. Too risky. Once he'd sunk a few, he'd forget who he was, tie his tongue in all sorts of wonderful knots, and there was no way Mick was going to let John sup lemonade.

Leo highlighted Sadie's number, then switched the phone off altogether. Maybe he would give her a few more days; calling her so soon would be a mistake. He could probably do with the extra time himself anyway, as he wasn't sure how to approach the situation in light of what he'd found in her diary.

Was Sadie through with him? Had she been waiting for John to royally fuck up so she could walk guilt free?

He showered until his fingers felt like bubble wrap, then stepped out and caught a whiff of the carpet. The smell of urine took him back to when he first entered John's body and to when he first tried to scratch his way out. As soon as he was dressed, he ripped the carpet up, threw it as far as he could into the knee-high wild grass at the back of the cottage, then went inside and scrubbed his hands with washing-up liquid. Why had he only just noticed the pissy carpet? What was wrong with him? He hadn't cleaned in days.

He switched his phone on and scrolled through his numbers again, highlighted Sadie, again, and switched the phone off, again. She worked Saturdays, anyway, and wouldn't be able to talk. He toyed with the idea of going to see her, telling her about his new position at Stamp & Son could work massively in his favour. He could turn up with flowers, tell her he loved her and that he hadn't stopped thinking about what she'd said. No pressure. Give her the flowers and walk away. Maybe that was better than a phone call, and definitely better than waiting for her to call him.

He switched his phone back on and called a taxi before the seed of doubt he was nursing grew into something big enough to spread roots.

2

Tarik drove away and left Leo standing on the side of the road, holding a bunch of yellow daffodils. Somewhere in the back of his mind he knew they were her favourites, but from where he'd dug that morsel of info he didn't know.

From the road, only the grey slate of the care home's roof was visible. The rest of the building was shielded by a row of conifers that were broken only at the entrance by two three-meter brick pillars that supported the open wrought iron gates and the sign above them reading: *Cliffdale Residential Care Home. The home from home.*

Once through the gates, his developer's eye blinked. He counted over thirty windows set into the vine-covered façade, and half expected a tweeded aristocrat with a shotgun broken over one arm to come bursting through the large wooden doors and chase him off his land. A fine example of Victorian architecture, Leo thought, and felt saddened that it would more than likely be diced into luxury apartments before the decade was out. He leant on the impressive front doors, but they were locked, and then a tinny female voice told him to push when he heard the buzz.

The reception area was contemporary in design – with not an old person in sight, if you didn't count the woman sat behind the reception desk.

'Can I help?' the women asked, smiling at the daffs and then at Leo.

'Yeah.' Leo cleared his throat. 'Sadie Howard?'

The woman glanced at the chrome clock hanging behind her. 'It's a bit early for visits,' she said. 'Some of the residents will still be having breakfast.'

'Oh no, she works here.'

'Ah, I thought I was going mad then.' She picked up the phone and tucked her silver hair behind her ear. 'We never get anybody come in for staff – not that it's against the rules – hi, it's Linda, is…' She held the handset to her bosom and looked at Leo. 'Sorry, what was the name again?'

'Sadie Howard.'

'Sorry, Cat, is Sadie Howard on today? There's a nice looking young man here to see her.' She paused for an answer.

Leo supposed John *was* a nice looking young man.

'Thanks, Cat.' The woman put the phone down. 'Sorry, she's not on today. She swapped shifts with Sandra, apparently.'

The woman looked embarrassed, but Leo couldn't tell if it was for him, for her, or for the both of them.

'We've probably got our wires crossed somewhere,' Leo said.

'Easily done – beautiful flowers though.'

'Thanks.' He turned to go, but stalled. 'I couldn't have a word with Sandra, could I?'

'Sure,' the woman said, and repeated the process. 'She'll be down in five. Take a seat.' She pointed at a small waiting area to Leo's right: stylish chrome and leather chairs lined up behind a low, matching coffee table with the home's brochures fanned out on top.

A few minutes later, Sandra was buzzed in through the large wooden doors, but without the instruction to push. The woman behind reception pointed, and Sandra made her way towards him, and at that moment Leo realised he didn't know how to greet her and hoped she would give him a clue.

'Hi, John,' she said with an easy confidence that gave nothing away.

Leo caught stale tobacco and recognised the telltale lines around her bright pink lips. This woman had been smoking forever, adding ten years onto what he thought was about forty-five.

'Hi, Sandra,' he echoed.

'Sadie's off today, didn't she tell you?'

Leo struggled to answer, but Sandra saved him the embarrassment by slapping him hard on the shoulder.

'Probably drunk again, weren't ya – typical bloke. Are those for me? You shouldn't have.' She winked and gave him a smile that shed those extra ten years, then removed a packet of cigarettes from the waistband of her navy uniform and shook them. 'Can we go outside? I'm gasping.'

She led him around the side to a tarmac car park, took a seat on the bonnet of a faded green Fiesta and lit her cigarette.

'So she didn't tell you she'd swapped shifts then?' she said between igniting puffs.

'She probably did, and I probably was drunk.' Leo shook his head and was about to shuffle out of the smoke cloud forming around her when a gust blew it away. Sandra's highly-combed hair didn't move. *Did women still use that much hairspray?* he wondered. After some of the silly rules and regulations he'd read in Sadie's diary, he was surprised her hairdo hadn't been outlawed as a fire hazard.

She shook out the match and let it fall to the tarmac, took a long hit on her cigarette and blew a white stream from the corner of her mouth. 'Sadie mentioned you were interested in the Walker kid. Knew him, did ya?'

'You say that like he's already dead.'

'As good as. Specially now they know it's the same bloke.'

'They'll find him.'

'Oh yeah, they'll find him, alright. In a shallow grave like Ryan Oliver – I knew his mum, you know? She's in St Clements, now.' Sandra curled the crazy finger round her ear. 'Poor cow.'

'Shallow grave?'

'In some woodland on the outskirts of Mundey.'

Leo's stomach bunched. 'How did he…?'

'Molested. Throat cut.'

Leo turned his face against the wind.

'Ignore me, John. When you've got a love life like mine, you learn to look on the pessimistic side of everything. The Oliver kid was gone three weeks before he turned up. Billy's only been gone two. Still a week to find him.'

Leo nodded, looked down at the daffs and held them out to Sandra. 'You may as well take these.'

'No,' Sandra said. 'I'll put them with her others.' She flicked her cigarette away with a pained expression on her face.

'What others?'

She slid from the car bonnet. 'I've really got to go.'

'No, you really have to tell me. And it's too late for bullshit.'

She sighed. 'It's probably nothing. You're all friends, right?'

'All?'

'Yeah. You, Sadie, Leo. He is your mate, ain't he?'

'Leo sent her flowers?'

'Well that was the name on the card.'

'What else was on the card?'

'Didn't get a chance to read it. Sadie put it in her bag – look, you won't tell her it was me, will you?'

'When was this?'

'Yesterday. Promise me, John.'

'Don't worry. I wasn't even here.'

Sandra smiled uncomfortably and walked away, her hair immoveable in the stiff wind. It was like watching a carnival float at Mardi Gras.

3

Before he even reached the street he'd called Sadie twice: the first time just rang. Second time she cut him off.

'Fuck!'

Leo opened a text box, but what was he going to say to her? *Leo's not really Leo, he's a murdering demon called Reuben. He abducted Billy Walker and plans to kill him just like Ryan Oliver, and for some strange reason I think he was in Mundey nineteen years ago because…*

The more Leo thought about it, the more he was convinced. Stephen Mercer, Ryan Oliver… Davey. They'd all died the same way: Molested, throat cut, then buried in a shallow grave. How many kids had Reuben murdered whose bodies still hadn't been found? Nineteen years was a long time, and that was assuming Davey was the first.

Leo needed to find Michael, had an idea he wasn't telling half of what he knew. But if he wasn't at the barn watching Reuben or sitting in the booth at the Crown, Leo didn't know where to look, and that left only the waiting game. A game he wasn't good at.

4

It was the first time Reuben had noticed how grimy the kitchen was. Filthy, in fact. He stacked all the crockery and cutlery by the sink and set about disinfecting the cupboards inside and out. With the cupboards smelling lemon fresh, he filled the sink with hot soapy water and started scrubbing plates, his mind wandering to the downstairs toilet he'd forgotten to bleach before going to bed.

The phone rang. Reuben looked at the blue rubber gloves he was wearing. He ripped them off and threw them in the bin, reached the phone just as it died. It rang again and he lifted the receiver.

'It's starting already, Simian.'

'Well of course it is, Ruby. You're getting stressed.'

'We need to leave. Give me the boy.'

'We've got time for one more. Then we'll leave.'

'No. Give me the boy.'

'You need to calm down. Relax. The more you stress, the quicker the transformation will occur. Focus on what you are supposed to be doing, and you'll have plenty of time for the boy.'

'How long?'

'I'll have the details ready soon, but in the meantime, I've left you a little something in the shed that will hopefully take your mind off the boy. The body has started to decay already, I'm afraid, but I'm sure you know what to do with it.'

The phone clicked, and Reuben replaced the handset, went through the kitchen and opened the back door into the garden.

The shed was small and lined with rusting hand tools, old tins of paint and a lawn mower with two wheels missing. At first, Reuben couldn't see anything out of place, but then he smelled it. He pulled the mower forward.

On the damp floor was a hessian sack, stained in a colour he knew well. He lifted the bundle and cradled it like a baby to his chest, rolled back the neck of the sack and peeked inside.

'Oh, Simian,' he said, and took the bundle inside.

5

Leo stepped off the bus at the bottom of the thoroughfare and walked up to the Crown. Michael wasn't there. He sat in his booth for half an hour, nursing a pint and watching the streets and the people that filled them, then headed towards the taxi rank at the station.

Fifteen minutes later he was standing on the brow of the hill that overlooked the barn. He'd seen Michael skulking in the trees opposite his driveway before, but he wasn't there now, and Leo started to wonder if he would ever see him again.

The wind had blown in a cover of grey cloud, making the barn dark inside. Leo would've had some lights on under this cast, so he guessed Reuben was either out or sleeping, and with his nocturnal habits being what they were, he supposed sleeping was the safer bet.

As he walked back to the cottage, his mind began to churn. What if Reuben *had* killed Davey? What if he knew beyond doubt?

The blood cloud rumbled at that moment, and Leo decided that maybe it was better to never know. Knowing meant that he would have to do something about it, and that road only led to one place.

As soon as he stepped into his kitchen he plucked the Chinese menu from the fridge door. It was only four o'clock, but he craved grease and cold beer. He ordered more than he knew he would eat, planning for breakfast as well, and a case of beer to go with. He barely noticed the washing-up he'd left that morning as he cracked a fresh one from the fridge and drank half in one gassy hit.

All he wanted now was to be comatose and to prove the person who'd said you wouldn't find the answers at the bottom of a bottle to be full of shit.

He went into the spare room and put his beer on the computer desk, knelt at the paintings and flipped through them to one he'd noticed earlier. It was a dark work, angular and jagged and devoid of colour. He set it on the easel, grabbed his beer and left the room.

He drank three more beers in quick succession, staring out the lounge window at not much at all, then pulled Bond from behind the sofa and set him on the mantel.

'I think Reuben killed Davey,' Leo said, and fetched another beer.

I'm fine. How are you?

Leo came back and resumed his post at the window. 'And he sent Sadie flowers.'

So what are you after? Help? A sympathetic ear?

'Michael seemed to think I was brought back here for a reason, a higher purpose.'

But all you can think of is killing Reuben to avenge Davey and protect Sadie?

'Not exactly the righteous path, is it?'

Well... you know the drill.

Leo nodded, set his beer on the windowsill and sat on the sofa.

Immediately the room began to change. Pale blue blotches infected the walls, grew and devoured the dowdy wallpaper of the cottage. Moore and Connery appeared above the TV set. Birthday cards materialised on the chest of drawers.

Leo was sobbing on his bed, could feel the slime from the branch eating into his hands like oil, like tar. He turned to his bedroom door when Simian entered, sat up and cuffed his tears.

Simian walked around the room with his hands clasped behind his back, as though he were browsing in a museum. He lingered in front of the two Bonds for the longest time, cocking his head from side to side so his ponytail swung like a pendulum.

'Your mother's taken your father to A and E. He's going to be fine. Now… ' Simian turned to face him. 'If you had to choose one, right now, which would it be?'

Leo sniffed. Swallowed. 'Mum.'

Simian smiled, aimed a thumb at the posters. 'I mean which Bond. There can only be one.'

Leo's mind was sprawling. Only twenty minutes ago he nearly bashed his dad's brains in. 'I like Roger Moore.'

Simian raised his eyebrows, then sat next to Leo on the bed.

'Do you ever think about dying, Leo?'

Leo sat up straight against his headboard, hugged his knees to his chest. 'Sometimes.'

'Do you ever think about where you'll go when you die?'

'Sometimes.'

'Heaven or Hell, do you think? Bearing in mind what just happened in the woods.'

Leo shrugged, and one eye spilled a tear.

'Where would you go if you died right now?' Simian clicked his fingers in Leo's face.

Leo flinched and shook his head.

'That's what I think too,' Simian said. 'But it doesn't have to be that way… if you're willing to change. Are you willing to change?'

Leo nodded, a single sob jolting his shoulders.

'Good boy. Now look at these hands of yours.' Simian took Leo by the wrist, twisted it so Leo could see his own palm. 'Look how filthy they are. They're black. Stained with sin. Go and wash them. The Devil lurks in the dark, and every good boy knows that cleanliness is next to godliness.'

Leo jumped from his bed, ran to the bathroom, crying and wailing. The water was steaming, but he scrubbed his hands till they hurt. He lathered them with soap, scratched at the skin with his nails. They would never be clean enough. Never.

When he returned to his bedroom, he held out his red-raw hands for inspection.

Simian turned them over, nodded. 'Better.' He let Leo's hands fall and went back to studying the Bond posters. 'It's funny. Your father would never tell you, but he's quite the Bond fan himself – of course, he's a Connery man – as I think you'll find most true Bond fans are.'

Simian went to leave but paused in the doorway. 'But even if you're not a true fan, there can only be one Bond, can't there?' he said, and left.

Leo stood in front of his posters, eyes jumping from Moore to Connery, Moore to Connery, then finally settling on Moore. He reached up with a painful hand and tore him down, scrunched the poster up and stuffed it in his bin.

He sobbed on his bed for what felt like hours, holding his sore hands to his bony chest, and at some point, he couldn't tell when, he began to hear a soothing voice:

There, there, Shtamp. There, there.

6

Leo went back to the lounge window and finished his beer; neither of them had anything left to say. He took Bond from the mantel and slipped him behind the sofa.

By the time the Chinese arrived, he'd lost his appetite. The case of beers would do fine, though. He sat in the armchair, bouncing channels till the news came on, then wished he hadn't bothered.

The police announced the scaling down of their investigation which, for anybody with a spark of intelligence, said that Billy was dead. But Leo knew better. Reuben had him; as sure as he knew that Reuben had killed Ryan Oliver and as sure as he knew Reuben had been to this part of the world before and taken Davey from him.

Leo hurled his bottle above the mantel, where it exploded in a plume of green glass. The person who had said you wouldn't find the answers at the bottom of a bottle was wise, but full of shit, all the same.

He wanted to help Michael now, but it looked like he would never get the chance. The best he could hope for was that Reuben moved on, grew tired of the climate, his new face. But who would save Billy, then?

Maybe God would step in and do the right thing for a change. The buck stopped with Him after all.

Leo pulled himself out of the armchair and trudged towards the bedroom, glanced at the dark canvas as he passed in the hall. He drew the bedroom curtains while he kicked off his boots and got into bed with his clothes on.

Maybe God would do the right thing after all and take him in his sleep.

CHAPTER 19

Leo was lying on a forest floor, looking up at the moon through a canopy that was being stroked by a midnight breeze. An owl hooted, and the trees whispered their lullaby, and in the distance, footsteps approached.

The footsteps grew louder, until Leo could hear twigs breaking near his head, and then the silhouette of a man crossed the moon, and the footsteps disappeared.

The man's outline was clear; tall and lean in his clothes, his jaw-line shaven smooth. A match was struck, and a lantern lit. Leo's own face illuminated before him.

Reuben placed the lantern on the ground, temporarily hiding his features until he bent over to bury his spade in the soft forest earth.

The first spadeful buried a foot, the second a knee. By the third, Leo was screaming the silent scream of dreams.

More footsteps approached as the earth continued to pile. Leo's limbs began to constrict.

Several more silhouettes surrounded him now, their faces illuminated in the lantern's glow as they bent for their handfuls of peaty soil. John's first handful dusted Leo's face from up high, as did the old German's. Jimbo's handful did likewise, only with maggots in the earthy mix. Steve Mercer and Ryan Oliver pushed earth on to his chest with little hands, while Reuben tamped down their work with the back of his shovel, *thump, thump, thump*.

The last handful was thrust into his mouth and held in place by Billy Walker, only it wasn't Billy he was looking at, it was Davey. Davey glared into his eyes, daring him to protest, but all Leo could do was choke on the dirt.

Before long, only an eyeball remained, and beyond the silhouettes that had all linked hands around his grave, the moon peered down through the canopy like a Husky's eye.

When Leo woke, he knew it had been a dream, but that didn't stop him from screaming and kicking the quilt to the floor in frenzy. The digital clock read two pm, and he had to check his wristwatch to believe it, then he stripped off his sweat-soaked clothes and hit the shower.

He scrubbed dry beer stains from the wall and mantel and swept up as much of the glass as he could be bothered to find, then ate cold chow mien straight from the foil container. He was just starting on a greasy chicken ball when there was a knock at the kitchen door.

Through the obscure glass, Leo could see Michael's unmistakable outline, and almost hit himself in the face he opened the door so quickly.

'Where the fuck have you been,' Leo said, still chewing the chicken ball.

'Watching Reuben.'

'Come in, I need to talk to you.'

'You need to see something first. Meet me on the brow of the hill that overlooks the barn.' Michael turned to leave.

'Wait, I'll come with you now.'

'Nein.'

'Why not?'

'I'm already there.'

Michael leant forward, as if about to sprint, then shot into the air.

Leo almost coughed up his chicken ball.

2

He climbed the hill, clutching his chest with indigestion. Michael walked down to meet him.

'Reuben is behaving very strangely.' Michael handed Leo a pair of binoculars and led him to a flattened area of grass a little ways back from the crest of the hill.

He focused the binoculars, panned left and right before training them on the kitchen. Reuben was opening a bottle of wine, and Leo couldn't help being disturbed at the sight of himself. 'He's opening wine.' Leo took the binoculars from his eyes to frown at Michael .

'In that case, it's their second bottle.'

'*Their* second bottle?'

Leo refocused, saw Reuben filling two glasses. He took the wine through to the main living area and handed one of the glasses to someone sitting on the sofa. The corner of a kitchen unit was obscuring the other person.

'Who is it?' Leo asked.

'I was hoping you could tell me.'

'How would I know?'

'Reuben has no friends, no acquaintances, only victims. I've followed him for centuries and have never witnessed him playing the good host to anyone, even as a lure.'

Leo crabbed to his right for about ten feet and set up again. 'All I'm getting is the back of Reuben's head.' But then Reuben walked around the sofa and switched the desk lamp on.

A slender, dark haired woman was all Leo could make out at first, as her back was turned towards him, and the lamp was creating a corona around her, making it hard to see detail. But as she turned to her host, the light shone through her hair, betraying a subtle red tint.

Leo threw the binoculars aside and started running, but before he could reach anything like top speed (whatever that was for John) he was taken out on his left side by a flying rugby tackle from Michael. Leo writhed on the ground, spittle blowing through his teeth, and his arms levered painfully up his back.

'Calm yourself and think for a moment, ja?' Michael whispered in his ear. 'She's in no immediate danger. If Reuben wanted her dead, she would be already. But if you go charging down the hill like the cavalry, I guarantee an unpleasant end for the both of you.'

'Get the fuck off me.'

'I'm guessing that's Sadie, ja?'

'Ja. Get the fuck off me – you're breaking my arm.'

'Now are you going to help me?'

'I'm thinking about it. Now get—'

Michael pulled him up, and Leo brushed past him and walked back for the binoculars.

'Let's go to the cottage and talk strategies,' Michael said.

'I'm not going anywhere until she's out of there. That freak's been sending her flowers, and here she is. Don't tell me she's not in danger.'

Leo crouched and brought the binoculars up to his eyes. Michael sat down.

An hour later, Sadie pulled away in her banged-up Beetle that had been hidden from view behind the double garage. When she was safely away, Leo lowered the binoculars.

'I need to know something,' Leo said, 'before I agree to help you.'

'Anything.'

'You say you've followed Reuben for a long time?'

'Ja. Centuries.'

'Have you ever followed him here before? Mundey, I mean?'

'Why do you ask, Leo?'

'I think you know.'

Michael looked away. 'You want to know if Reuben killed your brother.'

'I deserve to know.'

Michael's mouth set in a thin line, and when he turned, Leo could see the truth in his eyes.

'Fuck!,' Leo said, the heel of his hand going to his forehead.

'I should've told you, but I couldn't risk you doing something stupid out of revenge for Davey.'

'You mean like trying to kill that freak?' Leo pointed at the barn. 'That fucker ruined my life.'

'I can see now that God wanted you to know. He's testing you.' Michael glanced at the barn. 'Down there is your damnation. Helping me is your redemption.'

They sat in silence for some time, just watching the barn, and then Leo spoke:

'What happens if I can't find the dagger?'

'We wait. Go in again. Search other places in the barn; it has to be in there.'

Leo sighed. 'That's not much of a plan, especially as we don't know how long Reuben's going to be here for.'

'I'd say we were good for another week at least. Reuben usually kills three adults before he starts on the children.'

'So another two to go?'

Michael shook his head. 'One. He's killed a teacher called Benjamin Frinton.'

'Frinton? He taught woodwork at my school. Was Davey's form tutor, I think. Jesus Chri—'

Michael cut him short and pointed. 'The barn. Look.'

Reuben was crossing the garden. He opened the shed and took out a spade, went to one of the few parts of the garden that still had grass and started to dig.

They watched him for half an hour before he returned the spade to the shed and went inside. Cut into the lawn was an oblong hole roughly three feet by two. The depth was hard to guess, but there was a healthy mound of earth piled at the side.

'Is that what I think it is?' Leo asked.

'Ja.'

'For tonight?'

'Nein, it's preparation for the boy. Look at the size of the grave.'

'What makes you so sure it's not for tonight?'

'He still has one more adult to go. Plus, Reuben's a creature of habit; he never drinks before he kills – dulls the senses.'

Leo thought back to the untouched glass of wine Reuben had left in the pub.

'Reckless, don't you think, leaving an open grave for anybody to stumble upon?'

'Reuben wants them to be discovered; he wants to appal, to sicken hearts.'

'Looks like you can kiss your 'week' theory goodbye,' Leo said. 'If you're right, then we've only got one shot in the barn, which brings me back to my first concern: What happens if I don't find the dagger?'

Michael didn't answer.

'So nothing, basically. Billy dies.' Leo shook his head, stood up and started making his way back to the cottage.

'Wait, Leo.' Michael chased after him. 'I have another plan.'

Leo stopped, turned around. 'I'm listening.'

'We capture Reuben, incapacitate him and torture him for the whereabouts of the dagger and the boy.'

'A moment ago you were concerned about my redemption. Now you want me to torture a man?' Leo walked.

'Nein, nein.' Michael caught him up. 'He would sense me, so you would have to go in first. Admittedly, yours is the most dangerous part, but once you've incapacitated him, I'll do the rest.'

'No. I don't like that plan. We'll do it my way.'

'You have a plan?'

'Yes, Michael,' Leo said. 'I have a plan.'

CHAPTER 20

Leo told Michael to take a seat, then locked himself in the toilet. He called Sadie's phone three times, and she cut him off three times. The most frustrating part was that he only wanted to hear her voice, but she couldn't know that. She was the only reason he was still alive. If anything happened to her…

When he came out, Michael was standing outside the spare room.

'He was very talented,' Michael said, gesturing at the canvas on the easel.

'If you say so.'

'Do you see John in any of them?'

Leo shook his head faintly. 'Just in the mirror.'

'You've chosen such a dark work to display. Is that also what you see in the mirror?'

Leo pulled the spare room door closed. 'Let's concentrate on Reuben.'

They went into the lounge. Michael took the sofa, and Leo dragged a dining chair out, reversed it so he could rest his arms on the back when he sat.

'What happens to Reuben if we find the dagger?' Leo asked.

'He'll be finished, trapped in your body until he dies of old age, then judged like the rest of us.'

'Because he can't commit suicide without the dagger?'

'Nein. It would be a sin. And ironically, because he would have lived a clean life, he'd go to Heaven.'

'So he'd live out the rest of his days in a luxury barn conversion with close to half a mill in his bank account? Doesn't seem right to me.'

'But no more murders, no more dead children.'

'You hope. He's a psychopath, Michael – you can't second-guess someone like that. What's to stop him killing Billy? Killing Sadie, for that matter?'

Michael took his time. 'So what do you propose?'

'I say we get him nicked.'

'Call the police?'

Leo shrugged and offered his palms. 'It'll work.'

Michael rose. 'I should go. I've burdened you.' He went to leave, thought better of it and turned back. 'We can do this, but that means doing it my way.'

'You mean torture?'

'An ugly tool, but I think the time has come to fight fire with fire, ja?'

'That doesn't work for me,' Leo said, and just as Michael went to open his mouth: 'Even if you're the one doing the torturing.'

Michael shut his mouth again.

'Look,' Leo said. 'Saving Billy Walker and keeping Sadie safe is what this is all about for me, but if that means I have to torture another human being to do it, even if that human being happens to be a psychotic serial killer, then I'm back where I started.'

Michael exhaled and dropped into his seat, and for the first time Leo noticed how haggard he looked.

'Ja, ja, you are right; I'm going mad. I haven't slept for

days and when I do there is only Reuben in my dreams.' He looked vacant. 'I've crossed the line.'

'You haven't done anything wrong.'

'I have. I tried to save you. I'm not allowed to interfere.'

'You did save me.'

'I tried to stop you from dying.' He looked up at Leo. 'But you weren't slowing down for anyone.'

'That was you in the road, the night I crashed and drowned?'

'All guides sense death, but my particular talent is for sensing the passing of Dark Hearts. Out of everyone on the planet, you were next. Reuben knew it, too. I wanted to see what would happen if I intervened, stopped him from coming through.'

'No harm, no foul.'

Michael gave a wan smile. 'I thought so, too. But then you re-emerge in John, not ten minutes from Reuben. You even managed to get back into the barn without him realising. That's when I started to think that maybe this wasn't an accident. Maybe fate had brought us together. But you're right, if God has plans for us, I don't think torture is a part of it.'

'I'd like to believe in fate,' Leo said. 'I have to believe in redemption.'

'Tell me more about this plan of yours.'

Leo stood up and swung his chair back under the table. 'Firstly, there isn't a prison on the planet that'll let you in with a weapon. That leaves us with three possible scenarios. Scenario one: Reuben's captured with the dagger on him. The dagger will get bagged and tagged and stored in an evidence room and eventually destroyed. Two: Reuben hasn't got it on him when they arrest him. If the police don't find the dagger when they search the barn, then you've got twenty-five years to retrace his footsteps and find it.'

'And three?' Michael asked.

'Reuben tops himself on capture, and the dagger's found beside his good-lookin' corpse – and again – it'll eventually be destroyed. It's Billy's best chance. The police are trained for this. If Billy *can* be found, he *will* be found.'

'One small question: How are you going to get him arrested?'

'He's a murderer, Michael. How fucking hard can it be?'

'Language, Leo.'

'Sorry.'

Michael went to the window, combed his hair back with his fingers. 'Your reasoning is sound – I don't doubt it – but you can't expect the police to turn up and arrest him on the basis of an anonymous tip-off.' He turned to Leo. 'That *is* your intention, I take it?'

'There's a bit more to it than that.'

'There would have to be.'

'You said he has one more adult to kill before he gets to Billy.'

'Ja.'

'So whatever happens, there's going to be one more dead body in Mundey. We can't change that, but we can use it. We watch until Reuben leaves, then you follow him, and I'll slip into the barn – I'll try and find the dagger, obviously – but let's assume Reuben will have taken it for the kill.'

Michael nodded.

'Then I'll take some personal items from the barn – driving licence, clothing, whatever – you tell me where he's left the body, and I'll plant the evidence and call the police.'

'So the police find the body, your driving licence, etc…'

Leo was nodding. 'And head straight for Reuben.'

'That could work,' Michael said.

'If I make it look good… it *will* work.'

'So what now?'

'Now we need to be watching Reuben twenty-four seven,' Leo said. 'We should do shifts.'

'It'll be dark in a few hours, and Reuben will be inactive now he has drunk. You get as much rest as you can and meet me in the morning.'

'Fine. But if Sadie turns up, you come get me. I'll be going in after her, no matter what.'

2

Beer was the only way Leo was getting any sleep that night, so he started early. He fried the last of the Chinese in the wok and ate it hot for lunch and cold for dinner. By ten o'clock, he was chasing one beer after another to little effect. He stood at the lounge window and stared out at the night, wondered how he was fitting into the grand scheme of things, wondered where Sadie might be at this moment.

He called her again, but her phone was switched off. He sent a text: I love you. There was nothing more he could say.

When he realised the beer wasn't working, he reached for Bond.

How may I be of assistance? Bond said, with nothing of his usual sarcasm.

'What's up with you?'

Nothing. What do you want?

'I want to sleep.'

Close your eyes, then.

'I want to show you a memory.'

I don't want to see anymore memories.

'Okay, *I* want to see it.'

You don't need me for that.

'Your way is better. It's like I'm there.'

Is that all I am to you now? An archive for your memories?

'Fine. Don't bother.'

No, let's get on with it. The sooner you're done, the sooner you can put me back behind the sofa.

Leo sat down, and the room began to change. Pebbles bubbled up from the carpet, and the walls fell away to grey

172

sky in every direction. A salty wind blew through the lounge
– but it was okay – his mum had bundled him and Davey up
in woollen hats and scarves, and cod and chips warmed his
belly – the best food he had ever tasted. Shingle Street beach
was deserted but for the upturned rowboats dotted along the
shoreline like sleeping seals. It felt as though the three of
them were the only people on the planet.

Davey kept pulling on his mum's arm; he wanted to take
a rowboat out onto the water. 'Please, please, please can we?'

His mum was laughing. 'We can't, Davey. They're not
ours.'

'We could build one,' Leo said. 'There's wood all along
the beach.'

'Yeah,' Davey said, pulling harder on her arm.

'We can't build a boat out of driftwood,' she said.

Leo rolled his eyes at her, then nodded at Davey. 'But we
could try, couldn't we?'

She winked back at Leo. 'Not a boat perhaps, but we
could build a raft from driftwood.' She smiled at Davey.
'Would that be okay?'

'Yeah!' Davey shouted. 'A raft. And when we've built it,
we can sail it out to sea.'

They combed the shoreline for over an hour, bringing
back armfuls of ashen branches and lining them up on the
shingle. By the end they had a good sized square but no hope
of binding it together.

'We can bring some rope back with us next time, Davey,'
Leo said.

Davey had his back to them. He was surveying the grey-
green North Sea on the horizon. 'But I wanted to sail it today.'

Leo went to him, put his arm around his shoulder and
walked him back to Mum. They all linked arms and headed
along the beach.

'Where would you have sailed to, Davey?' Mum asked.

'Somewhere secret that just the three of us knew.
Somewhere safe,' he said.

They walked along the beach in silence, with just the clacking of the shingle beneath their feet and the seagulls cawing in the wind. Leo tried to imagine where that secret place might be, guessed they were all trying to imagine it.

Leo stopped and groped the camera from his mum's coat pocket. 'I want to take a picture.'

Mum and Davey held hands, the shoreline stretching out behind them. Leo took their picture and wished he could freeze his happiness within the same moment.

3

Reuben couldn't find a single book in the house but counted over two hundred theatrical recordings that were stored next to the television. This he found indicative of the age, and he thought about smashing the large screen into a million pieces. He was looking in the kitchen for a utensil heavy enough to do the job when an envelope dropped through the letterbox. He rushed over and opened the door, but Simian had gone.

Inside the envelope was a photograph of a beautiful woman, her eyes the most enchanting he'd seen for some time. He wondered what they would look like with the life drained out of them.

Beauty was fleeting, he thought, a temporary gift from God – His to give and His to take. God had taken things from Reuben, things he could never have back, no matter how many bodies he stole. How long would God allow him to kill like this; what would be the number?

Reuben pulled his wandering mind back to the task at hand and began to read the document: absorb the necessary, discard the rest. When he was done, he burned the file at the hob but kept the photo for a little longer. He couldn't stop staring at those eyes.

CHAPTER 21

Leo called Sadie first thing in the morning. Her phone was switched off. He didn't like not knowing where she was, but if he didn't know, Reuben probably didn't either. The idea of her turning up at the barn again was a persistent maggot burrowing into his brain. If that happened, all bets were off.

He swung himself over the fence and started up the hill. The cuffs of his jeans darkened in the dewy grass, and he realised he would need a few things if he were going to spend any length of time out here.

There was no sign of Michael at first, but then the soles of his boots came into view. He was lying on his front and didn't show any sign of hearing Leo's approach.

'Michael?' Leo called in a harsh whisper.

He looked awkward on the ground, one arm up his back, the other not yet in view. Leo called again but still didn't get a reply.

As he drew closer he could see Michael's blonde head and his other arm; it was pointing at the barn. Leo crouched beside him, placed a hand between his shoulder blades and rocked him, but still nothing. Michael's hair concealed his face. Leo was about to part the golden curtain when Michael grabbed him by the throat. They both let out a cry of surprise, although Leo's was muffled by unwanted pressure.

Michael released his throat as quickly as he had seized it. Leo fell back, clutching his neck, remotely aware that his arse was now as wet as the bottoms of his jeans.

'What the fuck?' Leo managed to squeeze out of his choked throat.

'Sorry, Leo, I must have nodded off.'

'Nodded off? I thought you where dead.' Leo hawked and spat, still clutching his neck.

Michael moved to his side, examined his throat. 'It's an old reflex. Many years ago, you would have found me with my shield to my back and my cape atop, as it was more prudent for a thief to impale you first and rob you second. In these times, although equally barbaric in ways, I don't feel the need for a shield, but the old habits die hardest.'

Leo pushed Michael's hand away, stretched his neck from left to right.

'No harm done,' Michael said, and picked up the binoculars.

'How long were you asleep?' Leo asked.

'Honestly, I couldn't say – an hour – maybe more.'

'You don't even know if he's still in there – fuck – you don't even know if Sadie's in there, do you?' Leo trotted off to the far side of the field to see if her Beetle was behind the garage. It wasn't. He walked back shaking his head.

'Reuben fell asleep on your sofa,' Michael said. 'I thought I could shut my eyes for a moment.'

'Obviously not.'

Michael trained the binoculars on the barn.

'He's not in there, is he?' Leo said.

'We can't be sure.'

'I know for a fact he's not.' Leo jerked the binoculars away from Michael, tapped him on the shoulder and pointed. 'Just came out of the garage.'

176

Reuben was making his way back to the barn with two bottles of wine. Once he was inside, Leo focussed on the empty sofa and breathed a little easier, then panned around to the back garden.

'At least the grave is still empty,' he said, handing the binoculars back. 'He was getting wine from the garage, so perhaps he's having a night off. That doesn't mean you can go back to sleep.'

'Nein. It won't happen again.'

'I'll be here at five, and you can nod off for a couple of hours. You're working the nightshift as well, remember?'

'Ja. Five.'

Still crouching, Leo headed down the hill until he'd evolved to standing, just as Darwin had theorised.

2

John's work flask wasn't fit for growing garden vegetables in, so Leo took a walk into Mundey to buy a new one, along with the other items he needed. No way of knowing how long they'd be out on the hill, so better to be comfortable.

When he returned, he set about loading the supplies into John's old rucksack, which was also in a sorry state. John had taken it with him on his yearlong trip to Italy, so it had acquired travelling character. What had once been succulent-smelling dark leather had now mellowed to a milk chocolate that was soft and supple to touch. It made Leo feel a little sad about his own life: sure, he'd been rich – big house, nice car – but John had lived. Leo hadn't even been abroad.

The new blankets went in first, followed by the six-cell Maglite. He'd been promising himself one of these for a long while. Now seemed like the perfect time.

Last but not least was John's hipflask, still three-quarters full with Jack Daniels. It fitted into one of the side pockets as though it had been made for it.

Sandwiches and coffee were last minute jobs, so with the prep work done, Leo sank into the old armchair that seemed to be getting more comfortable everyday. He fired up the plasma with the remote which had found a permanent nest on the chair's arm, and turned over the idea that this could be the last time he ever sat here if things went bad.

The news came on, fed down through the satellite dish by karma, it seemed. The newsreader confirmed what Leo already knew: The weapon that had killed the old German guy had been the same weapon that had sent Ben Frinton above and beyond. Nobody would confirm that it was used by the same attacker or brandish the words everyone was thinking: Serial Killer.

Billy did get a mention this time, but only to rule out any possible connection to the other two murders. Leo wondered how he would feel hearing his own name on the news, branded a serial killer, because if things went well, that's what would happen. He could only pray that Billy would not be on his list of victims.

'Pin 9/11 on me, but not Billy.'

He killed the plasma and the remote fell to the floor. His fingers dug into the arms of the chair as he tried to focus the blood cloud on Reuben, but he could only find his own face. Perhaps that was karma, too.

He closed his eyes and his face resonated – multiplied again and again. Soon he was drowning in his own image, and then there was only black. When finally he pushed through the darkness, it was his own face that came through, and he was wearing it himself. He was in his place, the secret place he'd created long ago but had not visited for a while.

In the distance was the raft. It was unusual to see it from so far, and even more so to see two figures kneeling upon it. He tried to swim through the black gloop, but as always in this place, it was almost impossible. But as he paddled, it did seem he was getting closer, and then he realised the raft was moving towards him, slowly but definitely. Soon he was able to make out that the two figures were waving their arms, as if it were they who needed rescue. He scrambled hopelessly in the slick, tried to cover more distance, but knew the best he could hope for was keeping his head above the oblivion.

From across the impossible space he heard a shout, a scream maybe, but bitter experience told him sound travelled poorly in his place. The raft needed to come closer. It did.

In the hazy light that came from everywhere and nowhere, the two figures began to take shape. A male and a female, arms waving, and faintly, very faintly, Leo could hear his name being called. He tried to call back, but his open mouth only invited the suffocating slop.

The raft moved closer, and the figures took form, more than gender alone. The long hair of the female began to hold the minimal light, and gave it back the faintest red. The male figure wore a watch, the strap reversed so the face was on the inside of the wrist.

Again he tried to shout, but their names were sucked under the black tide. Then it was them shouting to him.

'LEO, HE'S GOING TO…'

Leo went under, felt himself being pulled down, but he fought for the surface.

'HE'S GOING TO…' they shouted again, but again the blackness barred his ears.

He pushed to break through. Then air rushed in, his final breath for sure.

'HE'S GOING TO KILL YOU BOTH!'

3

Leo woke in the grip of fear. Fearful of not returning to save them, fearful of forgetting the dream. He'd woken from many dreams believing his mother was still alive, expecting to hear her pottering in the kitchen. He'd lost her more than once. This recent dream was flawed in that respect: Sadie was still alive; it was only John he had lost again.

He touched his cheek, wasn't surprised to find it wet. 'Get used to it, Stamp,' he said, and went to the kitchen sink and drank deeply for a few seconds before shoving his head under. The cold water soothed, but was never going to wash away the contents of his mind.

From the corner of his eye, Leo saw the kitchen door open, and he bashed his head on the tap trying to stand quickly. With the water in his eyes, he could only make out the size of the figure, but the voice allowed his brain to fill in the blanks.

'Easy, boy, you nearly got my new shirt wet.'

'Fuck your shirt – I nearly wet my pants. Haven't you ever heard of knocking?'

Mick handed him a tea towel. 'I saw you sleeping in the armchair; I was going to give you the fright of your life.'

If Mick's grin was anything to go by, he seemed pleased with his plan.

Leo dabbed at his head with the tea towel. It wasn't bleeding, but he could feel a lump coming.

'Thanks, Mick.' he said, insincerely. 'Shouldn't you be at work?'

'Yep, I'm sure I should be, but Stuart drilled through some armoured cable this morning, and with no spark on-site, all I could do was switch everything off at the mains. Terry's been back for a couple of days now – thank the Lord – but he told me Leo Stamp could go and fuck himself if he thought he was going to knock-up plaster by hand. I didn't want to lose him again, so I gave him the rest of the week off on full pay. I didn't think it was fair to give one without the other, so gave Stuart and his lad the rest of the week as well – full pay of course. And if Leo Stamp doesn't like it, like Terry says: he can go and fuck himself.' Mick was still looking pleased. 'What do you think of my new shirt, boy?'

Leo studied it. It looked the same as all the other check shirts Mick wore – a bit cleaner perhaps. 'Versace?'

'Fuck off! I wouldn't wear anything of that bent sailor-boy's.'

'You're thinking of Jean-Paul Gault—'

'I know who the fuck I mean.' Mick pawed at the fridge. 'Got any beer?'

'Haven't you anything better to do on your self-made day off? Leo tossed the tea towel in the sink.

'Nope.' Mick swung the fridge door shut. 'Can't believe you haven't got anything to drink, even the shite you was drinking the other day would be something. Let's go round to Leo's; I bet he's still got a mother lode left over from the work do. We can talk about the good ole days when he was a boozer instead of a bender. All those pretend muscles. Not a real day's work in him. Not like you and me boy, aye.' Mick patted his round stomach. 'Now go and do whatever you got to do, and we'll be off.'

'I hope you're joking about going round Leo's – and lay off with the name-calling, okay? He's still my best mate.'

'I wouldn't waste a day off with him – hiding away from everybody like that. He should start acting like a real man, like his dad. He done everything for that boy, and look how he turned out. Pitiful.'

There wasn't a hint of playfulness in Mick's voice now; the big man's fists were clenching and unclenching as he spoke. Leo was vaguely aware of his own fists. They were doing the same thing.

'I told you, Mick, he's been having it rough—'

'Don't you be defending him, John. He doesn't deserve it. He doesn't deserve good people around him; they only end up getting hurt or worse.'

'What the fuck is that supposed to mean?'

'He's poison – knew it the first time I laid eyes on him.'

'Get the fuck out, Mick; just get the fuck out. You haven't the first clue about him.'

Mick took a step closer, and Leo could see the early signs of the geyser, but his own anger felt like bubbling lava by comparison.

'It's like he's cursed – evil or something. Like that Damien kid. Everyone knew Leo hated his father, and lo and behold, he ends up dead.'

Leo started to laugh, could make out the crazy cackle in it. Maybe he hadn't woken up yet. Maybe he was still in the chair trying to hold onto that dream but could only manage this sick play.

Mick took another step closer, too close.

'Maybe he hated his mother, too. Look what happened to that poor bitch.'

Mick's hot breath should have made Leo blink, but all it did was give the blood cloud a tailwind. Leo drove his fist into Mick's face, and whether it was the force of the blow or the sheer shock of it, Mick went down. He sat on the bare concrete floor, red faced, holding his jaw. He'd shunted the fridge a fair way too, so it was half blocking the kitchen door. Whatever was going to happen next was going to happen inside.

Leo's fists were uncurling as they were shaking, and the shakes made their way up his body and forced it to shudder.

Mick slowly got to his feet, looked down at his new shirt, which had lost a button in the fall. 'I wish you hadn't done that, boy.' He turned and shuffled the fridge back into position, opened the kitchen door and closed it gently behind himself.

Leo stood trembling, thought about running after him to apologise, but wasn't quite ready to do that. Mick's words were still razorblades in his head.

4

Leo woke fully clothed on his bed. His hair was dry and his pillow wet, and every muscle in his body ached, even his heart.

The digital clock read six-thirty pm; Michael would have to do without his sleep. He tried Sadie's phone again and wasn't surprised to find it switched off. He wasn't in the mood to talk anyway.

He made the coffee strong, and double-checked the rucksack's contents before zipping it closed. He switched off the lights and left.

The sun was down, and Leo couldn't resist trying the torch out for the first time. Better to know it didn't work now, rather than later. The moon had deserted the night sky days ago, which made the Maglite even more potent. The trees looked different in artificial light, malevolent almost. He switched the torch off and made his way to the top of the hill in the dark.

Michael was snoring. No arm up his back this time, which led Leo to believe it was an unscheduled nap. He didn't try to wake him, just lowered the rucksack to the ground and reached out for the binoculars Michael had let fall from his hand. He retrieved them without getting choked.

The desk lamp was the only light on in the barn. Reuben was seated next to it. He was drinking from a mug, but more importantly, he was alone. Leo set the binoculars on the ground and started to unpack the blankets, tried to keep the noise down so Michael could sleep, but he'd already begun to stir.

'Sorry,' Michael said, dry-washing his face with his palms.

'No need to apologise; I was late. Anyway, Reuben's still home, so no harm done. Go back to sleep, if you want. He's only drinking coffee.'

'Let me see.' Michael gestured for the binoculars. Leo passed them over and continued unpacking.

'Don't get settled, Leo. I don't think he'll be staying home for long.'

'What makes you say that?'

Michael put the binoculars down but continued to stare at the barn.

'If he is not drinking wine, he is active. We could have our chance sooner, rather than later.'

Leo snapped his fingers for the binoculars. 'In that case, he could show us where he's been hiding the dagger. If he hasn't got it with him when he gets busted, we'll know where to look.'

'Unfortunately not.'

Leo sighed heavily through his nose. 'Why unfortunately not?'

'Because there are certain rituals he performs before he kills, and if he means to kill tonight, and I think he does, he will have performed them earlier, which means the weapon is already on his person.'

'Well? Did he perform any rituals?' Even in the dark, Leo could make out chagrin. 'Unfuckingbelievable! You've probably had more sleep than me.'

'Again, I must apol—'

'Don't you *dare* apologise to me again. Un-fucking-believable!'

'Langua—'

'Don't say it.' Leo pointed at him.

Michael closed his mouth and looked towards the barn.

Leo threw the binoculars in front of Michael and started jamming the blankets back in the rucksack, muttering under his breath: 'No fucking wonder he's still got the dagger.'

'Leo?' Michael whispered.

'Don't, Michael.'

Michael gripped the rucksack to get Leo's attention. 'Reuben.'

The desk lamp had been switched off, so Leo couldn't see much, but he heard the front door close, then heard footsteps on the gravel driveway.

After a few minutes, Michael lowered the binoculars. 'He's gone,' he said, throwing his jacket tail out to sit cross-legged on the ground.

'What are you doing?' Leo asked.

'Be quiet. I need to concentrate.' Michael drew in a deep breath, closed his eyes and did nothing.

Leo was about to prompt him to follow Reuben when Michael began to shimmer. The image reminded Leo of an old cartoon: Jerry Mouse would hammer the giant church bell that Tom had found himself under, and the poor cat would emerge ringing like the bell. That's how Michael appeared to separate, to double.

One of the Michaels stood up, presumably leaving the real one sitting in his meditative state, although it was impossible to tell the difference. The standing Michael opened his eyes and found Leo on the ground, leant forward onto one leg and shot into the sky. It was so sudden that Leo gasped 'Shit!' The seated Michael, eyes still closed, smiled thinly.

Ten minutes of silence passed before Michael's stone-face cracked. 'Go now,' he said without opening his eyes.

Leo didn't need telling twice. He grabbed the Mag and ran towards the barn, checked the grave to his right as he vaulted the fence. It was still empty. He caught his breath on the porch, the stygian mouth of the grave playing over in his mind, then lifted the brick and retrieved his spare key.

He'd already given some thought to the items he would take. There where several he could have chosen, but he'd narrowed it down to two, and one of them was in the safe. He swung the *Dr No* poster aside.

I need to talk to you, Shtamp.

'We'll chat later.' Not daring to use the Mag downstairs, Leo traced the combination out in the dark. He opened the safe door and felt around for his driving licence, found it, and slipped it into his back pocket.

There may not be a later.

Leo closed the safe and swung Bond back against the wall. 'I haven't got time for this.' He started searching for the dagger, but only half-heartedly; he knew Reuben had it with him. It was only then that the possibility of finding Billy came into his mind. Why hadn't he thought of it before?

The kitchen was the obvious place to start because of the cupboard space. He didn't want to find Billy in there. If Reuben was happy to go out and leave a twelve-year-old boy in a kitchen cupboard, he must be satisfied that he wouldn't be wriggling around and making noise, which meant Leo was only going to find Billy's corpse. But he still had to be sure.

The final cupboard he searched had much the same as the first: the usual pots and pans and long-forgotten juicers and blenders that had gone unused after a week. He breathed deep with relief.

When was the last time you took a holiday? Bond asked.

Leo went into the dining room, but there was no place to hide anything in there. Couldn't find the photograph, either. 'What the hell are you talking about?' he whispered.

I thought you'd never been abroad.

'I haven't.' Leo checked the toilet and the cupboard under the stairs.

After you showed me the memory of your mother and Davey at Shingle Street, you fell asleep.

'Yeah, thanks for that.' Leo started up the stairs.

While you slept, I had a wander.

'Fine. There's nothing left to hide anyway. Knock yourself out.'

Leo went into the study, pushed the door wide open. There was enough natural light in here to see the room was empty, and Leo wondered if he'd needed to bring the Mag at all, but then he felt the heft of the thing and realised it was more than just a torch.

I stumbled on a memory of Rome.

'I've never been to Rome.' Leo crept along the landing and checked the bathroom, pulled the shower screen back with his heart in his mouth. Nothing.

That's what I thought.

The second item was in Leo's bedroom, the most obvious place to hide Billy. He pushed the door open, satisfied himself there was no one hiding behind it. The bed had either been made or not slept in. Both scenarios were spooky. If there was enough space under the bed for his basket, there was probably enough space for a kid – definitely a dismembered one. With that sickening image etched onto the retina of his mind's eye, Leo jerked the duvet up, his reflexes locked and loaded for recoil. On the floor was his basket. Nothing else. Leo felt sweat trickle down his brow.

He went over to his walk-in wardrobe, opened the door with his reflexes on stand-by again.

At first he was blinded; the naked bulb that came on automatically burnt into his eyes and flashed neon beneath the lids. He quickly closed the bedroom door to stop light from escaping and went back to the wardrobe. Below the rails of hanging clothes were neat rows of shoes, boots and trainers – nowhere to hide a body. He felt his way through the jackets and shirts and only found bare wall behind. With no Billy, he made short work of obtaining his next item.

To his left hung a selection of old work clothes: jeans, jumpers and a boiler suit he used to wear for lagging and insulating. Next to them was his old Donkey jacket. He'd only worn it once to work, as fat Steve had started taking the piss, saying Leo wanted to grow up to be just like Mick. By the end of the day they were all at it, someone had even managed to write Mick Jr in the label. Fat Steve could be a real prick sometimes.

The jacket hung like new in a see-through suit-bag, apart from the label he'd cut out. He unzipped the bag, slipped his hand inside and unceremoniously ripped off one of the buttons.

Thanks to his movie addiction, Leo knew terms such as 'orgy of evidence' – where a glut of incriminating material made a set-up more probable than possible. Therefore, he had to apply subtlety to keep Reuben on the hook. There was plenty of other stuff in the place that he could have chosen, stuff for the novice copper to find. But Leo thought the licence would get them to the door the fastest. The button, however, was for the hardworking brains on the force, the ones that loved the game. Some hair fibres wouldn't hurt either, so he pinched a few from round the collar of the jacket and folded them into a ten pound note. He closed the wardrobe door, taking a moment to let his eyes readjust to the deeper dark, then slipped out onto the landing.

The second bedroom door was likewise pushed all the way open, and he could see the bed in here had been slept in. The hairs on Leo's neck stood up like a dog in a scrap, and he gripped the Mag. He wanted to run, but the thought of Billy held him in the doorway. There was only a chest of drawers in here, just enough room for all the junk he dared not throw out – mainly video tapes he'd since upgraded to DVD. But there was plenty of room under the bed: it used to be Cotton's favourite hiding place.

Leo crouched, but with the duvet hanging so close to the floor he couldn't see under. He thought about running again. Reuben could have turned back; there was no way for Michael to alert him; he could be on the stairs right now. Leo turned, fully expecting to see Reuben standing in the doorway behind him. 'Get a grip, for fuck's sake!' Leo uttered, and seemed to let out more air than a lung could hold.

With the Mag in one hand, Leo grabbed the hem of the duvet in the other and pulled it up. Before his eyes could rearrange the pile of washing, he was recoiling from Billy Walker's bloody corpse. He dropped the Mag, a dry scream caught in his throat as his brain solved the puzzle of clothes.

'Fuck sake, Leo.'

He shone the torch back on the bundle, recognised the shirts as his own. Judging by the huge crumpled pile, Reuben wasn't hot on ironing, and if the bloodstains were anything to go by, he wasn't hot on washing, either.

Leo was done.

He was down the stairs in a few skips and at the front door in no time.

Shtamp! Are you listening to me. If you've never been to Rome, whose memory was it?

Leo couldn't even think; he was already out the door.

5

Back at the top of the hill, Michael was still in his trance-like state. Leo crashed down beside him, panting, and took the flask of coffee from the rucksack. He needed a caffeine fix to slow his heart to merely racing, but before he had a chance to take his first mouthful, Michael was up and on his feet.

'You have the items, ja?'

'Got'em.' Leo gulped coffee.

'And the boy?'

Leo shook his head as he looked towards the barn and swallowed more coffee. 'Not in the house – damn, I should have checked the garage.'

'No time. Reuben's going to kill again tonight. You have to move fast.'

'Where is he now?'

'He's hiding in a copse of trees opposite a thatched cottage about twenty minutes walk from here. The cottage stands alone for about a hundred and fifty metres either side. It can't be a coincidence.'

'Twenty minutes that way?' Leo pointed at the country road to which his barn was adjoined.

'Ja.'

Leo shook the coffee dregs from his cup, didn't want to hear the answer to his next question: 'The cottage… could you hear wind chimes in the garden?'

'Ja, many of them. Do you know it?'

Leo felt a knot bunching in his stomach as he got to his feet. 'You wait here in case Reuben comes back.'

'Answer me, Leo. Do you know it?'

'Everybody knows it,' he said, and started running towards the road.

CHAPTER 22

Christine Castle had known more tragedy in her life than most people should. Although she had been dealt nothing but aces and kings when it came to her aesthetic appearance, when the beauty cards were set aside, and the Good Lord reached for the tragedy deck, the Devil chuckled, as he had already shuffled the deuces and treys to the top.

The first deuce manifested itself in the death of her baby boy, Thomas. Thomas was a little Houdini by all accounts, with perhaps an ounce or two of monkey blood thrown in. 'Uncontainable' was the word Christine had used to describe him in the *East Anglian*. Whether it be mother's arms, cot, or highchair, Thomas would liberate himself. Frightening enough for any parent to cope with, but making it doubly so was Thomas's blindness.

Unhindered by his affliction, Thomas would hunt for the sounds that blessed his dark world, and no sound blessed it more than when the breeze tickled the wind chimes that hung from the branches of the sycamore in the back garden. 'His eyes lit up when he heard those chimes,' Christine was quoted. 'It was like he was seeing for the first time.'

But it was the quote from Thomas's seven-year-old sister, Lucy, which had touched the hearts of the people of Mundey: 'Maybe Thomas can hear the chimes from Heaven and follow them home.'

At first, there was just a couple in the post, boxed, with a card of condolence, and Christine hung them on the sycamore with the other chimes Thomas loved so much. And as is always the case in small towns like Mundey, word spread.

People turned up on Christine's doorstep, asking if they could hang a wind chime on the sycamore for Thomas. Many people didn't even ask, just walked straight into the back garden (some with ladders as all the lower branches were taken) and hung a chime wherever they could find a space. Christine never objected.

Eventually, she placed an add in the local paper, thanking everyone for their support but asking them to stop bringing chimes to the house, as it was time for her family to grieve on their own. A few more chimes managed to find their way to the top of the tree, but by the end of the week, The Chime Tree, as it became known, yielded no more blossoms.

For the next three years, Christine would wake up on Thomas's birthday to find flowers beneath her bedroom window; the window that Thomas had escaped his sleeping mother's arms to climb through; the window through which Thomas would not find his blessed chimes, but only the cold, grey paving slabs twenty feet below. The flowers stopped appearing after the second deuce was dealt.

After beating Christine to within an inch of being reunited with her baby boy, Bruce Castle packed a case and left his bleeding and unconscious wife on the bedroom floor for his sick ten-year-old daughter to find the next morning.

Christine reluctantly gave an interview to the same local paper. She was photographed in front of The Chime Tree, her face in tatters, and her pale, sick daughter under her arm. The highlighted quote of the piece read: 'If he doesn't come back, I won't press charges'.

Whether through fear or shame, Bruce Castle was never seen again.

Leo overheard Mick and fat Steve talking about Christine a few months back. She'd become semi-reclusive since her husband had left, only venturing out for supplies and medicine for Lucy, who had become bedridden with illness.

Somebody had to die by Reuben's hand for him to be stopped – an unavoidable necessity that would save many lives, most importantly Billy's – but Leo couldn't allow it to be Christine Castle, even if her one life was outweighed by the many she would save by dying. She had been through enough.

Leo pumped John's legs as fast as they would go, the Maglite beam slashing the darkness up and down as he went, hopefully alerting Reuben and prompting him to abandon his target. On that thought, Leo began to slow. There was one person's life he'd neglected to think of: his own. What if he arrived at Christine's too late but not late enough, and Reuben was still there? What if Reuben wanted Lucy, too? If he turned up and found Reuben on the job, Leo would end up being his third victim of the evening. But unlike Christine and Lucy, Leo was less assured of where he was going in the afterlife. He slowed to a walk.

Upon death, Leo had been judged as a Dark Heart, but who was to say John had died before Leo; he may have been lying there for some time – died after Leo. In that case, John's death had not been weighed in Leo's judgement, and therefore Hell was still a real possibility. And what would happen to Billy Walker? Who would save him? And Sadie? Who would protect her if Reuben decided to put her on the list? Certainly not Michael.

Leo stopped walking and switched off the Mag. He had to get off the road. Reuben would most likely return the same way he'd come. All Leo had to do was wait for him to pass.

Up ahead was the neighbouring cottage to Christine's, and opposite that, if he remembered correctly, was a sizable head of brush: the ideal place to hide. Leo double-timed it to the cottage and worked his way into the middle of the bushes.

From here he could just make out the haunting whisper of the wind chimes, as if he wasn't freaked out enough. The eerie music seemed to move along the country road in search of something, or someone.

There was no light coming from the upper windows of Christine's cottage, and there was a high brick wall that would have blocked any light coming from the ground floor ones. This left the cottage almost invisible from here. He would have to wait for Reuben to pass him before it was safe to move, and he didn't have to wait long. Light appeared through the opening gate and then disappeared into sheet blackness again. Reuben was on his way.

Leo eased himself onto his knees, fearing he would topple in the bush or his ankle would crack at the wrong moment. Now he just had to worry about hyperventilating, as he still hadn't recovered from the running.

Reuben's footsteps began to drift along the road on a wave of ghostly chimes, and Leo's breathing seemed to worsen. There couldn't have been more than a hundred feet between them, and the more he thought about it, the more he struggled to get his breathing under control.

At around thirty feet, Leo could make out a silhouette, shades of black on black. He couldn't see Reuben's eyes, but they were looking right at him; he knew it. Reuben had some form of heat signature sensor, and Leo was flaring red like the burning bush of holy script. He started to panic, could hear Reuben's footsteps, Thomas's chimes. He could hear his own heart. Reuben must be able to hear it too.

Fifteen feet now, and he was never going to get it under control. He took a deep breath, clamped a hand over his mouth and held it tight.

Ten feet. Leo's head was banging from the lack of oxygen. He held his mouth tighter and gripped the Mag; it might be the only thing that would save him once he'd exhaled.

Reuben was directly in front of the bush Leo was hiding in when he stopped. Leo had only been holding his breath for thirty seconds, but it felt as though he was coming to the end of a world record attempt. He was going to puke, and while the vomit suffocated him, Reuben would open his throat and give him all the air he could ever need. Leo was just about to give into air and come out swinging the Mag when a light came on in the cottage opposite, moving Reuben on. Leo heard a dog being prompted into the back garden by a man. The blessed creature howled immediately. Leo counted off another ten seconds before sucking air into his deprived lungs. He rested in his bush long enough for the dog to defecate to his master's satisfaction and for the light to go out again, then waited a bit longer.

Eventually he climbed out of the bush, stretched the backs of his legs and cursed John's inflexibility as his palms came up well short of the road, then headed for the Castle cottage.

He hesitated at the gate, closed his eyes to the night and listened for footsteps or voices in the distance, but all he could hear was The Chime Tree.

The gate opened onto a narrow concrete pathway that hugged the side of the cottage in both directions. Leo turned right and headed towards the light.

The Chime Tree captured him in the back garden; he'd never seen it this close before. From the road it was only possible to see the top of the tree because of the high wall, and certainly no chimes. But from inside, they were all visible. There must have been over a hundred still hanging, all different shapes and sizes, all producing a different song, with more on the ground around the tree, their strings snapped and rotten. Leo wondered if there was a collective noun for wind chimes, and thought a 'symphony' wouldn't be inappropriate.

Further around the path was the back door and the source of the light. It was partway open, and Leo could see right through the galley kitchen and down a dark hallway. He stepped inside and crept heel to toe along the sticky lino, making sure not to touch anything. The dim strip-lights illuminating the cheap black worktop showed off the kitchen as clean enough, but the smell of cat piss made him think Christine had probably let her subscription to *Good Housekeeping* go with her husband.

The hallway was home to the stairs and one other door, which was ajar. A dim orange glow was daring to peek from behind it, as afraid to come out as Leo was to go in. He pushed it open with the butt of the Mag.

Cosy was his first impression as he edged inside. A dark bookcase filled more with knickknacks than books stood directly in front of him and reached all the way up to the low Artex ceiling. A painting of a country scene hung beside the bookcase, and further to the right was a TV with a small lamp on top: the source of the orange glow. He stepped fully into the room and jolted at the sight of Christine Castle sitting in an armchair, her eyes, a vibrant aqua despite the half-light, staring past him into space.

Even dead, she was a beautiful woman. Nothing like the picture they'd printed in the paper; her bruises had healed perfectly. Now, only the blood trickling from the side of her mouth could detract from her angelic face.

Her white blouse displayed a bloom of red, emanating from the centre of her chest. It didn't convey the savage attack Leo had expected. She looked peaceful. Maybe Reuben had wanted the girl as well, killed Christine quickly so he could have more time with the daughter. Leo thought briefly about searching for Lucy's body; perhaps she had put up more of a struggle. It would look better to plant the evidence on her. Christine looked as though she'd sat through the whole thing whilst watching her favourite soap, sitting up straight with her hands in her lap that way. But then Leo's mind was made up for him.

'Mum, I've been sick again,' came a weak voice from upstairs. It had to be Lucy.

Leo was startled into action and took the licence and the button from his jacket. He slipped the licence under the armchair and made a flimsy fist with one of Christine's hands and curled the button inside. It looked all wrong, but however it looked, she was dead.

'Mum? I've been sick,' Lucy called again.

Leo unfolded the ten pound note with the hair inside, held it in front of Christine's red chest and blew. The hairs stuck to the blood. He'd painted a surreal picture for the police, but it would lead them to Reuben.

He tiptoed back into the hall and out through the kitchen, had to step over a black cat sitting in the middle of the floor like a figurine. Poor Lucy called a final time, and he wanted to run to her and hug her and tell everything would be all right, but he couldn't.

Outside, Leo paused by The Chime Tree. 'Symphony' was all wrong, he thought. 'Misery' was perfect.

2

When Reuben arrived back at the barn, he knew something was wrong. All the doors upstairs had been pushed wide open. Not how he'd left them.

He took the bloody dagger from his waistband and opened his ears to the barn, stepped softly upstairs in the dark. It didn't take long to realise he was alone, but someone had definitely been here.

Every Dark Heart's body came with complications – usually in the form of friends and relatives. Leo Stamp had few of either, but it was still surprising to Reuben that he'd only encountered two: a bison of a man, and the beautiful Sadie. The man he could rule out: if he'd possessed a key, he would have used it the day he almost beat down the door. And as for Sadie… she was no longer a problem.

That left Reuben with only a name. Sadie had spoken of a John, and Leo Stamp had been thinking of a John the night he passed over.

196

Reuben went into the study. He was not comfortable around computers, but he was not ignorant of them. Perhaps there was something on file – a surname. He opened Word, clicked File to see what document the Dark Heart had worked on last. It was a list of accounts – twenty or so names and addresses. Reuben read through the list and found four employees with the first name John. Only one stood out, and it didn't take him long to remember why.

He went downstairs and switched on the lamp, faced the painting that hung on the solitary wall dividing the lounge and dining room. In the bottom right hand corner of the canvas was the artist's signature: John Kirkman.

Reuben walked into the kitchen, stared at the open grave through the glass. He'd finished the list and now it was his time; he wasn't leaving without the boy.

The phone rang: *three, four, dead.*

'I see you've had a visitor, Reuben. Are you sure you want to risk sticking around for the boy? There'll be other little boys.'

'I want this one. And don't worry, I'll make time. Now tell me where he is.'

3

No way Leo was taking the same route back to the cottage. The thought of Reuben hiding behind trees and bushes felt like termites beneath his skin. He decided to head into Mundey, stock up on some wine and try to clear his head on the walk back. The six-mile round trip plus the booze would give him a fighting chance of sleep tonight.

By the time he clinked through the kitchen door, his spirits were high. He could see an end to all of this. First thing in the morning he would find Mick, sort out that crazy mess. Of all the people to lose it with.

He poured a glass and went into the lounge. Bond was still on the mantel.

Ready to listen to me now?

'Can it wait? Michael will be back any minute.'

This is serious, Shtamp!

Leo sensed Bond wasn't joking. 'Fine. I'm listening.'

Good.

'Good.'

John's shpent time in Italy, hasn't he?

'A year.'

And you haven't, have you?

'What are you—?'

Have you?

'No.'

Then you've got some of John's memories in your head.

'I think they're just echoes. When I first entered John's body I had the same thing happen – memories of Sadie that weren't mine. I'll probably get them from time to time.'

This wasn't a fucking echo. I could have walked through the whole year if I'd wanted to.

'What are you saying?'

I'm shaying that more and more of John is bleeding into you everyday.

'I don't think so.'

You slept in those clothes.

'I've been dealing with some shit lately.'

There's washing-up in the sink from yesterday.

'I was too tightly wound to begin with.'

What time is it?

'What?'

Your watch. What time is it?

Leo looked at his watch. The face was on the inside of his wrist, just how John used to wear it.

That used to bug the shit out of you when John did that.

'It's nothing,' Leo said, and adjusted the strap. 'Probably did it without even thinking.'

You're damn right.

Leo put his wine down and picked Bond up. 'It's just another echo; don't worry about it.'

Something's happening to you, Shtamp, and I don't think I can fix it this time.

He slid Bond behind the sofa. 'You didn't fix it the first time.'

At that moment, his mobile buzzed in his pocket. Sadie had sent him a text message: Will call u tomorrow. Xxx.

'Hallelujah! Silent treatment over!' Leo stuffed his phone back in his pocket before temptation forced a clumsy follow-up call. Tomorrow was fine by him, he thought, then noticed Michael coming through the front gate.

Michael handed him the rucksack as he entered, and Leo passed him a glass of wine.

'A little premature to be celebrating, don't you think?' Michael said.

'Reuben's not wriggling out of this one.' Leo dumped the rucksack behind the kitchen door. 'My licence is by the body, and I placed an old button in her hand – even left some hair for the forensics. Is Reuben back at the barn yet?'

'Arrived just now.'

'We should make the call and get up on the hill to watch,' Leo said. 'I don't want to give Reuben time to even breathe on Billy Walker.'

'Nein. You've been at the crime scene. I don't want you anywhere near the barn when Reuben is taken. In fact, you should burn those clothes.'

'It's not my door the police will be knocking on, but perhaps I *should* steer clear of the barn.'

Michael nodded but looked uneasy.

'It's over. You should be pleased,' Leo said.

'Ja, ja.'

'Then drink up, this is ten quid a bottle – French shit!'

'In that case, you should have it. I want to stay focused, and I can see you're more in the mood for this than I'

'Is it because I said shit? I'm never going to swear again.'

Michael set his glass down. 'I want to ask a favour.'

'Ask away.'

'I want to be the one who makes the call to the police. Call it closure.'

'If you're sure…'

'I need to. I've followed Reuben for centuries, guided a countless number of his victims to a more deserving place, and to think that his reign could soon be at an end fills me with feelings that I do not quite understand, but I know that I will. I have you to thank for this, Leo. You have allowed me to be reborn, something I should have done for you, but I was weak.'

'That wasn't weakness,' Leo said. 'That was fate. If you had sent me back as a child, God alone knows how long you would have been chasing Reuben. This isn't ideal for me,' Leo looked down at the body that was now housing his soul, the body that used to house his friend's. 'But in a way, it's right. Every day I look in the mirror and see John Kirkman will be a reminder of what I was. This is my purgatory, and I need it. I'll make my peace with John in the next life, if I get the chance, but for now, I'm going to live mine the way I should have. What we've done here tonight is a good thing, and it wouldn't have happened if you had stuck me in a pram.'

Michael's lips formed a tight smile.

'Have one drink, and then go make your call.'

Michael took the glass, eyed Leo, and allowed a full smile to win back his handsome face. '*Salut*,' he said, and downed the lot.

'Use the public phone-box up the road,' Leo said. 'And keep it brief. You only have to get the police to the front door; the rest's taken care of.'

'Thank you, Leo.'

'Goodbye, Michael.'

Michael stepped outside, pulled the collar up on his coat and buttoned it. 'I nearly forgot. I have something for you.' He reached into his pocket, took something out and handed it to Leo. It was a book.

Leo read the cover: *Casino Royale* by Ian Fleming. 'It's a nice gesture, Michael, but I won't read it.'

'James Bond through the eyes of his creator? The purest Bond you will ever know.'

'Connery's Bond; *everyone* knows that.'

Michael smiled and walked into the darkness.

Leo closed the door, and despite his newfound affection for the big guy, honestly hoped he would never see him again. He fanned the ragged pages of the book as he walked into the lounge, then threw it in the trunk.

4

Billy Walker woke in the merciless darkness to the sound of his own screaming, but it didn't last long. The bitter pain in his throat reminded him that his terrified bellows did not bring his mother or father, and that the sound of his own screams only served to terrify him more.

He didn't know whether it was day or night, or how long he'd been here. He didn't know where *here* was. He *did* know that he had been here for a long while; his stomach told him that much. The last thing he remembered eating was the school lunch his mother had packed for him: a peanut butter sandwich, a packet of Twiglets, a Penguin, an orange drink and an apple. Billy ate everything but the apple, which he'd traded this time but usually binned. He now wished he could trade back the *Dr Who* stickers in his back pocket for that apple.

The insides of his legs were sore from wetting himself. When the man grabbed him around the neck and stuffed the stinking gauze over his nose and mouth, he couldn't help it. The next thing he knew was darkness.

He'd become the most vocal when he first woke, the most active, believing he could rip the heavy chain that was padlocked around his leg straight from the cold concrete in which it was embedded. But after his meagre lunch had been spent, his skinny muscles gave him no more. His exhausted lungs yielded screams for only a little longer.

The darkness was endless. He could have been in the middle of the school football pitch and wouldn't know. But his sobs didn't carry far, and his chains clinked mutedly on the concrete, so he guessed he wasn't in a big place.

He groped in the dark for something to throw – to prove to himself that there was a reality, something other than the floor, but he couldn't find anything within the chain's radius. Then Billy thought of his shoes, and began to untie one of his laces, still heeding his father's warnings about kicking them off at the heel.

Billy breathed as silently as his short sharp breaths would allow, and was contemplating in which direction he should launch the shoe when he heard a noise, and his breathing stopped altogether.

At first there was a bang – something wooden, he thought. Then a second and a third, followed by a creaking sound which seemed to tear the faintest bead of light along the floor about ten feet in front of him. Billy wanted to scream but couldn't. Even when the footsteps began to sound close, and the seam of light broke in places. At that point the only things he could expel were rasping pants and his last drop of hot urine down the front of his school trousers.

A key rattled in a lock, and Billy's eyes were assaulted by florescent tubes. He turned his head away from the painful light and saw a man's shadow on the floor. The shadow climbed the wall as it stepped closer, and although Billy's brain was locked in fear, he couldn't help noticing the cardboard egg boxes all over the walls. Then the door closed, and the room was blacker than before.

Billy hadn't realised he'd stopped breathing until he heard a bunch of keys fall to the concrete. Then he began to sob. Footsteps moved closer, and Billy slid away, retreating as far as he could before the chain bit into his ankle. He could hear the man handling a box of matches and prayed he wouldn't strike one; he wanted the dark now more than ever and pinched his eyes shut in fear of the light, but it came anyway. He could see the glow of the flame through his nipped lids. The man blew the match out, but the glow remained. Dead match scented the air.

'Billy?' the man spoke softly. 'Open your eyes, Billy, and let them adjust to the candle.'

Billy's eyes remained tightly shut.

The man picked up the keys. 'We'll get you out of these shackles, and you can put your shoe back on. We don't want you getting a damp foot, do we?'

Billy started to breathe a little easier, but still his eyes remained shut.

The man hunted through the bunch of keys. 'I'm going to unlock you now, Billy. There's nothing to worry about.'

The man took hold of the padlock and inserted a key, the lock popped open and the chain fell loose around Billy's ankle.

'Do you want to give that a little rub, Billy. It was on quite tight, wasn't it?'

Billy nodded and rubbed his leg, stole a suspicious look at the man, but the candle was on the floor, and the light didn't travel high enough to illuminate the stranger's face. He was glad of that.

'Do you want to put your shoe back on now, and then we'll see if you can walk, okay?'

Billy nodded and quickly put his shoe back on. He tried twice to tie his laces but his hands were trembling. The man took over and tied them in a tidy bow.

'Are you ready to go, Billy?' The man held out a hand to him.

Billy hesitated for a moment before taking it. The man stood up, helping Billy to his feet, then bent down to retrieve the candle. At full height, the man's face was visible.

'You've been a very brave little boy, haven't you, Billy?'

Billy nodded his tear-streaked face, and the man smiled. Billy smiled back and thought he didn't look scary at all.

'Very brave,' Reuben said. 'This will all be over soon.'

CHAPTER 23

Although he hadn't remembered to draw the curtains before going to bed, the room was still dark. The low, thatched eve and the apocalyptic sky beyond it lent themselves to the illusion of night, and all Leo wanted to do was set that sky to canvas.

It was a bizarre sensation, the feeling that he was about to create something. He could see the colours already in his mind – more than he thought he would ever need for a grey sky: Raw Umber, Gold Ochre, Prussian Green, and Indigo. He visualised mixing them on a palette with a painting knife, lashing great arcs across the canvas at speed. He swung his feet out of bed, convinced himself he was going to do it, but then he noticed his watch. At some stage during the night he'd turned the face back around to the inside of his wrist. It had to be the drink. Had to be. He removed the watch and put it in the bedside cabinet drawer.

Get some country miles in his legs, and he would be fine. That was all he needed. He hunted through the wardrobe for some running shorts, but he couldn't find any. Couldn't find running shoes, either. By the time he dressed, he'd made up his mind to buy new clothes today – a whole new wardrobe. He could tell Sadie the money came from his first paycheque as Site Manager at Stamp & Son. She'd go for that.

Where was she, for that matter? He thought she might turn up early to make him breakfast – there were three kisses on the end of that text after all. He checked his phone for messages, but there were none. Maybe she was running late or had broken down somewhere, and in that case, it would be perfectly fine to call her.

He made his way to the kitchen as he scrolled for her number, stopped outside the spare room and glanced in. The dark canvas he'd chosen days ago was on the floor, back among the rest, and a different canvas was now on the easel. It was predominantly pastel blue, with soft flowing lines of different shades sweeping here and there, as if moved by a breeze. In contrast to this serenity were two dark red tendrils reaching down towards messy blobs, ruining what was otherwise a beautiful picture. He couldn't remember changing the canvas.

Leo continued to stare at the painting as he dialled Sadie's number. Her phone rang, but he was hardly aware of it. The canvas disturbed him. It seemed to have a three dimensional quality. He was about to inspect it more closely when he heard the second ringing. He lowered his mobile to pinpoint the old-fashioned telephone, although he recognised it as a ringtone and not the kosher article. It was coming from the kitchen, or maybe the lounge. He pressed his mobile to his ear again; Sadie still hadn't picked up. He disconnected and the other ringing stopped too.

From the hallway, all Leo could hear were passing cars and his own shallow breathing. He redialled Sadie's number, but didn't hold the phone to his ear. The old-fashioned ringtone issued again and drew him into the lounge, where he found a pink Nokia quivering on the mantel. He disconnected the call, and the pink phone died.

He ran through the Nokia's numbers and recognised a few names: John, Sandra, even himself. Under the heading 'Me' was Sadie's number. It was the same number he'd been dialling. He rang it again. The Nokia came alive in his hand and the screen flashed 'John calling'. He ended the call.

'Sadie?' he called out, and stuck his head into the hallway to see if the shower room door was closed, but it stood open. He went to the lounge window but couldn't see her car. He then noticed the mantel and the envelope tucked beneath the scented candle.

Written on the plain white envelope were two words: *Lucky Charm.*

'Lucky charm?' He sat in the armchair and tore it open.

The letter was elegantly handwritten on two folded ivory sheets, and he could tell straight away it wasn't from Sadie. After reading her diary he was intimate with her style.

Dear Lucky Charm, it began.

'What's with this Lucky Charm shit?' Leo asked the dark reflection of himself in the plasma, and started again:

Dear Lucky Charm,

I am writing this letter in two minds whether or not to slit your sneaky throat open or leave you be. I believe, however, that to empty the bloody canals of my Lucky Charm could only serve to bring bad karma, and therefore I hope your God is watching over you tonight and grants me the strength to leave you breathing.

I now realise you and that guileless buffoon have been watching me, and for that reason alone I should bleed you, but all he ever does is watch. Your presence, however, has renewed my vigilance, as I've become sloppy and careless over the years – the consequence of having a faithful bloodhound such as Michael on my scent. But now it seems I have been selling the witless-wonder short, as he has found an apprentice in you, John.

Was it your idea to leave the licence and the button, John? Haven't had time to check if the button belongs to me, but I'm sure it does. And can you believe I'd left a treat behind? I didn't even know she was there, but then I told you I've been getting sloppy. That girl was sick, sick, sick, and I was quick, quick, quick.

You see you really are my Lucky Charm, and I give you fair warning because of it. After delivering this letter, I will take two personal items from you, and then I will place them, as you did, at the crime scene. I hope you haven't called the police, yet.

Now, I have had to wrap things up sooner than I had planned. The boy was a complete rush job – no pleasure at all, but I don't hold that against you. I have had it so good for so long that I've forgotten to enjoy my work. I thank you for my renewed appreciation.

Sadie will remain with me while I make my arrangements to leave, and for these few hours you will leave me in peace. You should be gone by then if you are sensible. But if you interfere, you have my word that her death will be anything but quick.

Sincerely yours, Reuben.

P.S. Hope you like the gifts. I picked them out myself.

Leo dropped the letter and buried his head in his hands, could hear his teeth creaking as the muscles in his jaw contracted. Within a moment he was on his feet, running into the kitchen. He flung the door open and it bounced back off the rucksack and nearly knocked him out as he darted through. His T-shirt caught on the handle and tore as he pushed on. He sprinted up the road towards the fence that gave access to the field, vaulted it, and powered up the hill. He could see Michael at the top, but he wasn't here for him.

Michael was sitting in his usual position, hunched over his Gameboy, when he turned towards Leo and sprung to his feet. 'What are you doing?' he said, holding up a hand to stop him. 'It's over; there's no need for this.'

Leo dodged around the side of him, but Michael grabbed his torn T-shirt and pulled. The shirt disintegrated, leaving only the collar and part of a sleeve, and as Leo drove onwards, they gave, too. But before he could pick up speed, the sight of the grassy hump in his back garden stopped him in his tracks. At that moment, Leo found unexplored dimensions of the blood cloud, could see Reuben's face in the spidery corners of his mind and feel Reuben's flesh rending beneath his fingernails. He went to set off again, but his head exploded in pain. He hit the ground face-first, the smell of dewy grass deep in his nostrils. Then the world turned black.

2

When Leo came round, the grass scent in his nostrils had been replaced by sofa dust. He could taste it on his teeth. Michael was sitting in the armchair, reading Reuben's letter. He turned to Leo, expressionless, and waved it at him.

'I should not have let you help,' Michael said.

Leo tried to sit up and winced at the pain radiating from his skull.

'I'm sorry about that, Leo, but he would have killed you. You *and* Sadie.' Michael waved the letter again. 'What does he mean by *gifts*?'

'What?' Leo cupped the back of his head.

'Reuben says here that he has brought you gifts.'

'No idea.' Leo stood and walked slowly towards the door.

'Where are you going?'

'Calm down, I'm just getting a flannel for my head.'

He came back wearing yesterday's T-shirt and holding a wet flannel to the mole hill beneath his scalp. He paced up and down, double-checking the flannel for blood, but it was clean.

'Did you call the police last night?' Leo asked.

Michael frowned.

'Fuck! I've got to get out of here – need time to think. What the fuck are we going to do?'

'Cut out the language for starters – it's not helping.'

Leo glared at him.

'We may have more time than you think,' Michael said. 'What items has he taken?'

'Haven't looked.' Leo checked the flannel again, saw it was clean and tossed it on the sofa.

'Is there anything with your name or address on it: bankcards, licence, that sort of thing?'

'Yeah, in here.' Leo knelt by the trunk and opened it, tilted the false bottom and took a quick look inside. 'It's all here I think.' He closed the lid.

'Well that only leaves fingerprints and DNA – nothing to bring the police here for a while, if at all.'

'What if he left the police a letter? My name's John Kirkman – come fucking get me!' Leo paced faster.

'If Reuben was going to set you up like that, then why would he send a letter telling you to stay away? Why not have the police at your door before you even wake? You couldn't interfere from jail.'

Leo stopped pacing. 'True, but then I could send the police straight around to him – say he was my accomplice. I'd do it, so he must expect it.'

'Then he would be a fool to stay there, and Reuben is no fool – bringing me back to my first point. Ja? Why would he send you a letter and leave one for the police? Believe me, we are safe for now.'

Leo slumped down on the sofa, put the flannel back behind his head and closed his eyes. 'Billy's dead. Did you see the grave?'

'Ja. By the time I'd made the call and got back to the hill, it was already filled. There was nothing we could have done.'

'He'll kill Sadie if we don't do something, Michael.' Leo stared at him.

'We will do as Reuben asks and let him move on. Perhaps he'll keep his word and let her go.'

'You honestly believe that shit you're talking?' Leo sprang to his feet. 'He's going to kill her if we don't do something, so you better start thinking, unless you are the buffoon Reuben says you are.' He threw the flannel and it smacked Michael in the face.

Michael turned red but didn't react, just folded the flannel and handed it back. 'If you recall, I had an idea, but you favoured the passive approach. Are you willing to go to the lengths necessary now?'

Leo sighed, took the flannel, felt bad for throwing it. 'Fuck,' he said and started to pace, then was struck with a sickening thought and headed for the spare room.

'Where are you going?' Michael called after him.

'I know where those gifts are.'

Leo stood by the easel in the spare room, studied the canvas. 'I knew it wasn't right.'

'What is not right?' Michael said from the doorway.

Leo waved him forward, then used the flannel to handle the dark red tendrils. From here, it was hard to believe he'd ever thought they were part of the painting. The two eyeballs had been stapled by their cords, and pulled free like week-old spaghetti, peeling pastel blue from the canvas along with them. Leo checked the irises, praying they weren't hazel, and to his relief found them a vibrant aqua. They were most certainly Christine Castle's.

P.S. Hope you like the gifts. I picked them out myself.

Leo folded the eyes into the flannel and dropped them in the waste bin by the computer desk, ignored a distant nagging that was telling him to go and scrub his hands.

'That sick fuck actually chose this painting to hang 'em on,' Leo said, and angled the canvas towards the window for a better look. 'What's going on in that psycho's mind?'

Michael didn't answer, but pointed at the back of the canvas.

Leo flipped it over, saw there was writing on the other side and hoped the dark red was paint. He set it back on the easel.

'It's a poem,' Michael said.

Leo read in silence:

I love God
And God loves me
Oh how happy we could be
If only I could stop
Murdering his flock
But he doesn't seem to care
It seems to me

'Well?' Michael said.

'Well what?'

'You didn't answer my question. Are you willing to go to the lengths necessary now?'

All Leo could think about was Billy Walker in that grave, and all he could see was Davey's face.

'I won't let him hurt Sadie,' Leo said. 'Whatever it takes.'

3

The getaway driver sitting outside the bank was just as culpable as the guy inside with the sawn-off shotgun aimed at the cashier. Leo wondered if God saw it the same way. He also wondered what would happen to Michael once he'd crossed the line. Trying to stop a Dark Heart from dying was one thing. Torturing somebody was something else. Michael must have some idea of what was going to happen to him; his days of being a guide would surely be over.

And what would happen to Leo if God decided he was the culpable getaway driver? He was walking a fine line as it was by being a Dark Heart, so taking torture to the judgment table along with John's death would certainly tip the scales in Hell's favour. Had Michael thought of that?

Leo looked out of the lounge window. Michael said they couldn't do anything until dark, but Leo was getting anxious. Reuben didn't have to wait until it was dark; he could kill

Sadie any time, if he hadn't already.

He set Bond on the mantel.

I shee you've put John's watch back on.

'No choice. Need it to synchronise later.'

So you're going through with it?

'It's gone too far.'

Torture? That's too far.

'I've done worse.'

No you haven't. All you're guilty of is being a mixed-up kid. Simian planted an evil seed in you that day, and you nurtured it and loved it and assumed it would love you back.

'You seem to forget that if it wasn't for Simian, I would have killed my own father.'

I don't believe that, and if I don't believe it, you don't either. Don't you shee how this works yet?

'Show me that rewind button and I'll press it. Put me back on the right side of the path and I'd do things different. But no one gets second chances like that. I can't bring John back. I can't save Davey. I can't stop my mum getting in that car. But I can try and save Sadie.'

So noble.

'Fuck you.'

Oh, I don't doubt you want to save her; it's jusht your motivations are all fucked up.

Leo grabbed Bond; the conversation was over.

You think saving her will make you feel better about yourself – same way you thought saving Billy would make you feel better about Davey.

'And how exactly do I feel about Davey?' Leo slammed Bond back down on the mantel.

You resented him for being your dad's favourite, and when Davey was killed you didn't grieve for him because you were too busy hating your father. Why do you think you can't bear to look at that photograph? Because it reminds you how selfish you are, and that perhaps you're not so unlike your father.

213

'We're nothing alike!' Leo shouted, and picked Bond up again and threw him behind the sofa. 'You don't ever see things from my point of view!'

Bond didn't answer.

4

When Michael arrived, Leo was in the kitchen, going through the rucksack.

'Reuben's taken my hipflask – which is engraved with John's name – and the Maglite – which has got my fingerprints all over it.'

'I have a torch,' Michael said.

'It was more than just a torch.'

'Don't worry, I have all you need.' Michael reached into his coat and pulled out a can of mace and a rubber cosh. 'Better than a torch, I think.'

Leo took the cosh and smacked into his palm, felt the sting. 'Where the hell did you get this stuff?'

'Pay attention, Leo. I haven't got time to explain this twice.'

They went over the plan and then Leo stood by the window and watched Michael leave. He half-expected to see the road filled with squad cars: lights flashing, dogs barking, the full works, but it was graveyard quiet.

In the shower room cabinet he found an old red lipstick of Sadie's, and in large letters above the mantel he wrote a short message for the police. If they did turn up here, and it did go bad at the barn, then he wanted some shit to rain on Reuben if he decided it was okay to stick around after all.

He checked his watch and didn't care that the face was on the inside of his wrist. Felt better that way. He zipped his jacket up to the neck and stepped outside the kitchen door.

As promised, the heavy clouds began to release their cache, and a drum-roll of thunder tumbled across the dark sky. Leo couldn't help thinking that the last time he'd left the cottage on a night like this, he had ended up dead.

214

CHAPTER 24

A forty-minute trudge through soggy fields and clawing bushes and Leo was finally in position. He was crouched down about ten metres from the side of the road opposite the barn, not far from where he'd first seen Michael.

The front aspect of the barn had traditional windows, rendering Leo virtually blind to what Reuben was doing inside. But that was okay. Michael was positioned on the hill and would be his eyes, and as soon as he gave the signal, Leo would make his move. Until then, all he could do was wait.

With no torch of his own, Leo couldn't see much of his surroundings, but he was still getting a double scoop of déjà vu. It couldn't have been far from this spot that he'd found his dad unconscious all those years ago. He cut the movie-reel right there; no need for a rerun of what happened that day.

The rain was relentless, appeared to have a tangible density that made Leo doubt he'd be able to see the signal at this distance. He couldn't even separate the hill from the night sky – everything was a grainy-black, but then it came:

two flashes was Leo's cue to move. He scrambled out of his hiding place and ran for the barn, didn't need to worry about the noise of the gravel, as he could barely hear his footfalls over the rain.

Under the cover of the porch, Leo struggled to dig the key out of his rain-soaked pocket but finally managed, and slid it into the lock. If this was timed right, Reuben would be in the toilet. Before he could think about what might happen if he wasn't, Leo entered, put the latch on the door and closed it behind him.

The toilet was obscured by the partition separating the lounge and dining room, and he had to walk to the foot of the stairs before he could see it. The door was closed, but the light was on. He made his way over there as quickly and quietly as he could and backed against the wall, hinges side of the door. He took out the mace and the cosh, noticed his hands were shaking and new it wasn't from being cold and wet. If there were ever a time in his life he'd been this scared, he couldn't remember it.

The toilet flushed. Leo held the cosh tighter and adjusted his grip on the mace. The door opened and what used to be his body stepped through. Reuben looked confused when he noticed the puddles on the floor, but his expression soon changed.

Leo levelled the mace to his eyes and sprayed. Reuben recoiled, coughing and spluttering and holding his arms up in useless defence. Leo pumped him with more, and Reuben fell to his knees and retched.

Charged and empowered, Leo felt brave enough to stop spraying. He kicked Reuben in the stomach. Reuben puked. Leo backed away from the mess and noticed the front door opening. Michael strode over and snatched the cosh from Leo's hand.

'I showed you where to hit him,' Michael said, then dealt Reuben a single, thudding blow to the back of his head. Reuben stopped moving.

Michael grabbed Reuben by the collar and dragged his limp body to the breakfast bar, took a handful of plastic cable ties from his coat and bound his wrists behind the base of the static barstool, then bound Reuben's ankles.

'Leo, wake up!' Michael shouted.

Leo dropped the mace and it clattered on the floor, jolting him from his trance. He walked over to Michael.

Reuben was propped against the barstool, his chin slumped on his chest and tilted to the left. Leo couldn't see his face from this angle and was thankful of it.

Michael stood in front of Reuben, arms folded with his jaw gripped in one hand. He turned to Leo. 'How badly did you spray him?'

'Enough to put him down – four, maybe five good squirts.'

Michael nodded. 'Well done.'

'I'm gonna check upstairs for Sadie.' Leo said and turned to go.

'Leo?'

'Yeah?'

'When Reuben regains consciousness, he will say anything. He will try to manipulate. He is evil, the likes you have never known.'

Leo nodded, then trotted up the stairs.

The first sweep was cursory, a systematic opening of doors and flicking of light switches that only revealed empty rooms. He tried to stay positive, told himself he was never going to find Sadie lounging on a bed with a book or playing Solitaire on his office PC, but it was hard. He was heading back to the bathroom to repeat the search more thoroughly, when a thunder-boom erupted outside that quaked his bones and blew all the lights in the barn. He stood there in the dark, suddenly gripped by the irrational fear that Reuben was somehow responsible, then rushed to the balcony and looked over.

'Michael?' Leo called down.

'Everything's fine, Leo,' came Michael's voice in the dark, and then lightning flashed, and Leo glimpsed them both. It looked as though Reuben was coming round.

3

'What's going on?' Reuben croaked, and started coughing.

Michael took Leo aside. 'Have you any candles?' he whispered.

'Why are you whispering?'

Michael didn't answer, but looked impatient.

Leo nodded. 'Some in the kitchen.' He trod cautiously in the dark, opened a drawer and grabbed a handful of plain white candles. He tried to light them on the hob, but the electric ignition was out, and then something heavy hit the breakfast bar and slid towards him. It was a chunky metal lighter, not something he imagined Michael would own.

'Thanks,' Leo said, and flicked the lid open with a *ching* and held flame to wick. Hot wax dripped onto the granite worktop, and he stuck the candle to it. He lit and mounted another four the same way. The exposed oak beams and candles gave the barn a gothic feel. Church-like, almost.

'You want money, is that it?' Reuben spluttered again.

Leo walked around the breakfast bar to look at him. He had a strange accent – a mixture of many, but with nothing definable coming through. When Leo emerged, Reuben locked streaming eyes on him and tracked him until he was at Michael's side.

'Go while you still can,' Reuben said. 'I have a friend watching this house. If he shows up, I can't help you.'

Leo stepped closer. 'Where's Sadie?'

It was unclear if Reuben was wincing or grinning at him. Either way, he didn't answer.

As the blood cloud gathered, Leo realised he wasn't just going to be the getaway driver. He kicked Reuben in the ribs.

'Where the fuck is she, you freak?' He gave him a second shot before he could answer and was about to deal him a third when Michael gripped his shoulder and eased him back.

Reuben was coughing again, hacking up strings of blood-laced saliva, and it was several minutes before he recovered and began to breathe easier. He stared up at them both, hawked and spat at Michael's feet, and then: 'How would I know where she is?'

Michael took three steps and gave Reuben the boot Leo had promised. There was an audible *click*, like a branch breaking in another room, and Reuben slumped to his side. Michael walked back to Leo with his hand inside his jacket and produced a small leather case. He handed it to Leo.

'What is it?' Leo asked.

Open it, Michael mouthed, then disappeared into the dining room.

Leo opened the case. Inside was a syringe.

Michael returned with a dining chair, positioned it in front of Reuben and came back to Leo.

Leo turned the syringe over in his palm, tried to find a label or something.

'Sodium Pentothal,' Michael whispered.

'Sodium what?'

Michael leaned in and whispered directly into Leo's ear. 'Truth serum.' He tapped Leo's neck with two fingers and nodded in Reuben's direction.

Leo eyed the syringe, then Reuben. Michael hadn't said anything about Truth Serum, but Leo could see why he wanted to try this first.

He plunged the syringe a little and the straw-coloured liquid spurted in a fine arc. He moved slowly towards Reuben, unsure of how to proceed with something he'd seen a hundred times before in films, but as he got closer, Reuben's lolling head presented him with a clearly visible vein in his taut neck.

He pressed his hand on Reuben's sweaty head to keep the neck exposed, but Reuben shook him off, fixed his bloodshot eyes on the loaded needle.

'What is that?' Reuben asked.

Leo turned to Michael for help with the answer, but Michael only had eyes for Reuben. Leo couldn't see the harm in telling him.

'Truth serum.'

'There's no need for that,' Reuben said. 'Ask me anything. I won't lie to you.'

Leo held fire. 'Okay, where's the dagger?'

'How do you know about the dagger?'

'There's a lot I know about you... Reuben.'

Reuben's eyes opened a little wider.

'Like I know you murdered my brother, you fucking freak!' Leo started pounding the side of Reuben's head with the heel of his fist. It was the sickest feeling, thumping his own face, but it also fulfilled some deep-seated, self-destructive need. He kept hitting and hitting, trying to get through to the thing inside, the thing that had killed Davey. Then Leo felt Michael's hand on his shoulder again, and he almost broke down and sobbed.

'I'm fine,' Leo said, panting. 'I'm fine.'

Reuben's head lolled to the side; he was barely conscious. Leo held him steady and pushed the needle into the proud vein in his neck, squeezed off the contents of the syringe and dumped the empty cartridge on the breakfast bar.

When he turned around, Michael was back in his chair, staring at Reuben. Leo went into the dining room and brought back his own chair and sat down next to him, feeling exhausted and wired at the same time.

The three of them sat in silence while the rain pelted the windows and the flickering candlelight painted the gallery-white walls in orange and shadows.

Reuben groaned, eventually managed to keep his head straight to look at them. 'How do you know of me?' he said.

Leo cocked a thumb to his right. 'This is Michael: the guileless buffoon. Your faithful bloodhound.'

Reuben looked at Michael. 'Am I supposed to know you?'

Leo looked at Michael. 'How long before the serum kicks in?'

Michael shrugged.

'What do you want from me?' Reuben asked. 'Money? I can get you plenty of that.'

'Where's Sadie?' Leo said.

'I get it now,' Reuben said. 'You're the jealous boyfriend. John. But I don't get how you know of me or the dagger.'

Leo cocked his thumb to the right again.

'Yes.' Reuben nodded. 'Michael the guileless buffoon – you told me already.' He turned his head to the window, leaned forward until his bonds would let him go no further.

'Expecting someone?' Leo asked.

Reuben sat back. 'So… Michael. Have you come to take me back? Replace me? Or do you want the dagger for yourself? Who sent you?' Reuben glanced up into the vaulted ceiling. 'Him?' Then down at the floor. 'Or Him?'

Michael didn't answer.

'Guileless buffoon.' Reuben coughed a one-syllable laugh from his nose. 'Retarded mute.'

'Why do you do it?' Leo asked.

'Why do I do what?'

'Kill people.'

'You wouldn't understand,' Reuben said, closing his eyes. 'I'm not sure I do.'

'You're probably right.' Leo slouched forwards, elbows on his knees. 'How could I begin to understand the mind of a man who goes round killing children.'

Reuben opened his eyes. 'I would never harm a child.'

'You molested and murdered my brother. He was thirteen.'

Reuben shook his head.

'When you were here nineteen years ago – remember?'

Reuben continued to shake his head.

'Sure you do.' Leo got up and went to the wall safe, swung Bond aside and punched in the code. He came back with his scrapbook and knelt beside Reuben. 'Let me jog your memory.'

Reuben turned away, but Leo grabbed his hair and turned him back.

'Look at it.' Leo fumbled the pages over with his other hand. 'Not just my brother – remember this kid? Stephen Mercer? I remember Stephen. I'll never forget him, and do you know why?' Leo shook Reuben by the hair. 'I told him to fuck off one day because he kept following me around – a week later you abducted him, molested him, then cut his throat open and buried him.'

'That wasn't me,' Reuben shouted. Leo could see tears in Reuben's eyes, and it made him sick.

'Just like you didn't kill Billy Walker?'

'I told you, I would never kill a child. '

Leo dropped the book, and with both hands began to bash Reuben's head against the base of the stool. 'Then how do you know Billy Walker is a child?'

'Because I saved him!' Reuben shouted.

'Don't lie to me. I've seen the grave in the garden, you child-murdering sack of shit.'

Reuben shook free of Leo's grip. 'Dig it up if you don't believe me. Dig it up!'

Leo fell back, panting, staring into Reuben's eyes.

'Dig it up!' Reuben shouted again, writhing in his binds. 'I would never kill a child. I never killed your brother. Dig it up!'

In that moment, Leo had to know, had to see Billy's face. He scrambled to his feet and rushed through the kitchen, opened the door to the deafening rain and ran up the garden. He groped inside the shed and found the spade, took it to the grave and started to dig.

The loose earth moved easily, and he was two feet deep in no time, scooping the dirt aside in tight arcs. Before long he was on his knees, soaked to the skin and paranoid about sinking the spade into something other than sodden soil. He dropped the spade and used his bare hands, dug at a frantic pace until he felt a coarse fabric on his fingertips.

He scraped around it and revealed the corner of a hessian sack, grabbed it with both hands and pulled. It came partway, but the ground wouldn't yield. He stood astride the grave and heaved until he thought his back would split in half. The sack came free, and Leo flew backwards, landed on his arse with the hessian bundle on his lap. He freaked, brushed it aside as though the lightning would reanimate the corpse within, and a child Frankenstein would rip free and lurch toward him. But how could it? The bundle was too small to be a young boy – a young boy in one piece, that was.

The mouth of the sack had been stitched, so Leo worked his fingers through a hole in the seam and ripped it apart. Inside were flower-heads and petals of all colours and varieties, the smell of incense and floral perfume overpowering even in the rain. He swallowed, delved his hands into the mix and locked onto a solid, hairy mass beneath the flowers. His stomach dipped as he lifted only God knew what.

It revealed itself by degrees as question marks multiplied in his head like bacteria. He tried to process what he was seeing, but his mind had already shifted focus to the spade rising in his periphery, then to the weight of it crashing into the back of his skull.

He collapsed face-first into the sack of petals, incense filling his nose, then a hand grabbed his ankle and dragged him across the wet grass.

The last thing Leo saw before he blacked out was Cotton's little body lying by the sack. She had ribbons in her hair.

CHAPTER 25

Mick was restless. Had been all day. His run-in with John had rocked more than his chin. He'd finished work two hours ago and should've been at the pub by now, but sewing the button back on his new shirt had taken longer than he'd thought – fingers too thick and nerves all shot to shit. Couldn't have mustered chit-chat, anyhow.

He fetched his bottle of Bushmills from the sideboard and poured three fingers into a tumbler, sat down at the kitchen table and nursed it for a few minutes. If he took a mouthful right now, his evening would live and die where he sat, but straight thinking was what he needed, even if whiskey-oblivion was what he wanted.

John's words played over and over in his head, and no matter which way Mick twisted them, tried to turn them so they meant something else, they kept pointing at the undeniable truth like a compass needle points north. If he was honest with himself, Mick had known the truth before he'd tried to push John's buttons; he'd seen it written on every wall the boy plastered, scratched down in the corner, where the skirting board would cover it.

2

The back of Leo's head was a forest fire of pain. He tried to reach up to out the flames with a soothing palm but his hands were stuck behind him somehow. He opened his eyes and saw that his legs were bound at the ankles, then he realised where he was.

'What happened?' he groaned, the fire spreading to his neck as he spoke.

'Simian happened,' Michael said.

Leo turned to his left and saw Michael bound to the stool next to him.

'What are you talking about?' Leo said.

'Simian is here,' Michael said. 'He was the one who hit you.'

'Simian? No. Can't be.'

Michael nodded. 'It's true.'

Leo tried to pull his hands free as he looked around. 'Where is he?'

Reuben had been obscured by Michael but now sat forward. His face was a bloody mess, worse than how Leo had left it. 'Sitting next to you,' Reuben said.

With that, Michael brought his hands out from behind the stool and got to his feet.

'What the fuck is going on, Michael?' Leo said.

Michael slapped him hard across the face. 'How many times do I have to tell you about that mouth?'

Leo's ear rang, but not before noticing Michael's accent had changed.

'Leave the boy alone, Simian,' Reuben said.

Michael ignored him and sat in the dining chair opposite.

A moment passed in silence, and the ringing and the pain in Leo's head subsided to bearable. He glanced between Reuben and Michael for some time, trying to work out what the fuck was going on.

'You two working together?' Leo ventured. 'Got me here to kill me?'

'I'm as in the dark as you,' Reuben said, and yanked at his bonds as if to make a point of it. 'What are you up to, Simian?' he said to Michael.

'Why the fuck are you calling him Simian?' Leo said, and caught movement to his right, just before the side of his face rang out from another slap. He looked up and saw Michael standing over him. 'Fuck you!' Leo shouted, and received a backhander that cut his cheek. Blood dripped down his neck.

Michael raised his eyebrows. 'Again?'

Leo couldn't take another hit, but the blood cloud needed release. A feral scream rose up from within him, laid him to waste in seconds. He fell back against the stool, spent and bewildered.

'If you can't keep a civil tongue, I'll cut it out,' Michael said. 'But I'm sure you have questions. I'm sure you both have.'

'You've had your fun, Simian, now cut me loose,' Reuben said.

Michael sat on the dining chair, took a cigar from inside his coat and flicked open the silver lighter. *Ching.* 'Make yourself comfortable, Ruby. We're going to be here a while.' He lit the cigar.

'That's not Simian,' Leo said to Reuben, casting his eyes back to Michael. 'I've met Simian; he'd be in his fifties by now.'

Reuben leaned over, the pain in his ribs showing on his face. 'I have spent nearly two thousand years with him. Believe what I tell you.'

'Why would I believe the word of a murdering sack of shit like—'

The side of Leo's face burned from another slap, this time so hard he smacked his head on the base of the stool, relighting that forest fire.

Michael knelt beside him, drew deeply on his cigar and blew the smoke in Leo's face. 'Would you like to try one, Leo?' Michael said, gesturing at the cigar. 'It's an absolute beast of a smoke.'

226

Leo stared through the haze of cigar smoke into Michael's eyes, then over Michael's shoulder at Bond.

It's him, Shtamp.

Michael followed Leo's gaze, turned back with a smile on his face. 'Only one James Bond,' he said.

'Simian,' Leo said.

Simian bit the cigar between his teeth and winked at Leo. 'The Simian you knew was just a junkie I used to borrow from time to time. Get him jacked-up and he never even noticed.' He swung his jacket off and cast it into the dining room in one fluid movement. 'This fellow,' he gestured to himself, 'I picked up in a crack den in Hamburg, and as I speak *every* language, seemed silly not to do the jas and the neins.' He produced an elastic band from his trouser pocket and deftly tied his hair back in a ponytail, á la Simian. 'What was in the grave by the way?'

'You sick freak.' The cable ties bit into Leo's wrists as he tried to free himself.

Simian placed his cigar on the chair and came towards him. 'You have no idea.' He reached above Leo for something on the breakfast bar, started spinning around with it as if he were ballroom dancing. It didn't take long for Leo to realise it was Cotton.

'You are insane,' Reuben said, but his words just seemed to make Simian dance with more vigour.

Cotton's head whipped from side to side with every turn, while Simian hummed a tune and hugged her limp corpse closer. He dipped her occasionally in Leo's direction and Cotton's swollen purple tongue lolled from her blackened mouth.

'You sick fucking freak!' Leo shouted, but even the f-word couldn't stir Simian from his dance.

Simian whirled, feigned conversation as if Cotton were whispering sweet-nothings in his ear, until finally he swung her around by her back legs and flung her over the breakfast bar, into the kitchen.

Leo heard her body hit the window and drop. The sound was sickening. When he looked up, Simian was coming out of an elegant one-armed bow.

'Don't look at me like that, Leo.' Simian put his cigar back in his mouth and sat down. 'You threw her up the driveway... and she was still alive. At least I showed her a good time first.'

'You killed my dog.'

'Technically, all I did was whistle to her – the car coming down the road did the rest.' Simian examined the tip of his cigar. 'Take solace in the knowledge, that if the Good Lord hadn't taken her then, she would have been in the belly of a fox by morning.'

Leo turned to Reuben. 'And you buried her to make me think it was Billy Walker?'

'Simian gave her to me,' Reuben said. 'He knew I would give her a proper burial. If you were led to believe it was Billy Walker, it wasn't by me.'

They both turned to face Simian.

'I stink of dead dog,' Simian said. 'I'm going to freshen up.' With that, he disappeared upstairs.

As soon as he heard the bathroom door close, Leo tried to free his wrists.

'Who are you?' Reuben asked.

Leo strained until the ties dug too painfully into his flesh and he had to stop. He glanced sideways, breathing heavy. 'That's my body you're in.'

'That's not possible.'

Leo laughed. 'You're sitting right in front of me.'

'I mean, you being in that body,' Reuben said, nodding in Leo's direction. 'How is that possible?'

'Ask Simian; he put me here.'

'What was supposed to happen tonight... Leo?'

Leo nodded. 'We were going to make you tell us where the dagger is – save Sadie.'

'Billy's safe,' Reuben said. 'I don't know about Sadie.'

'You'll forgive me if I don't believe anything you say.'

'I didn't lie about the grave.'

'You're still a murderer.'

Reuben hung his head. 'It's complicated.'

'You either kill people or you don't.'

'Of all people, a Dark Heart should know there are more shades than black and white.'

'Seems clear enough to me. Why else would you steel the dagger?'

'What makes you think I stole it?'

'Michael told—' Leo rolled his eyes. 'Simian told me about The Disciples.'

'And what did he tell you?'

'That there were two: an angel from Heaven and a demon from Hell, and that they decided to go their separate ways, so they hid the dagger.'

'And then I stole it?' Reuben asked.

'That's what he said.'

Reuben turned towards the window. The sky flashed a silent silver. 'I've thought many times of sinking the dagger into an ocean trench – to see what would happen.' He faced Leo. 'I don't think Simian would cope without me, though.'

'I don't know about that, Ruby.'

Leo looked up. Simian was directly above, leaning over the glass balustrade. He'd picked out a black silk shirt of Leo's. It looked too small for his bulk.

'I think you'd miss me more,' Simian said, and made his way to the stairs.

'What are you saying?' Leo asked Reuben.

'One from Heaven,' Simian said from the top of the stairs, then slid side-saddle down the banister and landed sure-footed near Leo. 'And one from Hell.' He licked the tip of his finger and pressed it to his arse. '*Tsss.*'

Leo couldn't speak. He looked at Reuben, at Simian.

'Oh come on, Leo. Do I need to sprout horns?' Simian shot both index fingers out from his forehead. 'Would you like Ruby to flap his wings?'

Reuben and Simian are The Disciples. You do understand, don't you, Shtamp?

'Yeah, got it,' Leo said.

Simian clapped. 'Bravo.'

'Told you it was complicated,' Reuben said.

'So you're from Heaven?' Leo asked Reuben.

'Once. A long time ago.'

'And the dagger was yours all along?'

Reuben nodded.

'Those people you kill… all sinners?' Leo could hardly believe it.

'Each and every one,' Simian said, closed one eye and affected a pirate's voice: 'I finds 'em, an' ee kills 'em.' He ran a thumb across his throat, made a ripping sound.

Reuben hung his head.

'Makes no sense,' Leo said. 'If Reuben is the one from Heaven, why does he have to do the killing?'

Simian glared at Reuben, held out an imploring hand. 'You see, Ruby? I've been saying that for years. Give me the dagger. If the time comes when either of Them try to bear a child to the earth, I'll gut the little brat from neck to naval; you know I will.'

'You've lost your mind,' Reuben said.

'And you haven't?' Simian went to the desk, pulled the drawer out and removed the ebony block – Leo's ebony block. He took it to Reuben and placed it in his lap. 'Tell me you haven't had enough of this; tell me you could go on for another thousand years or more.' He knelt beside Reuben, stroked his bloody cheek. 'Open the box for me, and I will send you home.'

Reuben spoke with equal gentility. 'That is not your choice to make.'

'The dagger's inside the ebony block?' Leo asked, but nobody answered him.

'They've forgotten about us. Can't you see that, Ruby?' Simian drew on his cigar and blew smoke into Reuben's face, extinguished the glowing embers on his chest.

If Reuben felt any pain, he didn't show it.

Simian went back to his chair, put the box under his seat and rolled up the sleeves of his shirt. Leo couldn't help staring at the tattoos on his forearms.

'Do you like them?' Simian said. I try to get something different every time – the luxury of having a clean canvas every few weeks, I suspect.' He knelt beside him and rolled his wrists around so Leo could get a better look.

Depicted on his left forearm was an army of skeleton soldiers, wearing horned helmets and carrying swords and shields. It reminded Leo of something out of Jason and the Argonauts. On his other forearm was an army of winged demons with claws and barbed tails: vicious looking things. The detail of both armies was remarkable, with each of their legions disappearing around the back of his arms until they were nothing more than needle pricks in a barren wasteland.

'Would have liked the battle depicted on my torso,' Simian said, admiring the work, 'but there is never enough time.' He sat down again. 'No imagination that one.' He pointed at Reuben with his cigar. 'Same ones every time.'

'What side were you fighting on?' Leo asked.

'Neither. To engage in war, you first have to believe in something, and that is usually somebody else's something.'

'So you believe in nothing?' Leo asked.

'I believe in pleasure.' Simian reached down and drummed his fingers on the ebony box.

'And what is your pleasure?'

'Tell him, Simian,' Reuben cut in. 'Tell Leo why you want the dagger so badly.' He didn't wait for Simian to answer. 'You see, Leo, Simian loves to kill people. If the term *serial killer* had been used two thousand years ago, it would have applied to him.'

The pride in Simian's smile was chilling.

'A serial killer who doesn't like foul language?' Leo said.

'He prays, too,' Reuben said.

Simian put his hands together. 'God grant me the serenity to accept the things I cannot change… '

'All this so he can kill again,' Reuben said. 'You are not fit for existence.'

'How can you trivialise it so? You've been killing for centuries; can you honestly say you don't feel the same things that I feel?'

'How can I?' Reuben said. 'I hate what I do; I hate what I have become.'

Simian went to Reuben and sat cross-legged in front of him. 'But that moment the soul leaves the body, do you still not find it exhilarating? It's like no drug I have ever experienced.'

When Simian scooched over to Leo, he seemed to have a child-like quality about him, as if they were going to swap ghost stories around a campfire.

'It's about being true to yourself, that's all,' Simian told Leo. 'A hunger should never be denied: it's your body telling you that you need something, no matter what that something is. Your body will tell you when you're happy or sad, and sometimes your conscience will conflict with those feelings, but that's just social conditioning. Your body never lies to you. Whatever guilty pleasures you may have are still pleasures, whether you feel guilty about them or not.' Simian glanced at Reuben and back to Leo again. 'Take reading for instance. When you finish that last page and close the book, your body gives you your opinion of it. It is unquestionably how you feel about the story – it'll be in your gut and in your heart, but not your brain. The brain cannot feel, it can only process feelings, and those processes are the product of a lifetime's social conditioning.'

'Like I said, I don't read.'

'That's right, you like films. But films are not always a solitary experience and therefore not as pure as books. Think back to a film you've seen at the cinema, a comedy perhaps. You've smiled through most of it, but no laugh, then during a scene that your body is telling you is particularly dull, the audience laughs, and you find yourself starting to laugh with them. Maybe you even find yourself telling your friends what a funny film it was, and that they should go and see it. Your brain has just overridden your feelings. I'm not saying that's always the case, but it can be.' Simian aimed a thumb at the *Dr No* poster.

'What?' Leo asked.

Simian leant forwards and pressed a finger against Leo's temple. 'Sean Connery.' He then placed his palm on Leo's chest. 'Roger Moore. You let your brain tell your heart who to choose that day, and you've been conflicted ever since. You don't need to change who you are to be happy; you need to embrace who you are.'

Leo could see Reuben shaking his head.

'You and Ruby are very much alike, Leo. Both conflicted with notions of right and wrong. You torture yourselves with your social conditioning, your religious beliefs, but it's not your fault. God is to blame. He punishes the good with conscience, and why? Because He Himself is conflicted. He created man in His own image. Every sin is His own. Why should we be punished for His sins?'

'Spoken like a true sinner,' Reuben said.

'When I was boy, I killed my first man,' Simian continued.

Reuben scoffed and turned away, as if he had heard the story too many times already.

'My younger brother and I were making our way home through the forest when we were taken by surprise. Before I knew what was happening, this dishevelled-looking character had a knife to Jacob's throat. He seemed to be under the impression we had monies to steal, but I think he was delusional from hunger. Poor Jacob was crying and pleading for my help, but I was paralyzed with fear. Anyway, the crazy fool, I think, realised his mistake and decided to make good his error. He cut Jacob's throat right there in front of me – no warnings, no threats – nothing. He let Jacob fall to the forest floor, stepped over him and came at me with the knife that was now coated in my brother's young blood... '

Simian paused, his eyes filled with tears, then spilled. He touched his cheeks and marvelled at his wet fingers as though they were the strangest things. He continued.

'Closer he came, but still I could not move, and even to this day it amuses me to think that I could have found a place in Heaven, if only his knife had been a few inches to the left, but the drunken fool stabbed me in the shoulder. I could smell the stink of wine on him as he fell backwards to the floor, leaving the knife in me. I didn't move, I didn't scream, I felt no pain. I was transfixed on the entity that had left the body of my brother; it was so beautiful – *he* was so beautiful, and then he was gone. I became aware of myself once more. I looked down at the fool on the ground and drew the blade from my shoulder. I returned it to him tenfold.'

Reuben was still looking away. Simian smiled at him.

'There was so much blood, Leo; it was all over me, intoxicating. When the murderous wretch's soul had finally left his body, I found it equally as intoxicating. It wasn't a beautiful thing as my brother's was; it was hideous, and it looked in great pain, even though there were no discernable features to behold, I could still see its agony, and I loved it.'

Simian took a puff on his cigar, pulled it deep into his lungs and released it in a sigh through his nostrils.

'I buried Jacob in the forest, washed myself in a stream and went home. My father received me with a drunken beating for returning without Jacob and promptly passed out. I cut his throat in his sleep and watched him die. His passing was no less enthralling than the thief's, and I knew there would be more to come. My path was clear. The more I killed, the more powerful I felt I was becoming. Not only could I see the souls of my victims, but on a few occasions I could follow them. Only a short way at first, but soon they were taking me to places I could not have imagined.'

'Heaven and Hell?' Leo asked.

'Of course not; I had no such knowledge of those places then. No, I only discovered the dreadful downside to my addiction afterwards.'

'You mean you discovered there was an actual 'downside'?' Leo asked.

'And more, as I found out on the day I died.'

'That's enough,' Reuben said. And to Leo's astonishment, Simian obeyed.

The barn lights flickered for a second, causing the vaulted ceiling to flash in Leo's eyes like a negative. A jagged bolt branched out across the sky to his left, and Simian stared at it, open-mouthed – a kid at the circus.

'Why am I here, Simian?' Leo asked.

Simian plugged his gaping mouth with his cigar, turned towards Reuben as if to check he was paying attention. 'You have your father to thank for that,' he said.

If Reuben wasn't paying attention before, he was now.

'What has he got to do with any of this?' Leo asked, unsure he wanted to know.

'I don't wish for you to feel second best, but your father was my first choice for this… task.'

Leo's muscles tightened at the mention of his dad.

'Your father was a Dark Heart, like you, Leo, but once that poisonous vulture sank her talons into him, he was no good to me.'

Leo twisted in his bonds. 'Watch your mouth, Simian.'

'Oh, calm down, Leo. I'm not talking about your mother. I'm talking about the harpy your father ran off to Spain with – Barbara Shields. You know who I mean, don't you? It was thanks to her I had to send Reuben after your father – caught up with old Ronald in a little backstreet in Spain, didn't you, Ruby?'

'Don't believe his lies,' Reuben said. 'Simian would not dare send me a Dark Heart to kill, only those deserving of Hell; those are the rules to which we abide. Simian may be many things, but he is no fool.'

'Indeed I am not, but kill him you did.' Simian took a pull on his cigar.

'My dad wasn't evil,' Leo said. 'He was a selfish bastard and more, but not evil.'

'Oh, please, Leo. You hated that man, and why? Because he didn't take you to the park for a kick-around? You knew there was more to it than that; you felt something in here.' Simian tapped himself in the chest. 'And you recognise that feeling because you feel the same way about yourself.'

'I didn't hate him; I don't hate him.'

'Then I'm anxious to know the source of your anger the day you almost split open his skull.'

You wouldn't have done it, Shtamp.

'If I hadn't stopped you that day,' Simian continued, 'you would have been lost forever. You see, you have me to thank for keeping you out of a really nasty place.'

You wouldn't have done it, Shtamp. Don't lishten to him.

Simian stood, paced around the living area, full of himself once more.

'That wasn't a good day for me, Leo. I saw so much potential in you that I neglected your father – and you're right, he wasn't an evil man; he just did an evil thing. Not that that buys any good graces with either of… Them.'

Simian went to Leo's collection of Bond DVDs, looked briefly at each cover before sending them spinning into the darkness of the dining room.

'What did he do?' Leo murmured.

Simian dropped the DVD he was holding and darted towards Leo's weak voice. 'What was that, Leo? Couldn't quite hear.' Simian's face contorted into an obscene grin.

'FUCK YOU! TELL ME WHAT HE DID?'

'Language, Leo.'

'TELL ME!'

'You know.'

'Tell me, Simian.' Leo was crying, sobbing almost.

Simian took him in with wide eyes that were filled with a sinister pleasure, soaking up every bit of misery Leo had to offer, before his expression changed to one of compassion. 'Daddy killed Mummy,' he said softly.

Leo surged forward, the cable ties tearing the skin on the backs of his wrists. 'YOU LIE!'

'Do I? Then see for yourself.'

Simian seized Leo's head in both hands and drew him close. Leo struggled, tried to shake free, but he was too strong. The barn began to fade to black, and the only thing Leo could see were the candle-flames reflecting in Simian's eyes. Then nothing at all.

CHAPTER 26

The smell of the leather in the Jaguar was mixed with furniture polish and lavender perfume. She looked beautiful in her yellow dress, but Ron Stamp didn't tell her so. He was impatient to leave.

She fumbled with her seatbelt, and he closed his hand over hers, told her it was broken and that she shouldn't worry. He'd been driving for years. He fastened his own belt and the Jaguar glided away. She reminded him that the last time they picnicked she had been pregnant.

The panorama now was luscious and green, the country road empty and winding. She asked him to mind his speed, as the Jaguar was deceptively smooth and the bends deceptively sharp, and he apologised with tears in his eyes, but the car crept ever faster. She gripped his leg when the Jaguar left the road and dropped onto the soft carpet of grass, and he told her again how sorry he was, but stood on the accelerator until the Jaguar met with the ancient and unyielding oak tree.

Patricia Stamp's breathing was shallow and wet. Her yellow dress now red. The indifferent oak played its part in holding her on top of the crumpled bonnet, a broken branch reaching through her stomach with intestines dripping from its gnarly fingers. A hellish hood ornament.

Ronald Stamp's breathing was laboured. He loosened his seatbelt and looked at his face in the rear-view mirror, didn't seem to like what he saw, and began to bang his head against the window. On the fourth strike, the glass turned to diamonds, and the side of Ronald's head turned to blood. He liked what he saw then.

Patricia Stamp's chest was still now; Ronald Stamp did not have to wait long. He took his phone from his pocket and was about to dial when he heard a car in the distance. He put the phone back in his pocket and laid his head on the steering wheel. He closed his eyes, and all was dark once more.

2

Leo opened his mouth to cry but had nothing left.

'It wasn't your father's idea,' Simian said, returning to his chair. 'Barbara Shields wanted what your mother had. All of it. And your father was so consumed by lust he would have done anything to please her – even kill your mother. Believe me, he wishes he hadn't.'

'What do you want, Simian?' Leo said, his chin on his chest, his eyes straining to look up.

'God kills with impunity. It is my right to do the same. Killing things on computer screens is a poor substitute for the real thing.'

'Break the box open if you want it so bad,' Leo said.

'Why didn't I think of that?' Simian rolled his eyes. 'At the moment it's a solid block of ebony; only Reuben can open it and reveal the dagger.'

'And I'm not going to do that,' Reuben said.

'I know, Ruby. That's why Leo is here.'

'You think I can open the box?' Leo said. 'Even if I could, why would I?'

'How did it feel when you thought you were going to Hell for killing John?' Simian asked.

'How do you think?' Leo said.

'But since then you've learned that murder is in the heart – John was an accident, and God judged you to be innocent of trying to kill your father, or you wouldn't be a Dark Heart. Had you even thought of that?'

'John could have died after I'd drowned, and whether or not John's death was an accident, I'm still responsible,' Leo said.

Simian smiled. 'Not so. What would you say if I told you that you never killed John, that I merely bumped his spirit from his body the moment he hit the floor, and that he is safe and well at the Way Station, on your raft, with Sadie?'

'Impossible,' Reuben said.

'Is it, Reuben? And why is that – because you cannot do it?'

'No, because it cannot be done.'

Simian stood up and started to pace.

'You see that is your problem, Ruby: you have no imagination. A gift is bestowed upon you, and yet you bear it like a cross. You've become so consumed by self-pity that you've missed glorious opportunities for self-expansion. Have you ever considered what the human spirit could be capable of, given a hundred lifetimes to evolve? Of course you haven't, but I have.'

Simian kicked the desk and sent the lamp and phone crashing to the floor.

'Not only have I imagined it, but I have encouraged it, and I have evolved.' He punted the lamp into the darkness of the dining area, ripping the plug from the wall, and marched straight for Reuben. 'So please don't tell me what I can or CANNOT DO!'

Simian bore down on Reuben, his cigar crushed in one fist. His other fist paused close to Reuben's chest like Bruce

Lee about to deliver a one-inch punch, and then his limp arm snapped straight, and his fist met Reuben's chest.

Reuben didn't recoil from a physical blow but merely collapsed into unconsciousness.

Leo fell on his side, instinctively trying to kick away from Simian, but only managed to tease his shoulder close to leaving its socket.

Simian stumbled backwards and collapsed into his chair, staring in wonderment at something above Reuben's head. 'Can you see it, Leo? Can you see how beautiful it is?'

Leo stared, but couldn't see anything above Reuben's head. 'You're crazy.'

Reuben jerked awake and scrambled backwards, realised his efforts were useless and became still, his breathing heavy but steady.

Simian lit another cigar with his chunky lighter and let the smoke pour from his mouth. He stared into the distance, limp and serine.

'Do you know, Leo,' Reuben said, struggling to sit up, 'that this strapping young stallion you see before you is, in his true form, a four-foot midget of a man with only three good teeth and as many good hairs on his head? His penis was so small that even with two consenting sexual partners, he remained a virgin until Lucifer opened his gates to him. Now every time we move on, he turns up in one of these ridiculous overcompensations. Pathetic, if you think about it. Don't you agree?'

Simian leaned forwards from his slouch, propped his elbows on his knees and stared at Leo. 'Reuben is hoping you'll join him in mocking me – hopes I'll lose control and kill you for it, because he doesn't know why you're here, and that frightens him. But I have Sadie and John. And if I lose control and kill you, I may as well kill everyone. Understand?' Simian cocked his head, glanced at Reuben. 'I'll lay this ridiculous overcompensation across Sadie and rape her for ten hours before cutting her in ways that would make Jack the Ripper wince.' He looked back at Leo. 'So think very carefully about the next thing that comes out of your mouth.'

'Believe me, Leo,' Reuben continued, 'this virgin would not last five minutes with a woman like Sadie. Tell him he should stick to sheep, but also tell him that fucking cattle and the like does not count towards the loss of virginity – he can be very persistent about that.'

Simian laid his cigar on the seat of his chair and walked over to the breakfast bar. When he crouched beside Reuben, he was holding a candle. He placed it underneath Reuben's wrist and pinned his arm tight to the stool, turned to Leo as Reuben's moans drifted up into the vaulted ceiling.

'Remember this, Leo,' he said. 'Ruby tried to get you killed just then.' Simian turned his attentions back on Reuben. 'Are you done? You smell done, but are you done?'

'YES!' Reuben screamed.

Simian replaced the candle and went back to his chair. 'What do you say, Leo?' He put the cigar between his teeth.

'To what?'

'To my cleaning your slate for you. Would you like your body back, your friends brought home? I can give you these things if you help me.'

'Why does the boy need to help you if his friends are safe?' Reuben said, his face twisted from the burn. 'We've established that he isn't going to Hell, and you, my friend, are not going to kill anyone, are you?'

'True, his friends are safe, and I'm not going to kill anyone, but the moment Leo injected you, 'my friend', you only had a few hours to live. So rest assured, he is going to Hell now.'

'What are you saying?' Leo asked.

'I am saying that you have killed Reuben; I am saying that you are damned.'

'More lies.' Reuben said.

'Yes, that's right, Ruby, more lies. Tell me though, do you feel an overwhelming need to speak the truth?'

Reuben glanced at Leo, back to Simian.

'Hemlock,' Simian said. 'It was good enough for Socrates.'

'You tricked me,' Leo said.

'That's right,' Reuben said. 'He won't go to Hell for a murder he didn't even know he was committing. In fact, you've just condemned yourself.'

Lightning branched across the sky and lit the barn for a second. Leo watched Simian taking pulls on his cigar, deep lines of concentration on his face.

'You haven't thought this through, Simian,' Reuben said. 'Now cut me loose.'

'Have you ever considered how you come to be here, Leo?' Simian said, gazing out of the window. 'I mean, sitting where you are right now?'

'You hit me with a spade.'

'So why didn't I hit you with a spade a week ago? You'd still be sitting there.'

'Does it look like I give a shit?'

'I'll tell you why,' Simian said, turning to face him, 'because I needed you to participate willingly. And who better to help me catch a serial killer of children than the brother of one of the victims. I must say, your idea of involving the police did throw me off for a while – had to get creative – but the overall effect was far better for it. The letter and the poem were especially nice touches, I thought.'

'I tried to save those children the last time we were here,' Reuben said, 'but we'd been here too long and had to leave.'

'Ruby agonises over those he cannot save, especially the children, but we only have so much time.'

'This changes nothing,' Reuben said.

'It very much does, Ruby. Murder is in the heart. When Leo arrived here tonight, it wasn't just to stop the man who'd murdered his baby brother, it was to stop the man who'd ruined his life, the man who had killed Billy Walker, the man who had taken Sadie from him. An evil man. A molester and killer of children.' Simian turned to Leo. 'When you were confronted with this evil man, did you not want him dead? When you were pounding the face of the man that had done those things to you – had wronged you so – did you not wish him dead? What will God find in your heart when you are judged?'

Leo stared at Bond, needed to hear something to contradict his own heart. Even a lie.

It isn't your fault, Shtamp.

'So, I'll be dead in a few hours,' Reuben said. 'I'll be back where I belong, and you'll be stuck here with a block of wood. I hope you have fun with it.'

'You underestimate me Reuben, but worse still, you underestimate my friend, Leo.'

Leo grinned through his tears at the word 'friend'. 'I would rather burn than help you.'

'Don't say things you don't mean.' Simian flicked ash on the floor. 'A little cooperation from you, and all three of us will have what we want.'

'He can't help you now, Simian,' Reuben said. 'Look at him, you have broken him. And whatever it is you think he can do, I'm the only one that can open the box.'

'It's ironic, Reuben, that of all the things we know of this world, of the souls and of the Gods that rule them, it will be human biology that opens the box.'

Reuben laughed. 'You can torture me all you like.'

Simian rubbed his forehead as if irritated by the remark. 'As you well know, when you first enter another soul's body you are not fully in control, in a mental sense, I mean. The body leaves behind certain thoughts, urges, compulsions, fears… memories. Fleeting, I know, but there nonetheless.' He looked at Reuben. 'I'm going to bump you from your body and put Leo back in, and for a short time, your residual memories will be Leo's. He will open the box for me.'

Reuben's expression changed, maybe for the first time realising Simian might not be mad. 'And why would he do this for you?'

'Yeah, why would I do that for you?' Leo could barely lift his head.

'Not for me, Leo – for you.'

'Go fuck yourself.' Leo waited for the slap, craved it.

'I understand. You feel that you need to spend some quality time with your father – an eternity in fact. Maybe over the centuries you'll come to understand why he murdered your mother and hated you so much. That's if you can find him. Hell's a big place and cruelly overpopulated.'

'Reuben will be dead in a few hours, thanks to me. I'm going to Hell, either way.'

'I can change that,' Simian said.

'He lies,' Reuben said. 'He is no God.'

'Help me, Leo. Open the box, and I will let you use the dagger to kill Reuben.' Simian stood from his chair and threw his arms up melodramatically. 'Kill him with the dagger, and YE SHALL NOT BE JUDGED!'

The front door blew open, and rain reached in a couple of feet. The candles flickered but stayed. Simian went to the door and kicked it shut.

'You think you know me, but you don't,' Leo said.

'Oh, I think I know you better than you know yourself.' Simian returned to his chair. 'Do you think you're here purely because you are a Dark Heart? This is a one-shot deal, so I had to be sure you would finish the journey with me. I've sent hundreds of your kind back to this earth and not a single one with your potential. Some become Dark Hearts through blind luck, totally unaware of themselves; others are like festering grenades waiting for that evil deed to come pull the pin. Some turn their lives around without even knowing they needed to. *You,* however, are totally aware of what you are. Both sides of your personality are locked in constant battle. The more you try to be good, the more your dark side fights against it, and yet you struggle on regardless. Whether or not you can turn it around is irrelevant. You believe you can.'

Leo turned to Reuben, who was struggling frantically to break his ties but getting nowhere.

'Do you understand what I am telling you, Leo? You can be free, your friends can be free, and after you have spent a good life on this Earth, you will be with your mother and Davey again.'

Leo glared at Simian. Is this what it had come down to: murdering for the sake of his soul? What kind of sick paradox was that?

'Well, are you bad enough to be good again?' Simian asked.

Don't even think about it, Shtamp.

Leo turned to Reuben, but was talking to Bond. 'I have to know how my life could have been.'

You won't be able to live with yourself.

'I deserve a second chance.'

Reuben struggled more ferociously. 'Think of the innocent people who'll die by his hand. The blood will stain your hands too, Leo.'

'Only those deserving of Hell,' Simian said. 'I promise.'

What would your mother and Davey think?

'God will know the truth,' Reuben shrieked. 'You don't have to do this.'

Simian walked over to Reuben and put a hand on his shoulder. 'Calm down, my friend; you will be home soon.' He looked at Leo. 'You have made the right choice, you know you have.'

CHAPTER 27

Mick pulled up outside John's cottage, windscreen wipers doing double-time. He'd seen the streetlights go out a couple of miles back, so wasn't surprised to see all the windows black. He grabbed his torch from the glove box, turned the collar up on his Donkey jacket and climbed out of the truck.

He knocked once on the side door but didn't hang around for a response; he was getting soaked. He opened the door and called out for John as he stepped inside, aimed the torchlight down the hallway and braced himself for shining eyes.

'Boy?' he called, groping for the light switch and flicking it on and off with no effect.

The lounge and spare room doors were open and the rooms empty. The bedroom and toilet doors were closed. Mick rehearsed apologetic dialogue in his head for when torchlight hit sleepy eyes or a constipated face, but he hadn't thought of what to say after that – wouldn't know where to start.

He knocked on the bedroom door. 'Boy?' Did likewise on the toilet door before opening it. Empty. He looked in the bedroom and felt relieved to find that empty too: the ensuing conversation would perhaps be better in daylight.

Mick went to leave, cast light into the spare room and lounge as he passed, but stalled before reaching the kitchen. He backed up two paces to the lounge doorway, threw light around inside until his eyes could make up their mind as to what had been odd the first time.

2

The wind cast nets of rain against the glass walls of the barn – a beautiful thing – but Leo was numb to it.

Simian placed the box next to Reuben and knelt beside Leo.

'When I bump you from your body you'll feel the urge to rush back in,' Simian told Leo. 'Be calm, and the feeling will pass. When I bump Reuben out, go to your body – it will almost be automatic; it's your body after all.'

Think of all the people he'll murder, Shtamp. You won't be able to live with yourself – I know you.

'When you are inside, I'll free your hands and give you the box,' Simian continued. 'I can hold Reuben off for more time than you'll need.'

'Did you kill the girl?' Leo asked. 'Lucy?'

'Of course not,' Simian said. 'Just went in for the licence and the button.'

'And the eyes.' Leo said.

'Yes. And the eyes.'

'Only sinners?'

'I promise, Leo. No women or children. Only the worst of the worst.'

Leo stared off at the rain cascading down the glass in waves. 'There's a tablecloth in the first drawer of the kitchen. Drape it over the picture for me.'

'The Bond poster?'

Leo nodded.

Simian shrugged. 'As you wish.' He went into the kitchen, came back with the tablecloth and went over to Bond.

'That won't stop the voices,' Reuben said softly.

Simian came back and knelt by Leo. 'Better?'

Leo glanced at the ghostly tablecloth suspended on the chimney breast. 'Get on with it.'

'When you first enter your body you'll be overwhelmed with feelings that are not your own: ignore them and focus only on those concerning the box, then simply open it. Are you ready?'

Leo bowed his head.

'Good.' Simian said, and brought his fist to Leo's chest.

As the gunshot victim never hears the bullet leave the gun, so to Leo never felt the punch that jolted him from John's body. He spun blindly into a black nothingness, rushing at some incalculable speed, and was then plunged into a near halt, a neutral buoyancy he hadn't felt since he was a child expelling air from his lungs until he floated near the bottom of the swimming pool – a gravity dead zone.

He floated that way for what seemed like a blissful age, and then colours and shapes stormed by him and circled him, and he realised he was suspended above John's body.

Simian had moved towards Reuben, and the image grounded Leo in the moment. He felt vulnerable in the open and had to fight the urge to rush back into the haven of John's body, but then he saw his own body, and the sight of it calmed and centred him.

Reuben went limp, and something appeared above Leo's old body. Not the beautiful apparition he imagined Simian had been so enthralled with, but just a man, thin and pale and frightened. Leo drifted towards him.

Simian's image split as it had on the hill, and his projected self rose up and engaged in a struggle with Reuben, but though they did not seem to be touching, a fierce confrontation was taking place; Leo could feel it.

As he drifted closer to himself, Leo began to feel an energy, a magnetic force that pulled gently but relentlessly. He didn't resist, and allowed himself to be sucked downwards, until he was rushing through the black nothingness once again.

At first there was only pain: his face and eyes burned from the mace, his chest and wrist aflame from Simian's torture. His head throbbed, his ribs ached when he breathed – but then all he could feel was an onslaught of thoughts and emotions he knew not to be his own.

A thousand faces of death flared in his mind, contorted and hideous, followed by the grim knowledge of a thousand more to come. So many eyes gazing into him as *he* gazed back. He could have died right there if he would only give in to it.

Leo felt his hands fall to his sides and the box placed in his lap. The box sickened him, and he wanted to cast it into the darkness, but instead he ran his hands across the top. A series of different shapes rose from the block, random to his eyes but so familiar to his touch. His fingers caressed the protruding nubs with the confidence and speed of a classical pianist, and the shapes sank back into the ebony as though they had never been there at all. A seam of light pulsed around the centre of the box as Simian took it from him, and then Simian's fist was at his chest once more.

Leo was plunged back into the gravity dead zone, re-emerging above himself. He felt the energy of the pale thin man rush past him, and looked down upon his old body and saw it reanimated.

Reuben tried to get up, but wasn't quick enough. Simian brought his boot-heel down onto his face, and Reuben dropped lifeless as a mannequin. Leo allowed himself to be drawn back into John's body in time to see Simian binding Reuben's wrists behind the stool. He stood when he was finished, and as he turned to Leo, the front door blew open again and extinguished the candles, plunging the barn into deeper darkness.

Simian's hulking silhouette was framed in the open doorway, the dagger turning over and over in his hand, lightning strikes catching along the blade.

'I always knew you would do it, Leo, but now the dagger's in my hand I can't quite believe it.'

Wind buzzed around the barn, cool on Leo's face.

'It's only right that you should go first, Leo.'

'Cut me loose. I did what you asked.'

'Waste of time. You couldn't kill an innocent man; you don't have it in you.' Simian looked at Reuben. 'Not many of us do.'

'Just let me go, then.'

'Again, a waste of time. You must've noticed John's biology taking over? His thoughts and impulses reasserting themselves? His memories reclaiming the space in his head? It wouldn't take long before there was no Leo Stamp left. How much repenting do you think you can do in a month – six weeks at best? Why do you think me and Ruby have to move around so much? *They* didn't want us to linger anywhere for too long, didn't want us to grow attached to anyone and lose focus on the task. Cruel, aren't *They*?'

Leo struggled to break free as Simian knelt beside him, got right down in his face, the smell of the cigar on his breath. It was the same disgusting smell that had drifted through his floorboards as a kid.

'If you were to ask me nicely,' Simian said, 'I could kill Reuben first. You could still go to Heaven. But you have to ask me nicely.' He put the point of the dagger under Leo's chin and offered his ear, but Leo knew there was no more bargaining to be done.

'Fuck you,' he whispered, the last of his tears spent on his cheeks.

Simian pulled away. 'Leo, Leo, Leo. That filthy mouth of yours.'

He could just make out Simian's bared teeth as he drew the dagger back to strike. Leo closed his eyes, heard a swishing sound, and felt a breeze on his face, followed by a dull *thonk*.

'You alright, boy?' he heard Mick say, but he couldn't open his eyes, fearing that Simian was playing one last sadistic game before cutting his throat open.

'Boy?'

'Mick?' Leo said, eyes still clamped.

'At least I know I'm not crazy; even that fella was calling you Leo.'

Leo opened his eyes and saw Mick standing there holding a pickaxe handle. The sight of him sent a judder of emotion through his chest as he breathed, and he struggled not to lose it.

'Don't you start with that, boy. You'll get me goin''

Mick took the dagger out of Simian's limp hand and cut the plastic ties at Leo's wrists, pulled him up.

'Sorry for what I said about your ma, boy.' He handed Leo the dagger. 'Had to be sure – not that I'm even sure now. It is you, Leo, isn't it, boy?'

The question didn't register at first. All Leo could think about was the weapon in his hand, how many lives it had taken.

'I am right, ain't I, boy?'

Leo nodded, found some hidden reserve of strength and put it to work on not falling down. 'Check the pockets of that jacket over there.' He pointed. 'Should be some cable ties.'

Mick didn't move. He was looking at Reuben but was undoubtedly seeing Leo.

'That's not me anymore,' Leo said, and slapped Mick's arm to rouse him from his daze. 'Need those cable ties before this guy wakes up.'

Mick looked down at Simian, then hustled to the jacket and came back with four cable ties and a cigar.

'There's a message at John's place saying you're a serial killer, that you killed that Walker kid.' Mick handed Leo the ties and put the cigar in his shirt pocket, then they grabbed an arm each and hauled Simian to the barstool.

'You need to leave, Mick,' Leo said, pulling the ties tight at Simian's wrists.

'I ain't goin' anywhere until you tell me what's goin' on. You been messing around with Ouija boards, ain't ya, boy?'

Leo removed the lighter from Simian's trouser pocket and relit the candles. 'You can't be here, Mick. There're things I need to do.' He paused, fought to keep a sob down.

'Like I said, I ain't goin' anywhere.' Mick took the lighter from him. 'Do what you've got to do, boy.' He shouldered the pickaxe handle and headed for the dining room. Leo heard a chair scrape along the floor, then a *ching* from the lighter. 'I ain't goin' anywhere,' Mick said again, and cigar smoke drifted above the partition like a spectre.

3

Reuben and Simian were still unconscious, but a glass of cold tap water brought them round in a snap. Reuben groaned, wiggled his nose and worked his jaw up and down. Simian shook the water from his hair, seemingly more concerned with his appearance than his physical wellbeing.

'Who hit me?' he said.

'That would be Mick,' Leo replied.

'Mick?' Simian looked around and shouted into the dark: 'Well, Mick, I owe you one, and I always pay my dues.'

'Whatever, boy.'

Leo bent down beside Reuben, could feel the mace working on his own eyes and had to back away.

'I can't untie you just yet, Reuben. Trick me once, shame on you – if you know what I mean?'

Reuben blinked as if to say he understood, then stared at Simian.

Simian sniffed the air. 'Is that giant leprechaun smoking my cigars?'

'Mine now, boy,' Mick said, and gave a soft, throaty laugh.

'Who do you think you are calling b—'

Leo pressed the dagger's blade to Simian's throat.

'Oh, please Leo,' Simian said. 'Do you actually believe you would have killed Reuben? You're no murderer.'

'Don't know how you can be so sure. I'm not,' Leo said.

Simian grinned, started struggling. He blurred before Leo as though his projected self was trying to break free, but was apparently bound by the cable ties as much as the flesh and blood Simian. Leo pressed the blade tighter to his throat until the razor-edge dented the skin, and both Simians stopped moving and merged into one.

'Careful, Leo,' Simian said, craning his neck away from the blade. 'That's sharp.'

Leo maintained the pressure for a moment before lowering the dagger from Simian's throat.

'You see?' Simian stretched his neck and swallowed. 'You're no killer, but even if you were, I'd just find another host.'

'If I killed you with a breadknife, maybe,' Leo said. 'But don't forget I've been inside Reuben's head, and I know the truth.'

'You know nothing of the truth.'

'I know if I kill you with this,' Leo held the blade to Simian's throat again. 'You'll go back to Hell.'

Simian pulled away from the blade. 'Aren't you forgetting something?'

'Sadie and John?'

'Only I can save them,' Simian said. 'If I don't bump you from your body, John has no way home. And there's still that little matter of you going to Hell for killing Reuben, and we both know you're not going to kill an innocent man.'

Leo half knelt, half dropped down in front of him. 'You're right, Simian, I'm not going to kill an innocent man.' He jabbed the dagger into Simian's stomach and felt hot blood splash on his hand, watched Simian's eyes widen. 'If God wants me to burn for Reuben, I'll burn, but I won't burn for you.' The blade slipped out easily, the blood black in the candlelight.

'You've just murdered your friends,' Simian said in grunts and breaths, slumping back against the barstool and exhaling a final time.

Leo stood up, sensed Mick in the doorway of the dining room, and not for the first time in his life felt shameful.

'Please, Mick, go back inside.' Leo's voice was syrupy thick.

He heard Mick's boots shuffle back inside.

'I'm sorry, Mick, this isn't a proud day for me.'

'That's alright, boy, I can think of more than a few days in your life that would give you cause for pride. They did me.'

Tears bled down Leo's smiling cheeks, and he fell wearily to his knees, turning the blade around to face himself. 'Cut Reuben free when I'm done.'

'Stop, Leo,' Reuben shouted. 'Cut me loose, and I'll end my own life. You don't have to do this – Mick, get in here now!'

'Simian told me that the body is the anchor for the soul. This is the only way I can get to my friends, the only way John can return.'

'What's goin' on, boy?' Mick emerged from the dark, wielding the pickaxe handle.

'I accept my fate, Reuben.' Leo said.

'Fuck God! Who is He to judge!' Reuben screamed.

Leo raised the dagger. 'It's the only way.'

For the third time in Leo Stamp's life, he attempted suicide. It was the first time he ever got it right.

CHAPTER 28

Mick crashed to his knees beside John's corpse, rage and bewilderment quickly dissolving into rampant grief.

'What have you done, boy? What have you done?' he said, not really knowing if he was grieving for Leo, John or both.

'Cut me loose,' Reuben said.

Mick's hands trembled near the dagger's handle. He wanted to pull it free but couldn't bring himself to touch it. 'What have you done?'

'Listen to me, Mick; there isn't much time. Cut me loose.'

'Cut you loose?' Mick said to the man Leo had just called Reuben. 'I should bash your brains in.'

'If you want me to save him you'd better do it quickly. Now pull the dagger from his chest and cut me loose.'

Mick looked down at John's body, at the blood. 'I can't.'

Reuben struggled in his binds. 'Do it!'

Mick wrapped both hands around the handle, closed his eyes and pulled. The blade slipped free.

Reuben offered his wrists around the base of the stool and Mick scrambled over to him and cut the ties, grimacing at the blood on the blade. Reuben took the dagger and freed his own ankles.

'I have only got time to say this once. Do you understand?' Reuben said.

Mick turned to look at John's body, and Reuben slapped him across the face.

'Look at me,' Reuben said, and Mick did. 'Do you understand?'

Mick nodded, his hands curled into fists.

'As soon as I've stopped breathing,' Reuben said, gathering the two halves of the ebony box, 'you pull the dagger from my chest and set it in here like this, do you see?' He offered the dagger to one of the halves. 'Place the other half on top, and once the box has sealed itself, you put it in the wall safe behind the picture – the combination is one, nine, six, two, okay?'

Mick didn't answer until Reuben raised his hand.

'You slap me again, boy, and you won't need that dagger to stop you breathing. One, nine, six, two – I got it. Do what you gotta do.'

Reuben didn't hesitate. He sunk the dagger fist-deep into his chest, coughed a thick tongue of blood over his bottom lip and down his chin, and collapsed onto his back.

Mick gagged and looked away, saw the pool of blood accumulating under John's body and gagged again. He shut his eyes and counted off five deep breaths, listened to the thunder and rain and tried not to think of the dead bodies lying all around him. When he'd regained something close to composure, he looked down at Reuben's body and could only see the boy he'd grown to love like a son. He watched for the rise and fall of Leo's chest, and when it never came, he counted off another five breaths, then started peeling the dead fingers from the hellish bone handle.

Leo felt like a leaf that had fallen from a lone tree on a mountain top, rocking gently to the valley floor in cerebral freefall. He seemed to dissolve in clouds of memories, absorbing them momentarily before passing through...

He saw Davey hunched dreamily at his desk, eyelevel with his Warhammer soldiers, battle cries and laser-blast sound effects drifting through his warriors on the gentle currents of Davey's childish whispers... he saw his dad on the hill against a blue sky, Cotton skipping circles around him... Mick tap dancing on dusty floorboards... John doing Tequila Slammers in a crowded nightclub, Sadie matching him drink for drink... his mum walking hand in hand with Davey along the beach at Shingle Street... his mum walking hand in hand with Davey along the beach at Shingle Street... his mum walking hand in hand with Davey...

The images dissipated as the matter surrounding Leo took on that all too familiar viscosity, and he was no longer sinking, but rising. The oily substance triggered an infant-like reflex in him to hold his breath, and although his rational mind told him this side of death did not concern itself with the trivialities of oxygen, he still gasped for air when he breached the surface of the oil-slick sea: the backdrop for so many of his dreams and nightmares, alike.

At first he panicked; there was no raft. The only flicker of doubt that had hobbled through his mind as he plunged the infernal dagger into his own heart, was that on his journey to Hell there would be no pit stops before The Pit, and he would never be able to save them. But as he manoeuvred to face the other direction, the raft came into view. It was empty.

His lack of desire to reach that empty place was only eclipsed by the thought of being sucked down into the underworld, but knowing his last – if not only – selfless act had been in vain, sent him into deep despair and made him crave the dark.

He tried to dive below the slop, but it seemed to push him back, deny him. He thrashed to the point of exhaustion, sent frustrated screams into the echoless, misty dome until eventually he could do no more than float there.

An immeasurable time passed before he could breathe without effort, and he realised there was only one course of action left until something else presented itself. He worked his way around to face the raft, mentally preparing himself for the arduous journey, then saw a male torso rise Dracula-fashion from the deck. A moment later, Dracula had a bride.

It was impossibly slow going, but with John and Sadie paddling to meet him, the gap between them closed. By the time he felt their arms around him, an age had passed.

They pulled him onto the raft, and the three of them hugged one another tightly.

'I'm so sorry for what I've done to you both,' Leo said, unable to look at their faces. Sadie clutched his hand, and it crushed his soul.

'This is not your fault, Leo,' John told him. 'No way, mate.'

John gripped the back of his neck and forced him to look up, but Leo's heart couldn't bear their understanding or forgiveness, and if it weren't for the immense task he had to fulfil, their compassion would have paralysed him. He took John's hand from behind his neck, and with Sadie's hand in his other, he brought them both to their feet.

'Listen to me.' Leo became aware that he was back in his old body; he was six-two again and looking down at both of them. 'You're going home.'

'Michael said he was the only one who could get us back safely,' Sadie said, fear mapped out on her face as she pointed at the black water. 'That there are things in there that would hurt us.'

Leo squeezed her hand. 'Michael's dead, and I know I'm asking a lot, but I need you to trust me. That's the only way back, and there is nothing in there that will hurt you, I promise, but you have to go now. I don't know how long this place can exist without me.'

'What do you mean, without you?' John asked.

'Doesn't matter now, John.' Leo tried to pull them both towards the edge of the raft, but John pulled his hand free.

'Yes it fucking does. What do you mean?' Tears ran down John's cheeks. 'What do you mean, Leo?'

Leo put his arm around John's neck, pulled Sadie in for more of the same and kissed their cheeks. 'I love you both,' he said, then pushed as hard as he could.

John groped for Leo's arm but with no luck; he and Sadie hit the slick and were sucked down, into the black. Within seconds they were gone, and Leo was alone.

3

Mick wrapped both hands around the bone handle, praying to God he wouldn't faint, and pulled. The blade slipped out, chased by a gurgle of syrupy blood that stirred his guts.

Reuben had told him to put it straight in its box, but Mick felt compelled to rinse it under the tap first. He took it into the kitchen, one hand cupped beneath the blade to catch the drips, and glimpsed the mangled dog-corpse by the draining board. The smell of decaying meat hit him deep in his lungs; his dinner of pork chops and mashed potato hit the sink soon after. He retched until he was empty and his eyes bulged and streamed in their sockets, then got out of the kitchen with the blood-gunged dagger.

He stepped over the blonde fella's legs, slipped on something wet and went down heavy on one knee. He groped in the dark and gathered the two halves of the box, did what he should have done straight away, and sandwiched the dagger between the blocks. Light pulsed around the centre and blinked out, leaving seamless wood in its place. Mick couldn't believe what he was seeing, but the seam had disappeared whether he believed or not.

A tablecloth had been draped over the James Bond poster. Mick tore it away. It took a while to locate the catch and to suss its workings with his thick fingers, but the picture finally swung out on its concealed hinges, revealing the wall safe.

The combination worked just like Reuben said, and the door opened with a *click*. He placed the box inside, closed the safe and swung the picture back in place.

His work done, Mick returned to the dining room to finish his cigar; the smell of sick in there was marginally more agreeable than the blood and dead bodies on display out here. He relit the cigar with shaky hands, inhaled a stinging lungful and imagined it to feel like a junkie's first fix of the day. But before the aromatic smoke had even scratched the surface of calm, he heard John screaming Leo's name in the other room.

4

Leo sat at the edge of the raft, his knees drawn up to his chest, staring at the spot where John and Sadie had disappeared beneath the black sea. He had no idea how long he would have to wait until someone came for him or something happened to signify the beginning of his journey to Hell, but he was ready to go.

Why are you always in such a hurry to condemn yourself, Shtamp?

Leo pinched a fleck of bark from the raft and flicked it into the black. 'Didn't think I'd ever hear your voice again.'

Look at me when I'm talking to you.

Something tapped Leo on the shoulder and he almost fell into the water as he jerked around to see what it was. Bond was stood behind him, taking a cigarette from a thin, gunmetal case. He tapped the filter on the case and slipped the cigarette into his mouth, fingered a stylish black lighter and lit up.

Nineteen years I've waited for this. He drew on the cigarette. Exhaled. *Delicious.*

'What are you doing here?' Leo said, getting to his feet.

Came to say goodbye, and maybe finish a conversation that doesn't end with you draping a tablecloth over my head.

'Sometimes you just wouldn't shut up.'

Sometimes you jusht wouldn't lishten.

'I'm listening now.'

Now *you don't need me to tell you; that's why it's time to say goodbye.*

'You mean I'm cured?'

Bond's cigarette drooped from his bottom lip while he tugged at his white cuffs and adjusted his black bowtie.

More a case of realising there was nothing wrong with you to shtart with. He drew on the cigarette and blew a stream of smoke into the mist. *It's your guilt that defines you as a good person, not the bad things you've done that define you as bad.*

Leo stared off into the near distance.

And don't feel bad for choosing me when you really wanted to choose Roger Moore. I'm over it.

Leo turned back. 'I didn't—'

Bond was shaking his head. *Why do you think I gave you such a hard time over the years?*

'It was *me* giving me a hard time,' Leo said dreamily.

Bond's face brightened, though his cocky slant remained.

Leo heard a deep rumbling behind him, could feel a tremor in the soles of his feet.

That was a brave thing you did for John and Sadie, Bond said, reaching into his jacket for his cigarette case. *Your mother and Davey would be proud.* He tapped a fresh cigarette on the case and placed it behind Leo's ear. *For later.*

The rumble became a roar, and Leo turned, the shuddering raft almost spilling him to the deck.

They'll be safe with me, Bond whispered into his ear. *Goodbye, Leo.*

A geyser exploded from the black about twenty metres out, sending a wave under the raft. Leo dropped to his hands and knees and countered the seesawing deck, eyes locked on what seemed to be a ball of white feathers riding the tip of the geyser. When the oil-slick column fell back to the surface, the feathery mass remained fixed in the mist, and Leo recognised the object for what it was.

The giant wings snapped open, beat twice in quick succession before stretching out in a ragged fan of mottled greys and whites. Stray feathers tumbled down to be swallowed by the black, and Leo wondered how such a sorry pair of wings could hold even Reuben's papery frame in the air, assuming this was the same frail man Simian had exorcised from Leo's body earlier at the barn.

Reuben circled the raft in sweeping arcs, displacing the mist in his wake, and swooped low to the water before rising above Leo's head and tucking in his wings. He seemed to be descending too fast, and Leo feared Reuben's bony legs would snap on impact, but his wings reached out at the last moment and his bare feet found the deck with all the grace of a ballet dancer.

'So this is your Way Station,' Reuben said, his pale, drawn face turning in all directions. 'Haven't visited one of these places in nearly five hundred years.' He opened his wings to examine them and more feathers cascaded from the tattered plumage. 'Not as I once was.'

'How can you be here, Reuben?'

'Simian is not the only one with talent; I just choose to keep mine in check.' He folded his wings behind his back, his skeletal nakedness both natural and ghastly at the same time. 'But I couldn't sit idle and watch this happen.'

'My choice.'

'All of us are capable of hideous things – what mother wouldn't kill for her child? – but most of us never have to answer those questions. If you hadn't crossed paths with Simian, you wouldn't have needed to make those choices.'

'I tried to kill my father. Simian had nothing to do with that.'

'And that should've been your only cross to bear. I can't erase the things Simian has done to you, but I can give you a second chance… perhaps a bit more.'

'What do you mean?' Leo said, exhaustion hanging on his shoulders like sacks of grain.

'Simian is fastidious about the information he finds on those I send to Hell, but the things he knew about your father went far beyond that. It never occurred to me at the time, but of course, now I realise Simian befriended him.'

'You're not making any sense, Reuben.'

Reuben opened his wings. 'Better if you see for yourself.' With a gentle flap, he lifted from the raft. 'Simian broke the rules and showed you things you shouldn't have seen. It's only fair I do the same.'

Reuben banked to the left and rose into the mist, circled back and clapped his wings just short of the raft. The powerful gust lifted Leo into the air, sending him up and out over the black. He twisted in the mist, caught sight of the raft as he began his descent in what seemed like slow motion.

His mum and Davey were sitting by the edge of the raft: Davey in his bobble hat, skipping pebbles across the water; his mum smiling and happy in her yellow dress. Bond stood in the middle of the raft in his black dinner jacket, a cigarette hanging from his mouth as he tied the white tablecloth to a central wooden mast. And sitting on his own in the corner was Leo himself, though he looked different in a way he couldn't explain. Bond tied the final knot, and the tablecloth-sail ballooned with an invisible wind, and the raft drifted beneath the mist curtain and was gone.

Leo hit the black water and was drawn down into the dark, only for his mind to flood with colours and images. He soon realised that the raft was not what Reuben had to show him, but a parting gift from his Way Station.

5

John had managed to sit himself up against the back of the sofa by the time Mick reached him. He was staring at the bloody hole in his chest and hyperventilating.

'My chest, Mick! Look at my fucking chest!'

In Mick's eyes, it didn't look half as bad as it had earlier, and unless he was going full-on Irish crazy, the wound appeared to have clotted, and in some places even scabbed over.

'Don't move, boy.' Mick rushed into the kitchen, flung drawers open until he found tea towels. He returned to John and compressed one over the gory hole. 'Hold this,' he said, and placed John's hand on top, only for it to drop lifeless by John's side again.

'He's gone,' John said, staring over Mick's shoulder.

'Don't be so sure. *You* weren't breathin' a minute ago – now hold this.'

John held the tea towel to his chest, and the lights in the barn flickered.

'There must be a first-aid kit somewhere,' Mick said, and was about to get up when John grabbed his new shirt, ripping the newly-sewn button off again.

'Shit, Mick,' John blurted. 'Sadie's in the garage, locked in the boot of her car. Go – I'll be fine.'

The rain came down in diagonal sheets as Mick ran across the driveway to find the garage door locked, but the frame splintered easily under the weight of his shoulder, and the door crashed open.

The lights were out in here too, but Mick could still see the Beetle's wheel arches jouncing in the dark. Then above the thunder and rain he heard muffled cries and placed an ear to the cold boot and knocked.

'Sadie?' he shouted, and felt the car rock and her cries strengthen 'Hold on, girly.'

He tried the car door, but it was locked; his elbow made short work of the window. Mick leant in and popped the boot.

6

Patricia Stamp was bathed in sweat, hair slicked to her forehead, her skin rosy and smooth.

'Push, love,' Ronald Stamp said, squeezing her hand tight. His hair was dark and curly, how Leo remembered in old photographs. 'Nearly there; you're doing brilliant.'

'Keep pushing, Pat,' the midwife said, hunched at the other end of the bed. 'The head's showing.'

Patricia Stamp pushed, her knuckles white in her husband's hand, and then the cry of new life filled the delivery room.

'A soprano if ever I heard one,' the midwife said, and cut the umbilical cord. 'Hold your son, Pat.'

Patricia cradled her baby boy, and Ron kissed his tiny fingers with tears in his eyes and a look on his face Leo had never seen before.

'This is Leo,' Ron told the midwife, the pride in his voice undeniable. 'If the first was a boy, he was always going to be called Leo.'

'Well, take your son, Mr Stamp,' the midwife said. 'Pat has more work to do.'

Minutes later, another child was born.

'A boy or a girl?' Ron said, Leo caterwauling in his arms.

'What's wrong with my baby?' Patricia said. 'Why is my baby that colour?'

The midwife didn't answer, only lifted the newly born child off to the side and laid its little blue body on a tray.

'What's the matter?' Ron Stamp said.

A time passed before the midwife turned. 'I'm so sorry.' She placed the child in Patricia's arms. 'You should hold him for a moment… both of you.'

'A boy,' Patricia said. 'Connor.' She cried with her baby at her cheek, beckoned for her husband to come to them. 'Hold him with me, Ron. Hold Conner.'

Ron shook his head, his face wide with disbelief. 'No.'

'You should hold your son, Mr Stamp… say goodbye,' the midwife said.

Ron Stamp looked down at the baby in his arms, slowly held the child further and further away. 'No. I can't.' He handed the wailing Leo to the midwife, his eyes an angry red, his lips trembling as he spoke. 'I can't touch them.'

CHAPTER 29

The pull of his own body was fierce, but Leo resisted and hung zombiefied in the gravity dead zone, not quite ready to be back in his skin.

The barn was a gothic shrine to bloody carnage: Simian and John sat facing each other in macabre symmetry; Cotton's tiny corpse lay hideous and angular by the sink, and Mick and Sadie cast long shadows across the room from the open doorway, Sadie's hair lank and wet against her head. Leo was glad he couldn't see her face when she started screaming and pointing at Simian, who was beginning to struggle in his binds.

Leo didn't hesitate and dived for his body. He emerged clutching his chest, eyes burning from the mace once again and his head reliving every fist and foot that had struck it. But the pain didn't concern him for long. He knew of these things now, thanks to the snippets of knowledge Reuben had left rushing around in his head like bees in a bell jar. The wounds would heal fast.

Mick had left Sadie cowering in the doorway and now had the pickaxe handle in both hands. Simian twisted and jerked as he tried to free himself, eyes never dropping from the pickaxe handle.

'Smash his face in,' John shouted. 'Do it, Mick.'

Mick stepped closer to Simian, raised the handle.

'*Bindet mich los!*' Simian blurted. '*Bindet mich los!*'

'Wait, Mick,' Leo shouted. 'It's not him.'

Mick hesitated.

'Help me up,' Leo said.

Mick lowered the pickaxe handle, stepped towards Leo and pulled him up.

'Don't you ever do that again,' Mick said, and didn't let his hand go until Leo complied with a nod.

'*Bindet mich los!*' Simian shouted.

'What *is* that… German?' John said.

'Why's he talkin' like that?' Mick said.

'It's not Simian anymore,' Leo said. 'Must be the guy whose body he stole in the first place.' He looked down at the guy, kicked his foot to get his attention. 'Speak English?'

The guy looked up with wary eyes. '*Lasst mich los!*' he said.

Leo bent down, dabbed two fingers into the guy's chest and showed him the blood. The guy's eyes grew large and his gaze dropped to the wound, then he began to pant, dry and sporadic.

'*Ich sterbe,*' the guy said, his eyes pleading with Leo. '*Helft mir! Helft mir!*'

Leo fetched a small serrated knife from the kitchen.

'Don't cut him loose,' Sadie said in a weak voice. 'He's the devil.'

Mick went to her and put his arm around her shoulder. 'It's fine, girly. He ain't no devil. Nobody's going to hurt you.' He guided her from the doorway, keeping the sofa between them and the German guy.

John struggled to his feet and snatched up the pickaxe handle. 'Be careful,' he told Leo, and widened his stance.

Leo cut the ties at the German's ankles, looked up to make sure everyone was ready, then cut the ties at his wrists and backed away.

The German didn't move at first, only dabbed his palm on his shirt and watched it come off red.

John tapped him in the foot with the pickaxe handle and the German looked up. John aimed a thumb at the front door. 'Go,' he said, and stepped aside to give him space.

The German got to his feet, stared everyone down and picked his way cautiously to the front door. As soon as he passed Mick, he bolted into the rain, gravel grinding under his boots until he hit the road and turned right.

Sadie ran to the door, slammed it shut and locked it. She stood there for a moment, dripping wet and breathing heavy. John took a step towards her as though to offer comfort, but Sadie raised a hand, and everyone seemed to hold their breath.

'I'm fine,' she said, without looking up, but her shoulders started jigging, and John and Mick went to her regardless.

Leo watched Sadie disappear into comforting arms, and all he could think was: *I did that to her, to them.* He reached out for a barstool to stop himself from falling and slid onto the seat, stared at the candle flame in front of him and tried not to think of Cotton lying dead beyond the glow.

When the first hand touched his shoulder, the candle flame blurred in his tears. When the arms wrapped around him and he felt hot faces on his neck, he wanted to die all over again.

Mick took the stool beside him and covered Leo's hand with a larger, callused one. 'It's done, boy,' he said. 'It's done.'

'It's done,' Sadie whispered in his ear, and kissed his cheek.

'It's done,' John said, and gripped Leo's arm.

It was the hardest thing he'd ever done, to accept their forgiveness, but he knew it was the right thing. He's own forgiveness wouldn't come so easy.

Leo edged out of his seat and walked around the other side of the breakfast bar. Sadie and John took the barstools either side of Mick, the candles up-lighting their faces, rendering them living ghosts. They stayed that way for some time, all lost in the flickering flames, and then Leo turned to Cotton. There was no bringing *her* back from the dead.

He cradled Cotton in his arms and took her out into the rain, laid her in the hessian sack with the flower heads and colourful petals, and unless his eyes were deceiving him, mottled feathers of grey and white.

As he tamped down the grave with the back of the spade, the lights came on in the barn. John, Sadie and Mick had begun to clean up. Leo couldn't have that.

Sadie was removing the candles from the worktop when Leo entered. He took them from her and shook his head, turned to Mick who was picking the Bond DVDs off the dining room floor.

'Leave them, Mick,' he said.

John picked the lamp up and returned it to the desk.

'It's my mess, John,' Leo said. 'I'll clean up when you're all gone.'

John's gaze lowered. He seemed lost. 'But I don't want to go just yet,' he said softly.

The silence at that moment had a physical weight to it – the dying storm the only thing daring to intrude. Leo didn't want them to go just yet but had no right to ask them to stay. They stood there for some time before Mick spoke.

'If you had to choose one,' Mick said, 'which would it be?' He was looking at the cover of a DVD. 'Film, I mean.'

Leo's favourite Bond film was in constant flux at the best of times; he wasn't about to give it consideration now. 'What you got there?' he asked Mick.

'Dr No.'

Leo shrugged, gave a flat smile. 'It's good.'

Mick walked over to the plasma, surprised Leo by finding the right button to eject the disc tray, and loaded the film. He sat down on the sofa and stared at the blank screen. 'Anyone know how to switch the TV on?' he said.

Sadie brushed past Leo and walked up to the plasma, thumbed the button below the screen. 'John has one the same,' she said, and sat next to Mick.

'I have a plasma?' John said, taking a seat next to Sadie. 'Sweet.'

Leo took a barstool, watched his friends cosy back into the sofa as the Bond theme tune issued from the surround sound. It was surreal, but it felt right. Their last goodbye.

Though every muscle in his body tried to defy it, a smile broke on Leo's face, and when it did, he felt something behind his ear. He didn't reach up to check what. He knew it was a cigarette.

2

Mick drove John and Sadie home in the truck. Leo stood at the front door and watched them go, grateful for the memory of those cherished last hours. The rain had petered and left a midnight blue sky. Everything seemed so clear in that moment.

He found Simian's silver lighter and placed it on the worktop next to the cigarette. Then set about his work.

3

By four in the morning, the barn showed no trace of the nightmare. Leo had scrubbed, scoured and bleached. Dusted, polished and buffed. He attended to every little chore that had seemed so important to him for so long: a smudge-free granite worktop, blemishless glass balustrade. The chairs around the dining table were aligned and equidistant, his

DVDs were returned and in their proper alphabetical order – everything the way it was… almost.

He stripped off his filthy clothes and stepped inside the shower. The hot water scorched his skin, made the scar on his chest tingle. He looked down his torso, noticed the entry wound the dagger had made was only a scab now – the cigar and candle burns gone. He stepped out of the shower, anxious to see how well his face had healed, remembering the mess he and Simian had made of Reuben. He armed the steam from the mirror and was pleased to see the bruises gone too. Then he noticed the tattoos and leaned in for a closer look.

On his upper right arm was the classical depiction of a wooden crucifix, apart from what appeared to be bloodstains where the wrists and ankles would've been nailed. His upper left displayed the slightly more disturbing image of what he recognised as the Devil's pitchfork, complete with entwined serpent. Incorporated into the scales of the snake were three sixes: the sign of The Beast. *Reuben's a mess, too,* he thought, *but who isn't, these days?*

When Leo arrived downstairs, the sun's corona was just peeking above the hill. He set the sports bag on the desk and swung Bond aside, punched in the code and removed the ebony box. In the desk drawer was brown parcel paper, an address tag already attached, just how Reuben had pictured it in Leo's mind. The dagger would soon be on its way to Turkey, and from there, who knew? Without Simian, Reuben could only guess the good from the bad, the risk of killing an innocent too great.

The sun was clear of the hill when Tarik pulled his White Mondeo onto the driveway. Leo placed the sports bag and the parcel on the back seat.

'I'll be a minute,' Leo said. 'Wait for me down the road a bit, would you?'

'Sure,' Tarik said, and pulled out of the drive.

Leo stood in his front doorway, tried to remember how the place had looked when he was a kid, but it was hard to focus on anything over the reek of petrol fumes. He lit Bond's cigarette with the silver lighter and took a long hit. He savoured the sting for a moment, then flicked the cigarette into the barn. *Fwoomp!*

Blue flame reached out along the polished oak floorboards like a pyrotechnic domino display, turned orange to climb the walls and engulf the blinds. The desk and lamp crackled and spat, the seats of the stools whistled and smoked. Within seconds it was almost too hot be so close, but Leo had to step inside and watch the flames lick around Bond's frame.

He closed the door, half expecting to hear Bond scream in agony, but there was only blessed silence.

The rain, it seemed, had been waiting for Leo to leave, and danced upon his upturned face. He walked out of his driveway and didn't look back.

'Bloody rain!' Tarik said as Leo climbed into the passenger seat

Leo rested his head on the cold window and looked up. 'You'd miss it if you couldn't have it anymore.'

'Wanna bet?'

Leo smiled.

'Where to?' Tarik asked.

'Mundey Police Station,' Leo told him. 'Via a post office.'

4

Colin Freeman felt the first few drops of rain on the back of his neck and cursed his wife. She'd insisted on buying the Spaniel pup, had insisted on naming her Lulu, too. But once Lulu had come through the other side of doggy-puberty (or whatever it was that signified the end of cute – Colin didn't know the technical jargon for it), his wife lost all interest. Now instead of enjoying his retirement with leisurely rounds of golf and indoor bowls at the K & F Club, his mornings and afternoons were spent babysitting a paranoid, neurotic Spaniel. He cursed his wife again.

As if to mock Colin's poor choice in spouses further, the rain began to thicken. He would soon be carrying a trembling Lulu home in his arms, which would only be slightly less embarrassing than holding her limp lead while she sat and pissed herself in fear of the perfectly natural phenomena falling from the sky.

This morning however, Lulu seemed oblivious to the trauma-inducing rain. She'd found something of far greater interest at the side of the country lane they walked at the start and end of every day.

Colin closed in on Lulu's excited black and white tail, which was sticking out of the brush. He reached in, clipped on her lead and gently coaxed her back. With Lulu out of the way, he could now see a shock of blonde hair and bright blue eyes. Colin's ageing heart tap-danced at the prospect of discovering a corpse in the Mundey countryside, and his heart stumbled a step when the blue eyes blinked.

'You alright, son?' Colin asked, but didn't receive an answer. 'Son?'

The young man held out a hand, which Colin took and began to pull on. Out of the bushes, the young man towered a clear twelve inches above Colin, and still had hold of his hand. Colin noticed a bloodstain on the young man's black shirt.

'Shit, you're bleeding,' Colin said. 'You been attacked, son?'

The young man pulled Colin close. 'Stabbed with moronic ineptitude, thankfully – but still no cause for profanity.'

Before Colin knew what was happening, he found himself spinning wildly into a black tunnel, and just at the moment he thought he would go mad with fear, he emerged into light and colour and realised he was looking down upon himself. The stranger was helping him to the ground.

Fear suddenly clawed at Colin, but before it could fully take hold, he was being pulled down once again into the tunnel. When he could see again, he was looking at himself. He was smiling.

Colin tried to scream, but nothing came. He looked down and saw the blood on his chest, felt it sticky and wet on his alien fingers, and then noticed the insane tattoos covering his arms. He found he could scream after all.

'Come on now, Colin, it isn't so bad. In fact you've had a pretty good deal if you ask me; you only had another thirty years at best. And don't worry about the wound; it missed all the vital organs and will be gone within a few hours, as should you, if you know what is good for you.'

Colin watched himself tap his greying head.

'That wife of yours is Hell to live with, and I should know.'

Colin watched himself walk away, watched Lulu follow before turning in confusion. Her eyes were telling her one thing while her canine senses told her another. But it seemed the eyes won the battle, and she trotted after the old man.

Simian looked down at his new companion. 'Hello, Lulu,' he said in a playful voice, then kicked her in the ribs.

Lulu yelped and skipped back towards what she now knew to be her true master, sat down beside him, trembling, and pissed herself. Colin fell to the road and did the same.

Simian shuffled away on ancient legs that disgusted him, wrapped in decaying skin that repulsed. 'Look at me! Just look at me!' He examined his beige attire with age-fogged eyes and felt like puking. 'Fuck you, Leo Stamp! FUCK YOU!'

CHAPTER 30

Leo memorised the page number of his dog-eared copy of *Casino Royale* and slipped it under his pillow next to the letter he'd received from Billy Walker's mother. He swung his legs over the side of his bed, rubbed his eyes, and looked round the never-changing cell which had been his home for the past four months and would continue to be for the next fifteen years, despite Karen Walker's pleas to the court.

His cell door opened and Mr Franklin the prison governor stepped in.

'You've made the big time, Stamp,' he said. 'There's a yank from Interpol here to see you.'

Franklin showed Leo to a room no bigger than his cell, with only a table and two chairs and a high barred window that didn't let in much light.

'Take a seat, Stamp.'

Leo sat down and Franklin disappeared. Two minutes later, a young prison officer showed in a well-groomed suited man with a briefcase. The man offered Leo a tanned hand to shake. Leo shook it.

'Hi, Leo,' the man said, his accent coming through thick in only two words – just needed the Stetson and a 'yee-haw' to complete the picture. 'I'm Agent Lance Deveraux, Interpol. I won't take up much of your time.' He popped the catches on his briefcase and sat down.

'I've got plenty,' Leo said.

Deveraux smiled politely. 'Could be worse. Three counts of first degree in the States woulda got you a little more than fifteen years.'

'What can I help you with, Mr Deveraux?'

'Are you a member of a religious cult, Leo?'

'No.'

'Have you ever been a member of a religious cult?'

'No.'

'Has anyone ever approached you or tried to recruit you into a religious cult?'

'What's this about, Mr Deveraux?' Leo sat back in his chair, sensing this wasn't going to be a short exchange.

Deveraux laced his fingers together on the desk, looked Leo dead in the eyes. 'In 1997 the SMT Database became standard procedure for the collation of data, but we've had databases going back to the early eighties doing the same thing.'

'SMT?'

'Scars, marks and tattoos. Any individual processed through a modern legal system will have their details fed into our databases – fingerprints, and so on.' He nodded. 'Your details made that same journey, which is why I've made the trip out here.'

'Don't they have agents in the UK?' Leo asked.

'They sure do, but this is my baby, so to speak.' Deveraux took a manila file from his case and laid it on the table. 'May I take a look at your tattoos, Leo?'

Leo's first instinct was to say he didn't have any. He forgot sometimes. 'Sure,' he said, and pulled off his sweat shirt.

Deveraux took a digital camera from his case. 'May I?'

Leo nodded and Deveraux took the pictures and sat down again.

'You're a unique case, Leo,' Deveraux said, putting the camera away.

'How so?' Leo pulled his sweatshirt back on.

'I've never seen those on a live person.'

'I doubt that,' Leo said with a snort of laughter.

'Not that configuration. Crucifixes – sure. Pitchforks – sure. But to have both is rare. Specifically, to have the crucifix on the upper right and the pitchfork on the upper left is rarer still. Add the bloodstains on the cross and the three sixes on the serpent's scales, and you've got yourself a Texan lotto winner. Were you ever told the significance of the symbols, Leo?'

'By whom?'

'Other cult members.'

'I told you—'

'Answer the question, please.'

'You want to know if I know the symbolic significance of a crucifix?'

'Want to hear my theory?' Deveraux said, his fingers laced again, eyes locked on Leo.

Leo shrugged.

Deveraux leaned forward. 'God is right. The Devil is left. You're in the middle.' He held Leo's gaze for a moment, then opened the file in front of him. 'You killed three people in cold blood and then handed yourself in and confessed – even brought in a gym bag full of bloody clothes which forensics linked to two of the victims.' Deveraux looked up from his file and whistled through his teeth. 'You're a homicide detective's wet dream.' He dropped his gaze to the file. 'They expedited your trial, so a lot of what I'm going to tell you now is post mortem.' He pushed over a photograph of the old German guy from the pub. 'Christian Fudickar. Why'd you kill him?'

'For his cash,' Leo said.

Deveraux gave a thin smile. 'So you said at the trial – even though Mr Fudickar's wallet was on his person when they found him.'

'I panicked and ran.'

'Mr Fudickar's house was cleared for sale two months ago. They found a secret room behind an old wardrobe – a shrine to the swastika.' Deveraux passed Leo another photograph, a black and white copy of a group of Nazi soldiers. In the centre was Adolf Hitler. Deveraux tapped a finger on one of the soldiers to Hitler's right. 'Recognise this guy?'

Leo angled the picture to the light at the window. The copy was grainy, and the face of the soldier very young, but there was no doubt that the man to Hitler's right was Fudickar.

'In the secret room they found a copy of Hitler's *Mein Kampf,* and a wooden box filled with gold teeth and pinkie fingers. Nice. You still say you killed him for his cash?'

Leo pushed the photos back, and Deveraux passed him another.

'Christine Castle. Why'd you kill her?'

Leo pushed the photo back; he didn't want to look at her eyes. 'She caught me robbing the place.'

'And again you leave empty handed. Not exactly Raffles are you, Leo?'

Leo shook his head absently.

'The police dredged the lake and found your Vanquish – nice car by the way – they also found Christine Castle's Ford Focus, the Focus her husband was supposed to have left town in. They found her husband, Bruce, in the trunk – breadknife sticking out of his neck.' Deveraux flicked through some pages, his finger in the air for Leo's patience. 'Lucy Castle?'

'What about her?'

'Made a miraculous recovery from her mysterious illness. Blood tests found traces of rat poison in her system, and forensics found similar traces on a few kitchen utensils and a saucepan at the Castles' home.' Deveraux eyed Leo. 'Pure conjecture on my part, but I'm thinking Munchausen by Proxy. Bruce Castle finds out about his wife poisoning his kid and beats the ever-loving shit out of her – winds up as a knife rack for his trouble. And who knows? Maybe little Thomas didn't fall out the bedroom window like it was reported in the paper. Still say you killed Christine because she stumbled on you robbing her place?'

Leo turned towards the window, saw Deveraux push over another picture from the corner of his eye.

'Ben Frinton,' Deveraux said. 'Taught carpentry at Berrington High School, where I believe you and your late brother Davey attended, if my records are correct.'

Leo didn't reply.

'My apologies for venturing into an area of sensitivity, but if you would allow me to continue?'

'Please do.'

'Why'd you kill Ben Frinton?'

'For his money—'

'A cash rich, successful property developer, murders a low-paid schoolteacher out jogging in a vest and shorts, for his money?'

'That's why I'm here.'

'I'll tell you why you're here. You're here because you murdered the man who, nineteen years ago, murdered your baby brother Davey.'

Leo shifted in his seat. 'What are you talking about?'

'Frinton owned a lock-up on the outskirts of Mundey. Police only found out about it six weeks ago. They found photographic evidence of seven children who had been held there – four of whom had been missing persons up to now.' Deveraux read from his file. 'Stephen Mercer, Ryan Oliver, and Davey Stamp were the only children whose bodies were recovered.' Deveraux looked up. 'Ben Frinton was a serial killer, and you killed him, Leo.'

Leo placed his hands on the table. 'What do you want from me? I confessed. I'm here.'

'I want the names of the people who helped you.'

'There are no people.'

'How could you possibly have known so much about the people you killed, their sins? The authorities didn't know. Where were you getting your intelligence from?'

Leo stood, and went to the window.

'This cult you're mixed up in is global,' Deveraux said, joining Leo at the window, 'and I know you're not okay with it, or you wouldn't have handed yourself in. Our records go back almost thirty years on this. I got a list of 257 suicides dating back to 1982, from every corner of the world, all with those same tattoos you're wearing. Some have been implicated in vigilante murders such as yours. That's one hell of a body count.'

Deveraux packed up his briefcase. 'You saved that kid Billy Walker, and you're in here pullin' fifteen because your conscience wouldn't have it any other way.' He handed Leo a card. 'When you're ready to do the right thing again, call me.'

2

Back on his bed, Leo stared at the only picture on his cell wall: the photograph of his mother and Davey holding hands on the beach at Shingle Street. He touched their faces, slipped his hand beneath his pillow and took out the letter from Billy's mum. In it she thanked Leo for sending her only child home safe and told him there was a place for him in Heaven, and that she would pray for him every day Billy was alive.

He replaced the letter, grabbed his dog-eared copy of *Casino Royale* and turned to his memorised page. Whomever Mr Fleming had envisioned as his Bond, Leo was reading him as Moore.

His mother had once told him that happiness was the anticipation of good things to come, and although he did not anticipate good things, he was hopeful of them.

One year later…

The cobblestones were wet from the recent downpour and shared a blurred reflection of the moon which hung above the descending street. Footsteps echoed off the sun-bleached render that lined the narrow street, and in the distance, the thrum of Latin guitar, muffled cheers and laughter.

The silhouette of a women meandered down the cobbles, the straight line eluding her. The woman's attention was drawn to a shadowy doorway by a low voice.

'You have very beautiful eyes, Barbara.'

'Who's there?' the woman said.

A young man stepped out of the shadows and into the moonlight.

'I'm sorry, Ms Shields; I didn't mean to startle you.'

'You were in the bar earlier.' She wagged her finger and winked. 'Saw you lookin'.' She moved closer. 'Like an older woman, do you?'

'The last time I saw Ronald Stamp was in this very street,' the young man said.

'You knew Ron?'

'I knew his son.'

'Leo?' she said, her smile disappearing. 'You're a friend of Leo's?'

The young man looked up at the moon. 'We were close once.'

'Well the next time you see that jumped-up little mummy's boy, you tell him he owes me big time.'

The young man looked both ways up the empty street and removed an object from beneath his white linen shirt. 'Do you know, Ms Shields, I couldn't agree with you more.'

The dagger slipped into Barbara Shield's chest without a sound, and he lowered her to the cobblestones, cradled in his arms like a lover.

'Look at me, Barbara,' Reuben whispered. 'You are the abyss.'

AFTERWORD

The town of Mundey is fictitious, but the places and locations within it are real enough. If you live in or around the Suffolk town of Woodbridge, you may well spot them. Leo's barn was imported from an old running route of mine and given an imaginary make-over to serve the plot, but John's cottage (though transposed from a different county completely) is a very real place, and I got to do more than just run by it. I lived there with my dad for a few years, and I have fond (and not so fond) memories of our time there. I stayed pretty true to the internal descriptions of the cottage for that reason, and just let John move in after we had left. I banged my head regularly on those low doorframes, and though the carpet wasn't pulled out of a skip, it didn't reach the edges of the room. At Christmastime we had to pile the armchair up onto the sofa (which was already blocking the front door) to make room for the drop-leaf table, but for the rest of that year, Ole Jimbo's armchair was my dad's, and I can still picture him sleeping in it.

The only thing I described differently about the cottage was the garden: John let it run to shit. My dad always kept it looking beautiful.

ACKNOWLEDGMENTS

Many thanks go to Andrew Sampson and Stuart 'Edge' Ellis for allowing me to pick their brains on police and prison procedure, to all the inmates of the Asylum for the loan of their time and considerable talent, to Chris Pitt, who kept telling me to rewrite the damned thing, and to Anna Torborg for giving me a shot. Biggest thanks of all must go to my longsuffering wife, Lesley, for her unwavering support and tolerance of her rain-dancing husband.